Donna Marchetti is a roma
Donna isn't burying her fac
at a keyboard writing her own, she can usually be found
spending time with her family and competing in agility with
her Dalmatian.

Donna currently lives in New York with her husband, her
daughter, and three dogs.

instagram.com/donnamarchettiauthor
facebook.com/AuthorDonnaMarchetti
x.com/DonnaMarchetti_

To Harper:
Never let a mean letter dull your shine.

HATE MAIL

DONNA MARCHETTI

One More Chapter
a division of HarperCollins*Publishers* Ltd
1 London Bridge Street
London SE1 9GF
www.harpercollins.co.uk
HarperCollins*Publishers*
Macken House, 39/40 Mayor Street Upper,
Dublin 1, D01 C9W8, Ireland

This paperback edition 2024
1
First published in Great Britain in ebook format
by HarperCollins*Publishers* 2024
Copyright © Donna Marchetti 2024
Donna Marchetti asserts the moral right to be identified
as the author of this work

A catalogue record of this book is available from the British Library

ISBN: 978-0-00-865467-2

Playlist

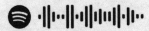

invisible string - Taylor Swift ♥
Now I'm In It - HAIM ♥
Mess It Up - Gracie Abrams ♥
Late Night Talking - Harry Styles ♥
Ghost of You - Mimi Webb ♥
Feel Again - OneRepublic ♥
Nonsense - Sabrina Carpenter ♥
get him back! - Olivia Rodrigo ♥
Someone To You - BANNERS ♥
I Wish You Would - Taylor Swift ♥
Motivation - Normani ♥
People Watching - Conan Gray ♥
Die For You - The Weekend, Ariana Grande ♥
Stuck In The Middle - Tai Verdes ♥
goodnight n go - Ariana Grande ♥
Kiss Me - Sixpence None The Richer ♥
Death By A Thousand Cuts - Taylor Swift ♥
Complicated - Olivia O'Brien ♥
Heaven - Niall Horan ♥
Back To You - Selena Gomez ♥
Paper Rings - Taylor Swift ♥
What if - Colbie Caillat ♥
This Love - Taylor Swift ♥

Chapter One

PRETTY GIRLS GET DEATH THREATS

Naomi

"I think this is a new record. It's only your second week on air and you're already getting fan mail."

Anne has this way of sneaking up on people, so when I hear her voice behind me, I swivel around in my chair, startled. I think it's her shoes. They're too quiet, even on tile. She smiles and waves a letter in her hand.

"I didn't know meteorologists got fan mail. Should I be concerned?"

"The pretty ones do," Anne says with a wink. "But, like I said, two weeks is a new record. Let's hope your new fan doesn't turn out to be a stalker."

I take the letter from her and turn the plain white envelope over. My name and the news station's address are handwritten on it. Anne watches me, not bothering to disguise her anticipation. I slide my finger under the flap and rip it open, tearing the whole envelope in half.

"Use a letter opener," Anne says. She looks annoyed.

"Who needs a letter opener? My fingers work just fine."

"You're going to get a paper cut," she says.

I don't care. I shrug. "I've always opened letters like this."

I reach into the torn envelope and pull out a single sheet of folded notebook paper. The letter is handwritten. Short, simple, to the point:

Dear Naomi,

I hope you get struck by lightning and die in the middle of your next weather report. Wouldn't that be ironic?

—L

I bark out a laugh before I can stop myself. I try to stifle it, but now that it's out, I can't stop shaking with laughter. Anne frowns, then snatches the letter to see what's so funny. I watch through tears as her eyes widen and her face turns red.

"Oh my God," she says. "I'm so sorry. I didn't know what this was. I didn't – are you okay? Why are you laughing?"

I take a deep breath to calm myself down, and then pick up the torn envelope. I'm disappointed to see that there is no return address.

"Where did this come from?"

Anne shakes her head. It's clear she's confused by my reaction. "It came in the mail this morning. No return address. Do you know who it is?"

I nod. I can feel the smile creeping back across my lips. "I haven't heard from this person in two years."

My responses only serve to confuse Anne more. "Is it a joke? Or do you have a psycho stalker we should know about?"

"It's a long story. It's kind of hard to explain."

2

Anne pulls a chair from the next desk and sits down. "I have time."

I stand up, gathering my things. I'm done for the day, and this isn't a conversation I want all my coworkers to hear. "I was about to head out," I say. Anne looks disappointed. "Come grab a coffee with me? I'll tell you all about it."

Dear Luca,

I am really excited to be your new pen pal. My teacher says that you live in California. I've never met anyone who lives in California before. I think that's so cool! Do you go to the beach every day? I feel like that's what I would do if I lived there. You must love it so much.

I live in Oklahoma. I've always wanted to live somewhere close to a beach so that I can go any time I want. There isn't a lot to do in my town, unless you count going to the mall or to the river, which isn't nearly as nice as the actual ocean.

What do you like to do in California? Do you have any pets? I have a hamster, but I really want a cat. My mom says that I can have a cat when I'm a little older, but she's been saying that since I can remember. I'm ten now, and I feel like I'm old enough to take care of a cat. Or a ferret. If I can't have a cat, then I really want a ferret. What about you? Do you like ferrets?

Love,

Naomi Light

I was in fifth grade when I wrote my first letter to Luca. My teacher made us choose pen pals at random by pulling names out of a hat. That's how I ended up writing a letter to a kid named Luca Pichler who lived in California. I was excited to be making a new friend who lived in another state. I had never had a pen pal before, and I wasn't sure how I was supposed to end the letter. My mother had always made me sign all my letters with 'Love, Naomi,' so that's how I ended this one. It wasn't until after I wrote it out that I wondered if it was weird to write 'love' to a boy I had never met. I had only ever written letters to family before.

It was too late to rewrite the letter, and I didn't want to scribble it out and make myself look sloppy. Mrs. Goble was walking down the aisle toward my desk, picking up all of our letters on her way. I stuffed mine into the envelope and handed it to her.

She explained that the letters would go out in the mail the next morning, and then it would be a few days before our pen pals received them. Then it would be a few more days before we heard back from our new friends in California.

We received the letters from our pen pals two weeks later. I was so excited to have mail addressed to me that wasn't from someone in my family. When I opened the letter, the first thing I noticed was that Luca Pichler's handwriting was atrocious. It took me twice as long to read it than it would have if he'd at least tried to write neatly.

Dear Naomi,

You sound really boring. My mom says that Oklahoma is in the middle of the bible belt, and you'll probably end up pregnant at sixteen. Also, ferrets stink. If you want a real pet, then get a dog because cats are boring. On second thought, maybe a cat would be a perfect fit for you after all.

Do you get tornadoes in Oklahoma?

Love,

Luca Pichler

The fact that I had to put in a lot of effort to decipher his terrible handwriting made it all the more infuriating. My letter had been so nice and cheerful, and he responded with … this? My chin quivered. I couldn't let Mrs. Goble see me like this. I folded the letter up and took a deep breath. I blinked away the moisture in my eyes. Then I unfolded the letter and read it again. He had closed it with 'love' just like I had. I wondered if that was something his own mother had taught him, or if he was just copying me. Maybe he had put it there to be ironic after writing such a hateful letter. Were fifth grade boys in California capable of that kind of purposeful irony? I doubted it. He was probably mocking me, just like he was with the rest of his letter.

I carefully ripped a clean sheet of paper from my notebook, picked up my pen, and wrote back.

Dear Luca,

   Your handwriting is terrible. I couldn't even understand what you wrote in your letter. It kind of looks like you said that you have five cats of your own, and your favorite thing to do on the weekends is clean their litterboxes. That seems a little weird. You should probably stop drinking so much salt water. Maybe it's a good thing I live far from the ocean after all.

   And yes, we get tornadoes here.

   Love,

   Naomi

His next letter was easier to understand. It was clear that he had taken his time, focusing on making his handwriting neater. That felt like a win, even if this one was meaner than the first.

Dear Naomi,

I wrote this one more slowly so that your simple Oklahoma mind can keep up. I'm sorry to hear that your parents are brother and sister. I've heard that incest can cause a lot of birth defects, which explains why you turned out the way you did.

I'm happy to hear that there are tornadoes in Oklahoma. If we're lucky, a tornado will destroy your house and keep your parents from breeding more of your kind.

Love,

Luca

I was furious when I got that second letter. I didn't understand how anyone could be so mean and disgusting. I folded up the letter and stuffed it in the drawer in my desk, vowing never to write to him again. I had thought that maybe he'd just had a bad day the first time, but now it was clear he was doing this because he was just a terrible, terrible human being.

"But you did write back to him, right?" Anne asks. "You said it's been two years since you heard from him. Did he just keep writing back to you all that time with no response from you?"

"I wrote back. Eventually."

"Did your teacher ever see his letters?"

I shrug. "No. She always gave us the envelopes unopened. I think as long as none of us complained, she just assumed all of our pen pals were behaving. It worked out in my favor, too, because I got pretty mean after that."

"Were you actually mad, or did you just do it for his reaction?"

I pause to think about it. "I was mad at first. I think as time went on, though, I started looking forward to his letters. I wanted to see how mean he could get. I made it my personal goal to be worse than him."

Anne looks down at the letter on the table between us. "Seems like the ball is in your court now."

I pick up the letter and look at it, my eyes skimming over his familiar handwriting. "No return address," I remind her. "How am I supposed to write back?"

"Try his address from two years ago," she suggests.

"I did. I tried it a year and a half ago. It came back undeliverable. Usually when one of us moved, we'd send the next letter with the new return address. This time, he moved without sending a new letter."

Anne purses her lips, thinking. "He's challenging you," she says after a minute.

"Challenging me?"

"To find him," she clarifies. "If you don't send a reply, then he gets the last word, ending a decades-old snail-mail battle. Are you ready to let him win?"

I shake my head. "Hell no. I'm tracking him down."

Chapter Two

BROTHERS AND SISTERS

Luca

I had thought the idea of writing to a pen pal was stupid. I had nothing to say to some kid in some other state. I was probably the only kid in my class who wasn't excited about it. While the rest of the class was reading their letters to each other, and talking about what they planned to write back, I sat in the back of the classroom, wishing I could be home playing video games.

It's not like this was a graded assignment. Mrs. Martin probably wouldn't even read our letters.

"Luca," she said, grabbing my attention. "Would you like to share your letter?"

I shook my head. "Not really."

She gave me a sympathetic smile. "Maybe just read it to Ben."

My friend Ben sat at the desk next to mine. He looked about as excited as I felt. I slid the letter across the desk to him. He read it, and then pushed it back to me.

"She talks about the ocean a lot," he said.

"I know," I agreed.

"What are you going to say?"

"I don't know. This is stupid."

"You think everything is stupid."

"Everything *is* stupid."

"You need to write back to her," Ben said.

"Why?"

"Because if you don't, she'll be the only kid in her class who doesn't get a letter."

I rolled my eyes, and with a sigh, I flipped my notebook to a blank page. I looked at Naomi's letter one more time, and then scribbled my own letter. When I was finished, I smirked. I ripped the sheet of paper out of my notebook and handed it to Ben.

"You can't send that," he said. "You'll get in so much trouble."

"Mrs. Martin isn't even going to read it," I whispered back.

"That's so mean," he said. "You're going to make her cry."

"So? I don't know her."

I took my letter back, folded it, and put it into the envelope our teacher had provided. I thought that would be the end of it. Naomi Light would ask for a new pen pal, and I wouldn't be expected to write to anyone.

But it wasn't the end. Two weeks later, Mrs. Martin handed out our new letters. I was surprised to see that Naomi had written another letter to me. Ben seemed surprised too. He waited for me to open mine before he even opened his own.

"What did she say?" he asked before I was finished reading.

Her letter made me angry. "She didn't even understand what I wrote last time, and she's making stuff up."

I opened my notebook and began to draft my response. I was halfway through my first sentence when I scribbled it all out. She was right. My handwriting was messy. Mrs. Martin was always asking me to write neater, and even my mom had told me I needed to work on it. I flipped to a new sheet of paper and started over. This time, I wrote slowly, careful to keep all my letters separate and readable.

I showed it to Ben when I was done. His brows shot up while he read it, and then he frowned at me. "That's gross," he said. "Do people in Oklahoma really do that? Marry their brothers and sisters?"

I shrugged. "Probably not."

I took the letter back and stuffed it into the envelope.

"Why are you still being so mean to her? She was probably excited about having a pen pal."

Ben looked around at the other kids in our class, and I followed his gaze. All of the girls had big smiles on their faces as they read the letters they had received, giving each other ideas for what to write back. I knew what he was doing. He was trying to get me to see Naomi as one of them: a real person, rather than just a piece of paper that came in the mail.

"I don't want to have to keep writing to someone all year long. If she's the one who decides not to write back, then it won't be my fault, and Mrs. Martin will leave me alone."

I sealed the envelope and wrote down Naomi's name and school address, and then dropped it off in the basket Mrs. Martin had designated for our letters. I was the first to hand mine in. She smiled at me.

"That was fast," she said.

I shrugged, and gave her what I thought was my most charming smile. "My pen pal is really easy to write to. I can't wait to hear back from her."

It was another two weeks before our pen pals wrote back. Mrs. Martin walked through the classroom, handing the letters out. When she reached my desk, she paused, flipping through the stack of letters in her hand. She slipped one out and handed it to Ben. She reached the end of the stack, and started over.

"Hmm," she said when it was clear there wasn't a letter for me. "I'm sorry, Luca. It looks like there isn't a letter for you this time. It might have been separated from the others. That happens sometimes. We'll probably get it in a day or two."

"Oh." I tried to sound disappointed, but I didn't have to try very hard. I was surprised to find that I actually *was* a little disappointed. While we waited for the letters, I had found myself hoping that Naomi would send another snarky letter in response to mine, so that I could fire back with something even meaner.

I knew that the whole point of writing mean letters was to get her to stop writing back, but I hadn't realized it would happen this quickly. Now I was the only kid in the class who didn't have a letter to read.

The following day, I stopped at Mrs. Martin's desk at the end of recess.

"Did I get a letter today?" I asked.

She shook her head. "I'm sorry, Luca. Nothing yet. Maybe tomorrow?"

But there was nothing in the mail the next day, either. Or the next day.

I had given up on hearing from Naomi by the time the next round of letters came in the mail. I didn't even look up at Mrs. Martin as she walked around the room, handing them out. I was working on a homework assignment when she dropped an envelope onto my desk. I looked up at her, surprised. She winked at me, then continued around the room, handing out the rest of the letters.

"I guess your plan didn't work too well," Ben said.

I ignored him and opened the letter.

Dear Luca,

I wasn't going to write back to you after what you said to me last time. I don't like to use bad words, but I want you to know that you're an asshole. I realized that you probably only said those nasty things to get out of having to write to me, so I decided that the best punishment is for me to just keep writing to you.

I feel like I should let you know that my parents are not brother and sister. I think it's kind of weird that you even thought of that. You must have some pretty disgusting fantasies. I hope that you don't have any brothers or sisters, but if you do, they probably wouldn't want to touch you with a ten-foot pole. You have an ugly personality, and I bet you're just as ugly on the outside too.

By the way, what's the weather like in California this time of year?

Love,

Naomi

Dear Naomi,

I'm actually not ugly at all. All the girls in my class think I'm hot. My teacher caught two of the girls in my class passing notes to each other, and that's what the note said. So, you're wrong. Also, I don't have any siblings. It's really gross that you think I fantasize about brothers and sisters. Why did you even think about that? Is that what you fantasize about? Gross.

The weather is pretty nice this time of year. It's almost eighty degrees today. I think I might go to the beach after school.

Love,

Luca

Dear Luca,

The girls in your class are wrong, because boys in fifth grade are not hot. When the girls in your class call you hot, they probably just mean that you're skinny. My older cousin says that boys don't get hot until high school. But, I guess, whatever helps you sleep at night.

I'm so jealous of your weather. It's really cold and cloudy here. I wish I was lying on the beach right now. Are you really tanned? I wish I could get a tan.

Love,

Naomi

Dear Naomi,

Stop trying to make friends with me by talking about the weather and tanning. It's not going to work. Also, you probably shouldn't lay out on the beach, because someone might mistake you for a whale. Next thing you know, a whole crowd of people will be around you, trying to help push you back into the ocean.

I don't care what your cousin says about boys. If she's older than us, then of course she doesn't think fifth-grade boys are hot. Besides, I'm not just skinny. I have abs.

Love,

Luca

By the time winter break started, I was one of the only kids in my class who was still consistently getting letters from my pen pal. Even Ben had grown bored with the letters. When we all went back to school in January, there was only one letter waiting for our return. It was addressed to me. The entire class turned around to stare at me when Mrs. Martin announced that I had received a letter from my pen pal. It was like they had all forgotten that our pen pals still existed.

I tucked the envelope into my backpack to read later without an audience. When I wrote back, I changed the return address to my home address instead of the school. I didn't want anyone to know that I was the only one still writing to my pen pal.

Chapter Three

NAMES ARE HARD

Naomi

"I feel like there's more to the story," Anne says. "It doesn't just end with you saying mean things to each other in fifth grade."

"There is more. A lot more. I told you it was a long story."

"Did you keep any of the letters?"

I shrug. "I'm sure I have them somewhere."

This is a lie. I know exactly where all the letters are. They're tucked away in a shoe box on the top shelf in my closet, organized chronologically. I even saved the unopened letters that were returned after Luca moved.

"I can't believe you've never told me any of this before," Anne says. "Aren't you supposed to tell your best friend everything?"

"I met you right after I stopped hearing from him," I remind her. "I guess it just never came up."

The truth is that I never told anyone about Luca. My parents only knew because they saw the letters coming and

17

going. My college roommate knew because she had seen me writing to him a few times, but we never talked much about it and she never read any of the letters.

I hear the café door open behind me, and Anne's eyes wander to whoever is walking in. Even as she's distracted, she doesn't drop the subject. "How are you going to find him?"

"No idea. Public record search? I don't really know where to start."

"You have his first and last name."

"True, but I don't know where he lives now."

"Look him up on Facebook."

I pull my phone out of my purse. "Of course," I say. "Why didn't I think of that?"

Her eyes go wide, and then she frowns. "You never looked him up before? Weren't you curious about what he looked like?"

"Of course I've looked him up before, but it's been a long time. He had one of those profile pictures with like five other guys next to him, so I couldn't be sure which one he was."

Anne's eyes wander past me again, toward the cash register. I turn around to see what she keeps staring at, and recognize one of my neighbors ordering a coffee. No wonder she's staring. Even facing away from us, Jake Dubois is a good-looking guy. He has dark hair and muscles that fill out his shirt nicely. His short sleeves hug his biceps as he reaches across the counter to pay for his coffee. We both take in the view for a moment longer before I face her again, returning my attention to my phone. I open Facebook and type in 'Luca Pichler' in the search bar. Several names and photos pop up.

"Think he's one of them?" Anne asks, leaning over the table to look at my screen.

I scroll through the list. "None of these guys live in

America. I don't know. I guess it's possible he moved, but I don't think he's one of them. I'll have to look harder later."

A figure looms over our table. Anne looks up at Jake first, covering up a squeal of surprise. "Hi," she says, her face flushing. I'm sure my face is just as pink as hers. I wonder if he noticed us staring at him a minute ago.

He says, "Hey," to Anne, and then turns to me. His ice-blue eyes never cease to startle me when he looks at me. They're the type of eyes that are impossible to look away from, and yet I feel like if I keep staring, he'll somehow figure out my darkest secrets. "I thought I recognized you," he says. "Are you all done reporting the weather for the day?"

"Wow. Two big fans in one day," Anne says. "Look at you."

I snort, and lift my coffee to my lips before I remember that my cup is empty. "Anne, he's my neighbor."

"Oh." She lets out a nervous laugh and glances away.

He's quiet for a moment. I realize that he's looking down at my phone, which is still displaying a list of all the Luca Pichlers of the world. I quickly close the screen, and he turns his attention back to me. "I wanted to ask if you'd like to have dinner with me sometime. Uh, maybe this weekend?"

I'm caught off guard by his question. It takes me a second to realize that he's asking me out. I've seen him around the building plenty of times, but we've only ever interacted twice. The first time was when he moved into the building about six months ago, and I held the door open for him on my way outside while he carried a box inside. He had said, "Thank you," and I responded with, "You're welcome."

The second time was only about a week ago. I was heading downstairs to check my mail just as he was coming up. He had stopped right in front of me, blocking me from exiting the stairwell, and said, "Hey, aren't you that weathergirl? Naomi Light?"

"Uh, yeah, that's me," I had responded.

I had stolen a glance at the name badge on the scrubs he was wearing, but I didn't get a chance to see where he worked.

"Cool," was all he said before stepping out of my way and hurrying up the stairs. I've seen him a few other times, but all either of us offer is a polite nod or smile, and sometimes we ignore each other altogether.

I realize now that it's been a moment, and I still haven't answered his question.

"Yeah, uh, sure," I stammer, sounding just as nervous as he had asking the question.

"Great," he says. His gaze lowers to my empty cup. "Can I buy you another coffee?"

This is already my third cup today, but I find myself saying, "Yeah, uh, sure," and then cringe at myself because this is exactly how I answered his last question. I force myself to snap out of my stupor. "Actually, I was about to head out."

"I'll get you a to-go cup then."

He turns around and heads back to the counter. I watch him over my shoulder, my heart beating fast. Anne clears her throat, but I avoid looking at her. I can tell by the way my whole body has heated that my face is probably as red as my hair. When I finally look at her, she has a big smile on her face.

"That was both the most awkward, and the most exciting thing I've ever witnessed," she says.

"Then you need to raise your standards for both awkward and exciting things." I wipe my hair away from my face, trying to cool myself down. "What's the big deal?"

"Naomi Light has a hot date this weekend," she says in a

sing-song voice, dancing in her seat. "And you didn't even need a dating app to meet him. What are you going to wear?"

I roll my eyes, fighting a smile. "I literally haven't had time to think about it yet."

"You never told me you had such a hot neighbor. You've only ever talked about the really loud one."

I shush her, then look over my shoulder again to make sure he can't hear us. He's swiping his card at the register. I turn back to Anne. "Why would I describe all of my neighbors to you?"

"You don't need to describe all of them, but..." She pauses, her eyes wandering back to Jake. "This one is certainly worth describing."

Jake is heading back to our table with a new cup of coffee for me. Anne and I stand up. She leans closer to me and whispers, "You have to tell me if you find Luca Pichler's address. I want to know what happens next."

"You'll be the first person I tell."

Anne leaves just as he's getting back to the table. I thank him, and then we head outside.

"I'll walk you home," he offers.

I laugh, glancing up at our apartment building, which is right across the street. "What would you do if I said no?"

He thinks about it. "Probably wait ten seconds and then follow you awkwardly."

"Fine. You can walk me home."

The way he smiles does something to me. I've seen him smile before, but when it's directed at me, my heart rate picks up and I think I might need to be carried across the street. I force myself to look away from his face, because it's the only way I can survive this walk home. My eyes land on his arm, and I imagine him carrying me, my head against that muscular chest… Okay, maybe I shouldn't look at him at all. I face the street, hoping that the effect he has on me isn't too obvious.

We wait for traffic to clear up, and then we head across the street. Without even looking at him, I'm acutely aware of every step he takes, how far away from me he is at any given moment, and every time he glances in my direction. I manage to make it to the other side without stumbling over my own feet. He holds the door open for me. As I step past him, I can smell his cologne, or maybe it's his body wash, mixed with the aroma of the coffee he's holding. I breathe him in for the fleeting moment that I spend walking past him through the doorway. I'm about to head for the stairs when I notice that he's stepping up to the elevator. I hesitate. The last time I took this, it broke down and I was trapped for thirty minutes before the fire department came and rescued me. According to other residents, it has been fixed since then, and most people in my building still use it, but I haven't taken my chances.

He watches me, eyebrow raised, as I turn from the stairwell back to the elevator. I'm not about to tell him that I'm afraid to take the elevator, so I try to play it cool. He hits the button, and the doors open. I take a deep breath before following him in.

"What's wrong?" he asks as he pushes the button for his floor.

"Nothing." I hit the button for the third floor, ignoring the fact that I can hear my own heartbeat drumming in my ears.

"Are you sure? Because you seem like you're afraid of the elevator."

"Nope. Not at all."

His brow wrinkles. "You're white as a ghost. Are you claustrophobic?"

"That's just my skin tone," I say, forcing a laugh. "Thanks a lot."

"Come on. We can take the stairs if you need to." He reaches for the button, but by the time he hits it, the elevator is already starting to move up. It shakes, and then stops moving halfway between the lobby and the second floor.

I let out an involuntary sound that's a mixture between a gasp and a shriek. I clasp my free hand over my mouth.

"Oops." He hits the button again, but it doesn't seem to help.

"This is exactly why I didn't want to take the elevator," I groan. "This always happens to me."

"This has happened to you before?" His eyes go wide. "Oh. That's why you were afraid." He looks back at the control panel. "And I just made things worse, didn't I?"

I back up against the wall and take a deep breath. I let it out slowly, calming myself. I pull my phone out of my pocket to check for a signal, but I know there won't be any. I was without a signal the entire thirty minutes I was trapped in here last time.

"Please tell me you have a signal."

He looks at his phone. "Nope. Sorry." He examines the control panel, then hits a button. There's a short dial tone, and then I recognize the voice of the security guard who sits in the lobby. At least they fixed the 'help' button since the last time I was trapped here.

"Hey Joel," he says. "We're trapped in the elevator."

"Is that Naomi in there with you?" Joel's voice sounds gravelly through the speaker. "Seems like she has bad luck with that elevator."

"So I've heard."

"I'll call for help," Joel says. "Hang tight."

The line disconnects, leaving just the two of us. The

elevator seems even quieter now. I wish there was some music to break the silence.

I look up at the ceiling, wondering if I can reach the second floor if I move a ceiling tile and climb up on top of the elevator. I didn't have this option last time because I wasn't trapped in here with someone so tall. I'm sure I could climb up onto his shoulders and...

"It's not going to work," he says, interrupting my thoughts.

I frown at him. "What's not going to work?"

He gestures with his coffee cup toward the ceiling. "You wouldn't be able to get the doors open even if you could reach them."

My mouth drops open. "Did I say that out loud?"

He laughs. "No. But I could practically see your plan forming just by looking at your face."

"I'm sure I could get the doors open. I'm strong."

"Maybe you could, but it's still not safe. What happens if the elevator starts moving while you're up there?"

I sigh. "I hadn't really thought about that."

"Let's just hang tight and wait for help."

I nod. I know that he's right, but I still feel anxious. I don't know why. It's not like I need to be anywhere.

"At least we both have coffee," he says.

"And each other," I add. "Last time I was in here all by myself. I thought I was going to go crazy."

"Are you going to be okay? You're not going to start hyperventilating and screaming, are you?"

I pace the length of the small box we're in. "I'll be fine as long as they get us out of here soon."

"I'm sure it's a simple fix. All I did was hit a button."

I can feel the panic creeping in. I take another deep breath to steady myself.

"What did you do last time you were trapped in here?"

I think about it for a moment. "I spent the first ten minutes trying to get a signal on my phone. Then I banged my fists against the door screaming for help until my throat hurt. After a while I gave up on ever getting out of here, and I was trying to decide which of my limbs I would need to eat to survive when the fire department finally pried the doors open."

His brow is wrinkled with worry, but a smile tugs at the corner of his mouth, like he's not sure if it's okay to laugh at my misery.

"It was a dark time," I add. "I barely made it out alive."

"That sounds rough," he says, still fighting a smile. "I think you'll be happy to know that I don't think either of us will need to resort to cannibalism today."

"It's great that you think that, but I'm not ready to rule it out just yet."

He snorts. "Okay. Remind me to never go camping with you."

The idea of camping with him makes me feel hot. I pull my shirt away from my stomach to cool myself down. "I can handle camping. There aren't any elevators in the wilderness."

His gaze lowers, landing on my stomach. I realize the way I'm holding my shirt looks like I'm about to take it off. I let go, clearing my throat while I pat my shirt back into place. He turns his head away, his ears turning pink.

"I can't believe I've avoided the elevator all this time just to get stuck in it again."

"You really haven't been in here since then?"

I shake my head. "I take the stairs."

He looks at the button for the third floor, which is still illuminated. "Two flights of stairs twice a day? You never get sick of that?"

I shrug, gesturing around us. "I feel like I would get sick of this a lot faster."

"True," he says. "I've heard I'm pretty intolerable."

I smack his arm. "That's not what I meant."

He pulls his arm away, acting like I've hurt him. "Ouch!"

I laugh. "That did not hurt."

"Yeah, it did. You're stronger than you look." He points at the elevator doors. "I bet you could pry them open."

I roll my eyes. I hand him my coffee cup, then step up to the doors and attempt to pull them apart. I already know that it's not going to work. I tried this last time.

"Nope," I say, taking my coffee back. "Guess I need to hit the gym more often."

"Nah. You don't need the gym. Just do a hand-stand your whole way up the stairs every day. You'll be strong enough in no time."

I almost snort out my coffee. "That would be a sight to see." I check the time on my phone. "Ugh. How long has it been?"

I take another sip of my coffee, which I regret, because I have to pee, and I'm not doing myself any favors by putting more liquid in my body. I lower myself to the floor and sit with my legs crossed in front of me. He sits down next to me. I suck in a breath. His closeness makes me forget how much I hate the elevator, if only for a moment.

I notice that he seems calm, like he's not anxious to get out of here like I am.

"So," he says. I turn to look at him, waiting for him to continue. The corner of his mouth tilts up. I pull my gaze away from his mouth to meet his eyes, which are fixed on mine. My breath catches. "I heard you and your friend talking about me."

My face heats as I remember everything that Anne said. I'm

afraid to know how much he heard, but I have to ask. "What exactly did you hear?"

He smiles. "I heard you have a loud neighbor."

I wish I could hide. If he heard that, then he definitely heard everything else.

"Can I see your phone?" he asks.

I pass it to him. "Why?"

"So that I can give you my number."

He starts typing in his contact information. I look over his shoulder. He puts himself in as 'Hot Neighbor'.

I roll my eyes. "A little full of yourself, aren't you?"

He shrugs as he hands my phone back. "Just accepting the title I've been given."

I send him a text message, and to my surprise it goes through despite the terrible signal in this elevator. "There. Now you have my number too."

I watch his face as the message pops up on his screen. He doesn't try to hide his smile.

"What are you going to save my number as? Weird Elevator Girl?"

He laughs. "Not a chance."

I look at his screen as he types 'Cute Weathergirl' to save my number in his contacts. I feel a smile tugging at the corners of my lips even as my face turns red.

"Cute, huh?" I tease him. "How many other weathergirls do you know?"

"A lot. You'd be surprised. I had to come up with a numbering system for all of the average weathergirls in my contact list."

I lean back against the wall. "I'm kind of disappointed I'm not one of them. Average Weathergirl Number Seven has a nice ring to it."

He shakes his head and waves his phone. "Nope. This name fits you better."

The elevator shakes, startling me, and then it begins to rise. "Oh, thank God."

We both stand up just as the doors open on the third floor. I step out into the hallway. He places his hand on the door jamb to keep it from closing. "We should do this again sometime," he says.

I look back into the elevator and cringe. "Not a chance."

He pouts.

"I'll let you take me to dinner as long as there are no elevators involved."

He smiles. "Deal."

Inside my apartment, I continue my Facebook search for Luca Pichler. I try narrowing the search to all the cities I know he's lived, starting with San Diego, where both his first and last letters came from before he disappeared. No results. I try again with the next city, and the next, with no luck. It seems like all the Luca Pichlers that came up in my initial search live outside the United States. I start checking their profiles, knowing it's possible he moved out of the country, but none of these men look promising.

My upstairs neighbor is stomping around. I hear something dragging – or maybe rolling? – before a loud crash on the other side of the room. I duck my head as if the sound is in my own apartment, and then I roll my eyes at both myself and my loud neighbor. It sounds like whoever lives up there has a bowling alley in their apartment. I turn on some music to drown out the noise.

Despite my loud neighbor and the infamous elevator, this isn't a bad place to live. It's one of the nicer apartment buildings in my area of Miami. We don't have a doorman, but we have Joel, the security guard. Sometimes when he's bored – which seems to be often – he likes to hold the door open for the people who live in the building. He's worked here long enough that he knows us all by name. He's one of the few fixtures I'll miss when I buy my house and move out of this building.

I make myself some lunch, and as I'm eating, my phone buzzes. I grab it and check the screen, hoping to see a message from Jake, but it's not him. It's Anne. She sent a link to a database called PeopleFinder where I can look up Luca Pichler.

Anne: *You have to pay to get access to his address and all that.*

I click on the link and type Luca's name in the search bar. The results are populated with a few different men with the same name. The free version of the website only shows their age and their city. I'm not thrilled with the results I have so far. One of the men is in his mid-fifties, one is in his early twenties, and the last on the list is close to eighty. Either my Luca Pichler isn't on this list, or someone got his age wrong. I decide to pay for the membership anyway. I can always cancel it after I get what I need.

The payment processes and the page reloads, this time with complete information. It turns out the geriatric Luca Pichler lives in a nursing home in Seattle. The mid-fifties Luca Pichler lives with his wife, his in-laws, and six children in Rhode Island. The younger Luca Pichler lives in a home for adults with disabilities. I sigh. None of this looks promising. Now I'm out twenty bucks, and my identity has probably been sold to the highest bidder.

> **Naomi:** *No luck. If I hadn't received that letter today, I might assume Luca is dead.*
> **Anne:** *Weird. I wonder if his parents still live in his childhood home. Do you still have that address?*

It's a good idea, and one that I was thinking of before she sent the link to PeopleFinder. I go into my bedroom and take the shoe box out of the closet. The most recent letters are on top, and the very first ones are at the bottom. I had written his return address on the back of every letter so that I'd always know where to send my next letter even if I threw the envelope away.

Using my phone, I take a picture of the San Diego address. I'm about to put the letters away when I have an idea. I skim through them, stopping at each one that has a new address, and take a photo. The first eight years of letters are all from the same San Diego address. After that, his letters had come from all over the country. He had moved frequently, but he always made sure I had his new address – until two years ago.

I know it's unlikely he's gone back to live at any of these old addresses, but it's a good place to start. Someone, somewhere, has to know where he is.

———————

I've already had two cups of coffee by the time Anne gets to the station with my third. I'm looking at satellite and radar data to prepare my weather report for the day when she sets the steaming cup next to me.

"Thank you."

Without taking my eyes off the screen, I reach for the hot cup and take a sip. I can hear her pull up a chair next to me and sit down.

"Don't you have some real work to do? Or did Patrick order you to watch me drink the whole cup?"

"I was just curious if you tracked down your penemy."

"My what?"

"Your penemy," she repeats. "Get it? Like a pen pal, but he's your enemy. Pen enemy. Penemy."

"Clever." I still haven't looked at her. I'm focused on my screen. I only have about ten more minutes before I need to be on air. "I already told you I couldn't find him on PeopleFinder. Short of driving out to San Diego, I'm not really sure how to track him down."

"Taking a break already, Anette?"

We both turn to see Patrick sauntering into the room with a stack of papers in his hands. He always carries the same stack of papers around the station when he wants to look busy without doing anything productive. He also has never called Anne by her actual name, but I guess 'Anette' is close enough that everyone knows who he's talking to.

"I was just bringing Naomi her coffee," she says.

"I didn't realize delivering coffee requires sitting down."

I turn back to my computer, rolling my eyes. She mumbles a quick apology and hurries off. As usual, her shoes don't make a sound on the carpeted floor. Patrick watches her go and then turns to me.

"I've been meaning to tell you that you're doing an excellent job, Naomi."

He's one of those people who pronounces my name like nigh-oh-me, even though I've corrected him countless times. I don't even bother anymore, but I wonder if he realizes that he's the only person at the station who pronounces it like that.

"Thank you, Patrick. I appreciate it."

"You're a natural on air," he continues. "And your graphics are impressive. Your predictions are spot on, too. Really great job. Emmanuel would have been proud."

"Oh. Thank you. Didn't you know that I was preparing the graphics for Emmanuel for the last two years? In fact, he didn't look at a single radar for the last year and a half before he retired."

"You've been here for two years?" Patrick says. "Huh. Doesn't seem like that long ago."

"Yep. Two years went by in a flash."

His whole face turns red. He wrinkles the pages in his hands. I smile at him to try to ease some of his embarrassment. He leaves the room, and not long after, Anne returns. I try to shoo her away.

"You're going to get in trouble," I warn her.

She rolls her eyes. "What's he going to do? Fire me?"

"Probably."

She laughs. "Tell me about San Diego."

It takes me a moment to remember what we were talking about before Patrick interrupted. "That's where Luca's first and last letters came from. I can only imagine he's probably still there."

"He watched your weather report."

"So? He could have accessed that from anywhere. You don't always have to live locally to get the local stations."

"What are you going to do?"

"I'm going to wait for him to send me another letter. Maybe he'll include his return address next time."

"What if there isn't a next time?"

Aside from the two-year gap, I never went longer than a month without hearing from him. The only difference now is that I can't write back. I wonder if it's intentional that he left off his return address. It has to be. Maybe he just wants to mess with me. Or maybe he doesn't want his wife to know that he's writing to me again. My best guess is that she's the reason I hadn't heard from him for two years. I don't blame her if she read the last letter I sent – the last one before the postal service started kicking my letters back to me. I would have felt the same way she did if I had read a letter like the one that I sent. I had never considered until after I sent it, and he never wrote back, that someone other than Luca might read it. No amount of returned mail could make things right. I spent the last two years feeling like a part of me was missing. Now it was back, but was it really? He wouldn't just send a letter like that after two years, with no return address, if he didn't intend to follow up.

"He'll send another letter," I say. I'm sure of it.

Chapter Four

THE HANGNAIL PREDICAMENT

Luca

A lot had changed in the three years between fifth grade and the end of eighth. I had kissed a girl for the first time the summer before sixth grade. I'd had seven girlfriends since then. My mom and dad brought a puppy home when I was in seventh grade. I named him Rocky, and he became my best friend. I had gone from being a skinny elementary school boy to what I imagined Naomi's older cousin called high-school-hot. Back in fifth grade, I had taken a long hard look in the mirror and determined that Naomi might be right. I was skinny, and had done nothing to earn the abs I was so proud of. My dad bought some home gym equipment that summer, set it up in the garage, and we started working out together.

A lot had stayed the same, too. Ben and I rode our bikes to school every day, and we had almost every class together. I was still living in the same house, in the same city. Sometimes when I stepped outside and smelled the salty ocean air, I thought of Naomi and smiled, knowing that she was jealous of where I lived. I was still writing letters to her. There was so much I could have told her in the three years that we'd been writing to each other, and yet none of what we wrote ever had any substance.

Instead, it had become a competition to see who could outdo the other. We weren't always mean. Sometimes I could tell that she was growing bored with writing to me, and her letter would be the most uninteresting thing I'd ever read. When she did that, I always returned a letter that was equally or – I hoped – more boring.

Dear Luca,

 I woke up this morning. I brushed my teeth. I went to school. I did homework. I went to bed. I ate meals in between.

 Xoxo,

 Naomi

Dear Naomi,

 I forgot to put the toilet seat up when I peed, and a little bit splashed onto the seat. I didn't clean it up.

 Xoxo,

 Luca

My parents were the only two people who knew I was still writing to Naomi. My mom thought it was sweet, but that's because she never read any of the letters. My dad never offered an opinion on it. Ben had asked about Naomi only once after we started sending the letters to our home addresses instead of the schools. I had shrugged and pretended I didn't remember what he was talking about.

I tucked the latest letter from Naomi into my backpack on my way to school one morning. It was the last week of eighth grade. My mom had forgotten to check the mail the day before and, curious about whether I had received a letter, I had checked the mailbox on the way out the door. Ben was rolling up on his bicycle when he saw me slip the unopened envelope into my backpack.

"What's that?" he asked.

"Nothing."

I zipped my backpack closed, slung it onto my back, and got on my bike. We were both quiet on the ride to school that morning. It seemed like Ben always knew when I wasn't in the mood to talk. I was tired that morning. I had been awake all night, trying to drown out the sound of my parents arguing by blasting music in my headphones. I had managed to drown out their voices, but I could still feel the vibration in the walls from the doors slamming as they made their way through the house, fighting in every room but mine.

When we were a block away from school, I started pedaling faster to outpace Ben. His bike was better than mine, though, and he caught up quickly. We locked our bikes on the rack in front of the school entrance and went inside.

"Is it your report card?" Ben asked.

"What?"

"That letter that you put in your backpack."

I frowned. "Report cards haven't gone out yet."

"What is it then? Why are you being so sneaky?"

"I'm not being sneaky. It's just none of your business."

"It's that girl, isn't it?"

I turned to look at him. "No. What girl?"

He rolled his eyes. "Your pen pal from Mrs. Martin's class. You never stopped writing to her, did you?"

"How do you even remember stuff like that? And no, I'm not still writing to her."

I could feel my face getting hot. I hadn't thought I was that easy to read.

"Bullshit," he said. "I asked you last year and you pretended you didn't know what I was talking about." Then, in an exaggerated imitation of me, he said, "Uh … uh … who?"

"That's not what I sounded like."

"You're a bad liar, Luca. I know you're still writing to her. Is she your girlfriend or something?"

My face turned even redder. "No. She's not my girlfriend. She just won't stop writing letters to me. And she's mean, too."

"Really? Why do you still write to her?"

The truth was that I didn't want Naomi to get the last word, but I didn't want Ben to know that I was that petty. I shrugged. "It gives me something to do."

We stopped walking when we reached our classroom. Ben blocked the door. "What does her letter say?"

"I don't know. I haven't opened it yet."

He raised his eyebrows, prompting me to open the letter. I sighed, shrugged off my backpack, and pulled out the letter. I tore open the envelope and read it out loud to Ben.

Dear Luca,

I hope that you wake up tomorrow morning with a small hangnail, and when you pick at it, it just gets bigger and more painful. I hope that it bothers you so much that you just keep picking at it, but it doesn't come off, and you end up pulling a really long sliver of skin off your finger. Then I hope it gets infected, and the only solution is to amputate your whole hand.

That would really make my day.

Love,

Naomi

Ben stared at me, wide-eyed. A few other students had gathered around us, waiting to go inside the classroom.

"You're blocking the door," I reminded him. He stepped into the room, and I followed him to our desks at the back of the class.

"Why would she say that?" he asked once we were both sitting. "That's..." He clutched his hand as if feeling a phantom hangnail after hearing me read Naomi's letter. "That's disturbing."

"She has a way with words." I tucked the letter back into the torn envelope and slipped it into my backpack.

"Does she always write 'Love, Naomi' at the end?"

"Sometimes. Why?"

"It just seems a little weird to end a letter with 'love' after writing something like that."

"I never really thought about it."

Actually, I had thought about it every time I read her letters. I usually copied whatever she had used to close her last letter, but sometimes I wrote something different.

"What are you going to write back?" he asked.

"I don't know yet." I was too tired to come up with anything creative, and I couldn't follow a letter like that with something boring.

"Luca. Ben." We both looked up at our teacher, who had already started the lesson while we were distracted with the letter. "Care to join the rest of us?"

Ben mumbled an apology, and I straightened in my seat. The rest of the school day was uneventful. We were going to be spending the rest of the week taking our state tests, so most of the teachers had us reviewing what we had learned over the year.

As I rode home on my bike that evening, my mind

wandered to Naomi's letter in my backpack. I hadn't decided what to write back yet. I felt like nothing I came up with could top what she wrote about the hangnail. I blamed my lack of imagination on my stress over the upcoming exams. I could probably come up with something better once school was out.

I was surprised to see my mom's car in the driveway when I got home from school that day. She wasn't usually home until after five. I parked my bike in the garage and went inside. I found her sitting at the kitchen table, reading over a document. The whites of her eyes were lined with red.

"What's wrong?"

She seemed startled when she looked up at me. I don't think she heard me come in. She shuffled the sheets of paper in her hand and stuffed them into a large yellow envelope.

"Nothing, sweetie. Everything is fine."

I wasn't convinced. "You look like you were crying."

She forced a smile. "I had just yawned before you came in. It must have made my eyes water."

Her eyes were too wet and red to be from a yawn, but I decided to let it go. I shrugged off my backpack and dropped it onto the floor.

"Homework?" she asked.

I shook my head. "We have exams this week."

"Go put your backpack in your room, then."

I did as she asked. When I returned to the kitchen, the envelope she had on the table was gone. She was standing by the sink, stirring a cup of tea.

"What's for dinner?" I asked.

She turned around and smiled at me. "We're going to order a pizza."

I frowned. "But it's not Friday."

"We'll make an exception," she said. "We can get whatever toppings you want."

"What about Dad?"

My dad didn't usually allow me to pick the toppings. It was always what he wanted.

"Dad won't be coming home tonight." She turned away from me as she said it.

"Oh. Why not?"

She shrugged, made herself look at me, and stretched her lips into a forced smile. "He has a work thing. He might not be home for a few days."

I knew then that something was up. My dad never had 'work things' that prevented him from coming home. That, and my mom was acting weird. I had never seen her try this hard to make it look like everything was normal when her red eyes told a different story. She picked up the cordless phone and handed it to me.

"Do you want to order the pizza?"

"Sure," I said, taking the phone from her. She began to walk away from me. I stared at the phone in my hand for a minute, and then turned to my mother's retreating back. "Mom?"

She stopped, turned slowly, and stared at me with a worried brow. I wanted to press her to be honest with me, but with her looking at me like that, I couldn't bring myself to do it.

"Can I get a soda?" I asked instead.

"Of course, sweetie. Order whatever you want. Tonight is your night."

———

My dad didn't come home the next night, either, or the next. I could have let his absence distract me, but instead I chose to distract myself by studying and working hard on my exams. Writing a response to Naomi's letter was the least of my concerns. I had almost forgotten about her letter until I was emptying out my backpack after eighth grade graduation. I had been disappointed to see that my dad hadn't shown up, but I guess I wasn't all that surprised. I knew that something was going on. I just wished that my mom would tell me.

I was sitting on my bed when I found the letter. Rocky was sitting by my feet. He was a large dog, and took up most of the space on the floor between the bed and the wall. I slipped the letter back out of its envelope and reread it. Coming up with something mean to write back seemed so pointless now. I didn't have the energy to waste on writing back to Naomi. I was in a terrible mood. It was ironic, I realized, that these letters had started because I was in a bad mood that day in fifth grade, and now I could only come up with something mean when I was in a good mood.

There was a light tap on my door just then. I set the letter on my nightstand, and said, "Come in."

The door creaked open. I was surprised to see my dad step into my room. For a moment, I thought that all of my fears and doubts had been unfounded, and that he really had been at a work function that was keeping him away from home for the last several days. I thought that maybe he was coming into my room to apologize for missing my graduation, and that now we could go out to dinner as a family. I had turned down an invitation to a party that Ben was going to in the hopes that my dad might come home tonight. Now I was glad that I had.

But then I saw the look on my dad's face. His brow was furrowed, his lips curved downward. He tucked his hands into his pockets. Any words of greeting that I had for him died before they could get past my lips.

He sat down on the end of my bed and stared down at the floor for a minute. Rocky stretched, stood up, and walked over to him, tail wagging, but my dad ignored the dog. I watched him, waiting for him to say what he came in here to say. It was a while before he finally spoke.

"Your mom said that I should talk to you."

"About what?"

"About what's going on."

I wanted to point out that not even my mom had talked to me about what was going on, but I was afraid that if I did, he might change his mind and not tell me either. He sighed, and then continued.

"Your mom and I are getting a divorce. I want you to know that this has nothing to do with you. Your mom and I— We just can't make it work anymore. We thought it would be best if we went our separate ways, so I, uh, I got a job in Montana. I came back to get my things, and I'm leaving tonight."

I fought the quiver that I felt in my lip. He had always told me that boys shouldn't cry, and even though I was angry with him, I didn't want to disappoint him.

"What about me?" I asked.

"You'll stay here with your mom."

I thought about that for a moment. "Why can't I go with you?"

"Your mom needs you here."

"Will you come back?"

He was quiet for so long that I knew what the answer was before he spoke again. "No."

"Why not?"

"I think that it would be best if I make a clean break. Things with your mom are just… I wasn't going to come back at all, but I needed some of my things. You know I'm not good at saying goodbye."

It occurred to me that in the time that had passed since he sat down on my bed, he hadn't looked at me once. He still hadn't looked at me when he stood up again and left the room. Rocky followed him into the hallway, wagging his tail even though he hadn't been acknowledged. I felt jealous of the dog, so blissfully unaware of how uncaring my dad was. When I heard the front door slam, I knew that it was over. My mother had packed his suitcase so that he wouldn't have to be here any longer than the few minutes it took to tell me that he wasn't part of our family anymore. I locked myself in my bedroom for the rest of the night.

I was angry. Mostly at my dad, but also at my mom for allowing him to leave like that. There were so many cruel things I could have said, but I knew that she was hurting too, and I didn't want to make things worse. I couldn't call Ben because he was at a party. I wasn't sure if I wanted to tell him, anyway. I looked at Naomi's letter on my nightstand. Writing about a hangnail seemed so immature, so stupid, so inconsequential. Then again, none of our letters ever had any substance. We had been writing to each other for almost four years, and it was all stupid, petty, mean, and boring.

I wondered if she looked forward to these stupid letters like I did. I wondered if it would hurt her if I stopped writing back. I wondered if she would comfort me if I opened up to her, or if she would only make fun of me for being anything but mean or boring.

Dear Naomi,
    I hope that at some point in your life there will be someone you

love and respect more than anyone else, if there isn't already. I hope that you think you can count on this person to always be there, and you can tell him anything. And then I hope that one day he decides to leave, and he doesn't even give you the choice to come with him. And he won't even look you in the eye when he tells you that he's leaving. He won't tell you that he loves you, and he won't even say goodbye. He probably never really loved you, and he's fine with not saying goodbye because it was all an act, and the joke is on you for believing it.

You have plenty of good memories with him, but he just shits all over them. Now you can't remember the good times without also remembering the way that he left, how he wouldn't even look at you or tell you that he loved you, because he didn't. Because you're such a shitty person that you don't deserve a real goodbye. And you'll be left wondering, for the rest of your life, if the people who claim to love you really do, or if it's all a lie and they're just going to leave one day like he did.

Don't be surprised if I don't write another letter to you. This is stupid.

Bye.

Luca

Dear Luca,

This must be the tenth time you've said that you're not going to write to me again so I don't really think I believe you. But just in case I don't hear from you again, I want you to know that if anyone ever did those things to me, it would be because he's a shitty person and he doesn't deserve me. Not the other way around. And if I saw someone treating one of my friends like that, I would kick him in the balls.

Love,

Naomi

Chapter Five

IN SEARCH OF BETTER BEACHES

Naomi

"You were right!"

Anne startles me yet again, and I can tell by the smile on her face when I turn around that she knows it.

"You need to invest in some louder shoes before you give someone a heart attack. What was I right about?"

She flings an unopened envelope onto my desk. It's been three days since we got the first one. "You said he was going to send another letter. You were right."

"I didn't expect it to be this soon."

I pick up the envelope, disappointed to see that he still hasn't included a return address. I rip it open.

Dear Naomi,

I can just imagine how annoyed you are that you can't write back to me. You always had to get the last word, didn't you? Maybe if you had accepted my invitation, you wouldn't be stuck wondering how to write back to me now. Oh well. Your loss.

Love,

Luca

Anne reads the letter over my shoulder. She raises an eyebrow when she gets to the end. "Love?"

"That's how he closed every letter. Well, almost every letter. I'm pretty sure he did it to be ironic."

"He didn't close the last letter like that," she says. "Maybe he's not trying to be ironic anymore. I mean, you were writing to him for how many years?"

"He's married." I realize that I've never said it out loud before. I hear the words come out of my mouth, but it sounds like someone else is saying them. The two words echo inside my head even as Anne continues the conversation.

"That didn't stop him from writing to you."

"Actually, I think that's exactly why he stopped writing to me."

"Maybe he got divorced."

I don't know why the idea of Luca being single makes my heart rate pick up. It must be because that means he can write to me again. I put on a smile so that Anne can't see my inner turmoil. "Oh, yay! Lucky me."

Anne rolls her eyes, still smiling. "What does he mean by accepting his invitation?"

"I'm not sure. He had dared me to meet him a couple times over the years, but it was always part of some dumb joke. He also asked if we could be friends on Facebook, and I said no. Maybe that's what he's talking about."

"He's taunting you. I think he wants you to figure out his address and write back."

"How am I supposed to do that? He must have known that

I would try to look him up after I got his last letter. He probably deactivated his Facebook before he sent it."

"Try his childhood home. You still have that address, right?"

I shake my head. "That's not going to work. I looked it up on PeopleFinder. Some other family lives there now."

"Maybe one of his old neighbors still lives nearby. If someone on his street was close with his family, they might know how to track him down."

"What am I supposed to do? Send a letter to every house on the street and wait to see if someone writes back?"

"That's one option."

"That's the only option," I correct her.

"Well…"

"Well, what?"

"You could show up in person and ask."

I laugh. "It's in San Diego, Anne. There are a few thousand miles between here and there."

She purses her lips. "I've always kind of wanted to go to San Diego."

I frown. "Why?"

"I heard their beaches are better."

"Seriously?"

She shrugs. "I just want to find out if it's true."

"I'm not driving all the way to California to get an address for an old pen pal. Sorry – penemy."

Anne looks taken aback. "Drive? Who said anything about driving? We could fly out tonight and be back before the end of the weekend."

The thought of flying makes me nervous, but I don't want to tell Anne that. "That sounds expensive."

"I bet it's not that expensive. Do you have anything better to do this weekend?"

"I have a date with my hot neighbor."

"Oh, right. I forgot. Where are you going?"

I shrug. "I don't know. We haven't talked about it."

"You guys live in the same building."

I think about how we were stuck in the elevator together. I had thought about sending him a text that afternoon, but I chickened out. I wonder if he's waiting for me to make the next move, or if my behavior in the elevator freaked him out.

"Do you think I should cancel? Will it be weird if the date doesn't go well and we still have to see each other in the lobby for the next month?"

"First of all, that's a really stupid reason to cancel. And second, you're buying a house next month. It's not like you would have to face him forever."

I stand up and gather my belongings, ready to head home. Anne is finished with her shift, too, so she follows me outside.

"You should probably figure out the details of your date," she says when we reach the parking garage.

"Yeah, probably."

"Or…"

"Or what?"

"Or maybe you could put it off until next weekend?"

"You really want to go to San Diego that badly?"

"It'll be fun. Plus, I need an excuse to get out and do something this weekend. All I ever have to look forward to is meeting men I have no chemistry with just because we both swiped right on Tinder. I could use some girl time."

I let out a sigh. I spent the last two years trying to get Luca out of my mind, and now he's back, front and center. I never knew it could be so hard to get over someone I've never met in real life. But that's the thing. He's only ever been words on paper. I know that if I track him down, it will never be the same. Maybe that's what I need.

I think of the date I'm supposed to go on with Jake. What terrible timing.

I reach my car and open the door. Anne stops walking, waiting at the rear of my car, watching me.

"I do need to figure out Luca's address," I say.

"Imagine how shocked he'll be when you send him a letter. I don't think he'll be expecting you to go all the way to San Diego to figure it out."

"You're right. If I don't figure it out, he'll just keep sending these letters to the news station, taunting me."

"He probably thinks he's already won after getting rid of his Facebook profile. Are you going to let him win?"

I shake my head. "Hell no. Let's go to San Diego."

Anne doesn't try to hide her excitement. "I'll call you when I get home." She jumps up and down like a little girl who's just been told she's going to Disney World.

I laugh, and get into my car as she heads to her own car. I love how invested she is in trying to find my pen pal.

When I walk into my building, I spot Jake checking his mail. He looks over his shoulder when he hears the front door, then does a double-take when he sees me. His mouth widens into a grin, making my heart rate pick up. It's been a long time since anyone has looked this happy to see me. His dark hair is a little bit messy. I have this weird desire to run my fingers through it. I tuck my hands into my pockets to keep myself from doing anything embarrassing.

He's wearing another T-shirt that hugs his biceps. I've never felt so jealous of a shirt. He closes his mailbox and turns his whole body to face me. I start to regret committing to going to San Diego this weekend. I wonder if it's too late to cancel, but I know that Anne is probably halfway done booking tickets by now.

"Hey," I say as I step toward the mailboxes.

"Hey."

He maintains eye contact with me as I step toward him. I notice that one side of his mouth lifts a little higher when he smiles. His eyes also seem bluer, but maybe it's just the lighting. It's hard to look away from him. I don't think I've ever met a guy as physically attractive as this one. I realize that we've been standing in front of the mailboxes, staring at each other without a word for several seconds. I clear my throat.

"So, uh, about this weekend." I don't realize how hard this is going to be until I'm forced to say it. "Something else came up. Can I take a raincheck?"

"Oh." His smile falters. Both sides of his mouth are now even with each other. The smile is still there, but it's not as bright anymore. "Yeah, of course. I hope everything is okay."

"Everything is fine. I'm just going on a last-minute trip to San Diego." I roll my eyes in an attempt to convey that the meaning of the trip is no big deal. "But we can go out next weekend. Or, I mean, whenever you're free."

"Next weekend should work. San Diego, huh? Is it a work-related trip?"

"Not exactly. Well, not at all, actually. I'm going with Anne." I don't want to make him feel jealous by telling him that I'm trying to find another guy, especially when I'm postponing our date because of this. I try to think of another excuse. "She, uh, she wants to see what the beaches are like. She thinks the beaches might be better there than in Miami."

It's a half-truth, but I still feel bad for saying it.

"Ah. So it's a research trip."

I laugh. "You could say that."

"I hear the sand is whiter here."

"I wouldn't know. I've never been to the west coast. I can't imagine they have as much seaweed on their beaches."

"You'll have to let me know what the consensus is."

"I will. See you around?"

The corner of his mouth tilts back up, completing his crooked smile. "I'll walk you upstairs. Unless you want to join me in the elevator?"

I laugh. "Not a chance."

We head into the stairwell. I don't realize until we're halfway up the first flight of stairs that I forgot to check the mail.

"It must suck having to go up and down these stairs carrying your groceries in," he says.

"It's better than the alternative. What if I got stuck in the elevator every time and all of my milk products spoiled?"

"Good point. But at least if you got trapped with all of your groceries, you would have something to eat besides your own foot."

"I don't have that many groceries anyway. I'm only one person. I can carry it all in one trip."

"Ah. You're one of those get-it-all-in-one-trip kind of people."

"I don't trust anyone who isn't." I turn to look at him as we reach the third floor. "Oh no. Please don't tell me you like making multiple trips. Do you only carry one bag at a time?"

He frowns. "Is that a deal breaker?"

I nod. "Obviously."

"Well, you're in luck then, because I practically invented getting it all in one trip." He ignores my eyeroll. "Try carrying in all the groceries for a family of six without any help."

I raise an eyebrow. "Okay, now you're just showing off. Big family, huh?"

He smiles. "Yeah. What about you?"

I shake my head. "It was just me growing up. I always wished I had siblings."

"It can be chaotic," he says, "but I wouldn't change a thing."

I find myself hoping that I'll get to meet his family. I know this is absurd, because we haven't even been on our first date yet.

My cell starts to ring. I pull it out of my purse to see who is calling.

"Need to take that?" he asks.

I sigh. "It's Anne. She's trying to plan our trip."

I hope that he'll tell me to cancel the trip and spend the whole weekend with him. I want him to tell me to forget about that guy who used to write letters to me and move on with my life. Even if he knew all this, I'm not sure I could. I need closure. I can't leave this thing with Luca open-ended.

"Have fun," Jake says. "I'll see you when you're back."

I watch him go up the stairs, and then I answer Anne's call, balancing my phone on my shoulder as I open the door to the third-floor hallway.

"So, I'm looking online and there's a nonstop flight to San Diego that leaves in four hours for less than three hundred dollars."

"That's not bad at all." For some reason I always imagined that plane tickets cost thousands of dollars.

"It's a pretty good deal," she says. "We'll get there tonight, and we can book a double room – unless you want separate rooms? – and then look for your penemy's street first thing in the morning. If that goes well, we can spend the rest of the day at the beach, then catch a redeye back home."

"Okay. What's a redeye?"

"Are you serious? All those years in college and you never learned what a redeye is?"

"Is it an airplane? I've never flown before, Anne."

I can hear her laughing at me on the other end. "It's an overnight flight. We'll get home early Sunday morning. That way we don't have to pay for two nights at the hotel."

"Count me in. How do I get my ticket? Do I buy it at the airport?"

"You've seriously never flown before?"

"If you keep mocking me, I'm going to back out."

"Fine. But no. I mean, you can buy the ticket at the airport, but it's quicker if you just do it online. I can send you a link."

My hands are sweating when I hang up the phone. Anne sends the link right away, and I click on it. I can't believe I'm about to go to an airport and try to get on a plane. I put my information into the form and find that it's surprisingly easy to buy my ticket. I'm worried that as soon as I hit the button to confirm my order, an alarm will sound, the screen will flash red, and I'll be denied my ticket. Maybe my apartment will even be swarmed with TSA agents. My finger hovers over the button. I'm getting palpitations. I close my eyes and tap the screen.

Nothing happens. No alarm sounds, and no one barges into my apartment. I open my eyes and see that my finger missed the button. I tap it again and wait, holding my breath, as the page turns white, then reloads with my ticket confirmation. I exhale heavily, and then remind myself that this was the easy part. Now I have to get through the airport.

Chapter Six

DEMONIC HUSKY EYES

I'm on the sidewalk outside my building, my backpack slung over my shoulder, waiting for Anne to pick me up. A young girl is doing cartwheels back and forth in front of me. I'm terrible at guessing ages, but I'd say this kid is probably five or six. Or maybe ten.

When she does a fourth cartwheel in front of me, I look around, wondering where her parents are. No one seems to be taking ownership of the young sidewalk acrobat. I watch with a raised brow as she stops cartwheeling and crouches down next to a bush lining the sidewalk. Then, as if knowing she's being watched, she stands up and turns around, facing me.

"Look at this!"

I have no choice but to look at the kid's extended hand which is suddenly a lot closer to my face than I'm comfortable with. On the kid's finger is what looks like a fake mustache. I frown, trying to figure out why the kid is showing me this, when I notice the mustache is moving.

"What's that?" I ask, taken aback.

"It's a caterpillar."

"Oh. Lovely." It's the hairiest caterpillar I've ever seen. I didn't even know caterpillars could be so hairy.

"Do you want to hold it, Gnome?"

It takes me a second to realize the kid is not calling me a gnome, but is trying to say my name.

"Maybe you should put that thing down," I suggest. "It might be poisonous."

"You're silly. Caterpillars aren't poisonous." The kid places her other hand in front of the caterpillar. We both watch as the caterpillar moves from one hand to the other. "This one is going to turn into a moth."

"Is that so?" I look around again. Anne should be here any minute, and I'm afraid that once I'm gone, this kid won't have any adult supervision. "Where are your parents?"

"My mom is cleaning the bathroom. She doesn't know I'm out here."

"You should probably go back inside before she realizes you're missing and starts to worry."

The kid grimaces. "Can I bring the caterpillar inside?"

I think about that for a moment. "Better put it back on that bush where you found it. That way it can build a cocoon and become a butterfly."

"Moth," she corrects me.

"Right."

Anne honks her horn as she pulls up to the curb. The kid runs back to the bush to release the caterpillar. I toss my backpack into Anne's backseat, then watch from the passenger seat as the kid disappears into the apartment building.

"Whose kid is that?"

"No idea," I say. "She lives in the building and thinks my name is Gnome."

"Gnome? I'll have to remember that."

"Please don't."

"Are you excited to fly for the first time, Gnome?"

"I'm a little bit nervous, Anette."

Anne cringes. "Okay, fine, sorry. Forget I ever called you that." We're both quiet for a moment as she drives us to the airport. "There's no need to be nervous, though. Do you know how rare a plane crash is?"

"That's not what I'm nervous about." As soon as I say it, I regret it. Being afraid of a plane crash is a lot easier to explain than what actually has me rethinking this trip.

Anne frowns at me. "What are you nervous about then?"

"Nothing. It's stupid."

"You brought it up."

"Let's just drop it. I'm sure everything will be fine." I don't actually believe what I'm saying, but I have to at least pretend to be normal.

"You're afraid you're going to get sick, aren't you?" she asks. "Do you get motion sickness?"

"Yeah, that's it," I lie. "I can't ride a rollercoaster without throwing up."

"You'll be fine. I used to throw up every time I flew. I can teach you what I did to overcome it."

"Thanks." Now I have two things to worry about. I hadn't even considered that if I made it onto the plane, I might throw up all over myself.

We make it to the airport, and Anne parks her car in the lot. I take a deep breath. I'm more nervous now than I was when I first got into her car.

"I forgot my passport," I say. "It's probably too late to go get it, right? We should just head back."

Anne rolls her eyes and grabs onto my arm, pulling me

toward the building. "You don't need a passport to fly to California."

I feel weightless as I let her drag me toward the sliding doors that open into the airport. I'm sweating and yet I'm cold at the same time. I'm sure that if she looked back at me, she'd be startled by how pale I've become. As we head into the security line, I watch the TSA agents ahead of us. When one of them meets my eye, I look away, hoping that I'm not drawing too much attention to myself.

I lean over to Anne as we reach the X-ray machines. "What if they don't let me through?" I whisper.

She laughs. It's clear she thinks I'm joking. "Do they have a reason to not let you through?"

"I don't know. Maybe. They're not going to, like, make me take off my clothes, are they?"

She scans the line ahead of us. "I don't see anyone else getting naked. I'm pretty sure that's what the body scanners are for. But I won't complain if that guy with the biceps tattoo tells me he needs to pat me down."

"What guy?" I don't remember noticing a tattoo on any of the TSA agents.

"Blue shirt," she says.

"He's not a TSA agent, Anne. He's…" I watch as Tattoo Guy unfolds a stroller and a woman carrying a toddler lowers the kid into it. "He's a passenger. *And* he's married."

"Still wouldn't complain."

I jab her in the arm with my elbow. "You're terrible."

I'm too entertained by Anne's inappropriate remark to realize that I've made it to the front of the line. I pass through the body scanner, then hold my breath when the TSA agent tells me to wait. I realize that all my fears are about to come true. Someone is going to pull me aside and arrest me or tell me that I need to—

"Okay, you're good to go," the agent says before I can even finish my train of terrified thoughts. I hurry to the conveyor belt and grab my things. Anne comes through the body scanner a moment later, and then we continue through the airport.

We stop at one of the restaurants for a bite to eat, and then we make it to our gate just in time to board the plane. We're seated all the way at the back of the plane.

My phone buzzes almost as soon as I sit down. I look at the screen and feel a jolt of excitement when I see a new text message from Jake.

Hot Neighbor: The elevator just shook while I was riding down. Made me think of you.

I smile. I wonder if he's making this up just for an excuse to talk to me.

Naomi: Did you get stuck?
Hot Neighbor: Nope. It only shook a little.
Hot Neighbor: Are you on the plane yet?
Naomi: Just sat down. They just announced that we're supposed to turn our phones off.

"How did Demonic Husky Eyes take it when you canceled?"

Anne's question snaps my attention away from my phone. I'm so confused by the combination of words she just said that it sounds like she's speaking another language. I frown, and when she doesn't repeat herself or attempt to clarify, I'm forced to ask.

"What did you just say?"

"When you canceled," she repeats.

"I heard that. I have no idea what the rest of that sentence meant."

"Demonic Husky Eyes," she says with a roll of her eyes. "You know. Your hot neighbor with the super intense blue eyes who you were supposed to be on a date with right now?"

"Oh." I shrug. "He took it fine."

"You did tell him, right?"

"Of course I did. I was just confused by what you called him."

"Come on. You don't think he has the eyes of a demonic husky?"

"I mean, now that you mention it, I guess I can see it. But does it have to be demonic? That makes him sound creepy."

"If you would just tell me his name, I wouldn't have to call him Demonic Husky Eyes at all."

"His name is Jake."

She looks over my shoulder at my phone. When she sees how I have his contact saved, she rolls her eyes. "Seriously? I'm sure a guy that looks like that doesn't need his ego stroked."

"I'm only planning on having a little fun with him until I'm out of the building. Besides, he's the one who saved his number in my phone like this."

"If you're gonna go with a nickname, Demonic Husky Eyes sounds better," she says.

"I don't like the Demonic part. Maybe just Husky Eyes?"

She purses her lips, frowning. Then she snatches my phone.

"Hey. What are you doing?"

I watch as she changes his name from *Hot Neighbor* to *Husky Eyes.* Then she powers my phone off before I can do anything about it. She hands my phone back to me, and then turns to the window.

"Look at that," she says. "We're in the air."

"Oh. Wow. You're right." I had felt when the plane lifted off, but I was too absorbed in my conversation with Anne to say anything about it.

"See? It's not so bad."

I watch the tiny houses and cars below us for a moment, and then I reach under the seat in front of me and open my backpack. I pull out a folder.

"What's that?" Anne asks.

"Reading material to keep us entertained for the next few hours." I open the folder, revealing a stack of letters that I've chosen to let Anne read.

Her eyes widen, and she picks up the first page. "These are from Luca?" she asks.

"These are all the letters he wrote to me in high school."

She reads the first one, frowns, and then barks out a laugh that turns a few heads in front of us. "What did you say to that?" she asks. She picks up the next page, disappointed to see that it's not my response, but another letter from Luca.

"He never sent any of mine back, so all I have are the ones from him. But I remember these like I just got them yesterday. I can probably tell you what I wrote back."

Chapter Seven

THE POOR BLIND WOMAN

Luca

The thing about Naomi was that no matter how mean I was, or how terrible of a mood I was in when I wrote to her, she always wrote back. And I was really, really mean. For a year after my dad left, I used her as a virtual punching bag. I never told her what happened because I didn't want her to pity me like everyone else did. If I vented to Ben or to my girlfriend, they would offer solutions that never worked or apologies even though they did nothing wrong. But when I vented to Naomi in the form of a mean letter – usually something that I wished I could say to my dad – she fired back with something equally mean or disturbing, and would often make me laugh.

We were in high school when the tone of our letters began to change. Gone were the innocent insults of children without the life experience to back up what we were saying. I'm not sure at what point we crossed that line, or who crossed it first, but neither of us was backing down.

Dear Luca,

I'm supposed to be working on an essay right now, but I can't concentrate because my cousins are in my room giving each other makeovers and trying to talk me into getting one. Courtney is tweezing Bella's eyebrows and Bella is screaming. It's really hard to write about the civil war with this going on, but it's making me think of you.

I would love to pluck each of your leg hairs one by one with a pair of tweezers. It seems like it would be really satisfying to watch you cry out in pain. Then I hope that you get an ingrown hair when it all starts growing back, and when you pick at it, it becomes infected and you end up losing your leg. Then when your doctor gives you a prosthetic, it's a couple of inches too short which gives you an awful limp for the rest of your life.

Love,

Naomi

Dear Naomi,

My mom tweezes her eyebrows and always talks about getting herself waxed. I don't understand why girls put themselves through that much pain. Just use a razor or something. You should let your cousins give you that makeover, though. I'm sure you really need it.

I want to know why you're so obsessed with my leg hair and the idea of me losing a limb. Is it because you secretly want to come to San Diego and take care of me? I'll let you tweeze my legs if it means I have you on your knees in front of me.

Love,

Luca

Dear Luca,

It's gross that you always have to make everything sexual. I guess I'm not surprised since you never get laid. You'll probably be a virgin until you're fifty and some poor blind woman at the nursing home accidentally fondles you because she thinks you're her husband. You're lucky that her husband also has a tiny dick, so she doesn't even notice the difference.

Love,

Naomi

Dear Naomi,

You're wrong. I'm not a virgin, and I actually have had plenty of girlfriends, so I'm not going to end up alone at a nursing home like you. You'll probably be that blind woman playing with the wrong micro-penis.

Also, I don't have a small dick. I can send a picture next time if you want to see for yourself?

Love,

Luca

Dear Luca,

You probably go through so many girlfriends because you're really bad in bed. Just because you have a big dick doesn't mean you're good in bed, and going through a lot of girlfriends doesn't mean you're not going to end up alone. Also, I'll pass on the dick pic. I don't want my poor mailbox to get chlamydia.

Love,

Naomi

By the end of my junior year of high school, many of our letters had turned a bit flirty like that. Or maybe I only imagined that she was flirting with me because I was a horny teenager. Ben had been dating Yvette since freshman year, and he spent all his time with her. We only had one class together junior year, so that was the only time we really saw each other.

Even then, it wasn't like it used to be. He had made new friends in other classes, and I started to feel like an outcast. I had never been any good at making new friends, and I guess I always counted on Ben to be my best friend.

Unlike Ben, whose relationship goals were for the long-term, I wasn't interested in dating any girl for longer than a week or two. It had been fun for a few years, but by junior year I had dated half the girls in my class. The other half either weren't attractive or I was off-limits to them because I had already dated their friend. I ended up spending most of the year alone. It was great for my report card, but it was lonely.

At the end of that year, it seemed like all of my friends were joining some website called Facebook that my mother had been a part of for years. I had been reluctant to join at first, but I hopped on the bandwagon and created an account. My profile picture was of me and Ben and a couple of his friends at the beach.

It was a mix of boredom, mostly, and a little bit of loneliness that had me typing 'Naomi Light' into the search bar late one night. I had been writing to her for years, and I wondered what she looked like. I hesitated before pressing 'enter'. I wasn't sure if I really wanted to know what she looked like. I had implied that she was ugly in many of my letters to her, but I had no idea if she really was. I was afraid that if I knew, it might change things. When I pictured her inside my head, I imagined her being cute. This was part of the reason it was fun to flirt with her. Would I still want to write to her if I knew she looked like an ogre?

I hit the key anyway and waited for the search results to populate. A few results came up – mostly old women – but there was one icon of what looked like a teenage girl who lived in Oklahoma City. I clicked on her profile, and found myself holding my breath. This couldn't be the girl I'd been writing letters to for years. I double-checked her profile, confirming that she lived in Oklahoma City and was in the same graduating class as me. Then I clicked on her profile picture to get a better view.

Naomi had golden-red hair and fair skin with a few light freckles dusting her nose. Her eyes were dark blue, her lips were full and pink, and her teeth were perfectly white and straight. She had dimples in each cheek when she smiled. I clicked to see the next photo. She was wearing a track uniform. She was fit, with toned legs, standing in the middle of a group of other girls. She stood out to me as the prettiest one. I felt my mouth drop open. I looked at the next photo, and kept clicking to see more. I wanted to see every photo she had ever taken.

I couldn't believe that all this time, I had been writing to *her*. She made the hottest girl at my own high school look like a mushroom in comparison. I suddenly wished that I could take back all the mean things I had ever written to her.

I considered sending her a friend request, but then she would know that I had looked her up. I wasn't sure why I didn't want her to know that. Instead of sending a friend request, I picked up a sheet of paper and a pen.

Dear Naomi,

I finally made a Facebook profile for myself. I'm pretty sure I was the last person in my class to jump on board. It's a little weird logging on and seeing all these random thoughts my mom is posting on there. She's always the first person to comment on all of my photos. Sometimes when I log on, I have fifty new notifications, and for a second, I think that I must be popular, but when I click on the icon, it's just my mom spamming my page with likes and comments.

I think my mom might be my only real friend. Isn't that a little pathetic?

Do you think we should be friends on Facebook? I mean, assuming that you have an account on there. Let me know and I'll look you up and add you.

Love,

Luca

Dear Luca,

What makes you think I would ever want to be friends with you on Facebook? Don't bother sending me a friend request. Don't even look me up, okay? Oh, and be nicer to your mom.

Xoxo,

Naomi

It wasn't the response that I expected. I had thought she would read my letter and then, out of curiosity, she would hop on Facebook and look me up. She would inevitably see that I was also hotter than any guy she went to school with and would send me a friend request or, at the very least, tell me that it was okay to send her one.

I was so bummed out by her letter that I put it aside and didn't write back for a month. I guess I kind of hoped that my lack of a response would make her change her mind, or maybe she would look me up and realize what she was missing out on. But that didn't happen.

Chapter Eight

HOW TO BECOME A STALKER

Naomi

"Why didn't you want to be his friend?"

Anne had just finished reading all the letters Luca sent to me during the first three years of high school, while I read over her shoulder and recounted to the best of my memory what I had written back.

I shrug. "I don't know. I guess looking back on it, it does seem pretty cold of me."

"Weren't you curious about what he looked like?"

I had looked him up after he sent that letter. I would be lying if I said that I didn't have a little crush on Luca at some point, but I would never admit that to Anne. His page was private, so all I could see was his profile picture where he stood with a group of other guys on a beach, all wearing sunglasses and crossing their arms over their chests like they thought they were hot shit. And they were – at least high-school-me thought they were hot – but that didn't matter.

"I had a boyfriend at the time that Luca sent that letter. I didn't really care what he looked like. His profile was private anyway."

I leave out the fact that I visited his profile many times, trying to figure out which guy in the picture was Luca, and hoping that he would change his settings so I could snoop a little more without him knowing.

"You're crazy," she says. "I would have accepted his friend request."

I think about it for a moment, trying to remember my rationale for rejecting Luca back then. "You read his letters," I remind her. "He was mean and offensive, and I didn't want him leaving comments like that on my Facebook page where everyone could see it."

There was also something about writing a letter and putting it in the mailbox that I enjoyed, and I was afraid that if Luca and I found a way to talk outside of those letters, it would be over. I wasn't ready to put an end to that era. I guess I'm still not ready, seeing as now I'm on a plane to find him after not hearing from him for two years.

"I guess that's fair. Still, I would have at least added him for a minute just to see what he looked like. In fact, I've Facebook-stalked almost every person I've ever emailed at work."

"Seriously? Why?"

"I like to put a face to the name."

"I admit that I'm curious now. Do you think he deleted his Facebook page just to make it harder to find him?"

Anne nods. "And probably paid to have his information removed from PeopleFinder. Either that, or Luca Pichler isn't his real name."

"It has to be his real name. That's the name the elementary school gave me when we started the pen pal program."

"True. If that's the case, then he really put in effort to make himself hard to find."

"That's okay," I say. "We don't need Facebook or public records to find him. We'll stalk him the old-fashioned way."

I kind of wish I had thought of doing this sooner, but I figured there was a reason behind him cutting me off: his wife. It probably would have been a little weird if some random woman (me) showed up at their door looking for Luca. Then again, maybe he's still with her. Maybe it will still be weird. I have no idea what I'm walking into.

"This is going to be so much fun," Anne says. She places the letters back into the folder and then tucks it into my backpack while we wait for the plane to land. There are still plenty more letters to read at the airport tomorrow night.

"What if this is a bad idea? What if he moved back into his childhood home, and when I show up at his door, he has me arrested for stalking him? Or worse. What if I get pepper sprayed?"

"Highly unlikely," she says. "Besides, I bet he had to do a little stalking of his own to figure out where you work now."

I think about Luca going through all the trouble that Anne and I are going through to find him. I wonder what his motivations are, and why I'm finally hearing from him after two years. Why now? It feels a little like whiplash to be forgotten for so long just to hear from him again and still not be able to write back. I guess 'forgotten' might not be the right word, though. We had both moved away and I imagined he had moved on with his life. Meanwhile, he was always lurking in the back of my mind in some way or another.

It doesn't seem fair that it's so hard to find him now. I imagine it was probably a little easier for him, seeing as my name and face are on the news every morning.

Anne got me up early to track him down, and now here we are at eight in the morning, standing in front of the house he grew up in. It's a pale blue house with white shutters. There's a mailbox on the corner of the lot. I wonder if this is the same mailbox that housed the countless letters I sent to this address over the years.

"It couldn't be that hard," I say. "All he had to do was look up my name and find every weather report I've ever done. He didn't have to fly all the way to Miami to figure that out."

"Well, he's not giving you much of a choice but to do it this way."

"I'm sure that will go over well in court. 'It's not my fault, your honor; he gave me no choice but to stalk him!'"

Anne rolls her eyes. "Calm down. The worst that will happen is he'll get a restraining order against you. And I doubt he'd even do that. Why go out of his way to find you and write to you if he was going to freak out and get a restraining order?"

I know that she's right, but I'm stalling. I take a deep breath and watch the house a moment longer. I try to picture Luca as a kid running out that front door and heading to the mailbox to see if there was anything for him. I wonder if he was excited to check the mail like I was. There were times when I wondered if he actually hated me. Some of his letters were so mean, and so personal, that I wondered why he even bothered writing to me at all. Sometimes he even threatened not to write to me again, but he never made good on those threats.

I wonder if he was just an angry kid. It sure seemed like it sometimes, but maybe he simply enjoyed messing with me. I picture him getting older and still coming through that front door to check the mail, looking for my letters. It's hard to imagine since I don't know what he looks like. I picture him differently every time he comes through the door. Sometimes he has blond hair, sometimes brown. Sometimes he's tall, and sometimes he's short.

"Are you scared?" Anne asks the question quietly, pulling me out of my daydream.

"A little bit."

"No one is going to pepper spray you. Just go up and knock. You're probably freaking them out just standing there and staring at their house."

I sigh, and force myself to take the steps up to the front porch. I ring the doorbell and hold my breath.

A woman appears on the other side of the screen door. She pushes it open and stares at us expectantly. "Can I help you?"

"Hi," I say, struggling to find my voice. "I was wondering if you know anything about the family who lived in this house before you."

She shrugs. "The Jones family? Are you from the census or something?"

"No, I just … how long did the Jones family live here? Was there someone named Luca? Luca Pichler?"

"No idea. I don't know them. Just get their mail sometimes."

"What about your neighbors? Do you know how long they've lived here?"

She sighs. I can tell she's impatient. "I don't know. I've only lived here a year. I don't really talk to the neighbors."

"Okay. Thanks. Sorry for bothering you."

The woman disappears back into the house, letting the

screen door close behind her. Anne and I exchange a shrug, and then step off the porch and back onto the sidewalk.

"I figured she wouldn't know anything about him," I say. "He hasn't written to me from this address since high school."

"There has to be a neighbor around who's lived here long enough to remember him or his family," Anne suggests. "Where do you want to start?"

"Let's start with the immediate neighbors first."

As we make our way down the block, my phone vibrates with a new text message. For a moment, I forget about the name change Anne did in my phone, and I'm confused about why I'm getting a message from someone named Husky Eyes.

Husky Eyes: How's San Diego? Better than Miami?
Naomi: It's beautiful here. I might never come back.
Husky Eyes: You can't make a big decision like that until after you've been on a date with me.
Naomi: You must be really sure of yourself to think one date can make me rethink such a big decision.
Husky Eyes: It won't be just one date.

I read his message again, trying to figure out how such a simple sentence can make my whole body feel warmer. I start to feel lightheaded, and I realize that I've been holding my breath. I don't know how I'm supposed to respond to a statement like that. I release my breath, and then I start typing.

Naomi: Oh? Someone is really confident. What if you end up hating me?
Husky Eyes: Not gonna happen.
Naomi: What are you doing today?

Husky Eyes: *Just hanging with my family, wishing I was walking on the beach with this really cute weathergirl I met...*

I'm startled when Anne grabs my arm, yanking me to the other side of the sidewalk.

"Earth to Naomi," she says. "Did you really not see that telephone pole?"

"What? Oh." I look behind us, realizing that she just saved me from walking right into a wooden pole.

"What were you smiling about?" she asks, gesturing toward my phone. Then her eyes narrow with a knowing smile. "It's Husky Eyes, isn't it? Is he sending you sexy pictures?"

I laugh. "No. I mean, yes, it's him, but no, he's not sending me pictures." My phone buzzes again. I slip it into my pocket without looking at it just in case he decides to contradict me. "Come on. Let's go to that house over there."

The last house on the corner has overgrown shrubs that make it impossible to take the walkway to the front door. We have to step around the hedge to get to the porch. We haven't had much luck with all the vacation rentals on this street, but at least this house doesn't look quite as meticulously maintained as the rentals, so I'm hopeful that this tenant has lived here a while.

There's no doorbell, so I knock on the wooden front door and wait. A small chirpy dog barks somewhere inside the house. A moment later, the door opens, revealing a frail older woman with glasses that make her eyes look huge. The dog is still barking from a back room inside the house.

"Good morning, ma'am," I say. "I hope I'm not interrupting you."

"Not at all," she says. She smiles, showing dentures that look a little too big for her small face.

"My name is Naomi, and this is my friend Anne. We're trying to find someone who used to live on this street. I was hoping you could tell me about how long you've lived here?"

"I'm Carol Bell," she says, shaking each of our hands. "I could tell you how long I've lived here, but I don't want to give away how old I am." She gives me a cheeky smile and a wink. "I've lived right here my whole life. My daddy built this house, you know."

Anne elbows me, and when I look at her, she's bouncing with excitement. I turn back to Carol.

"That's incredible," I say. "It's a beautiful house. I bet you love living so close to the ocean."

Carol nods. "I wouldn't have it any other way."

I turn and point to Luca's old house. "You see that blue house down there in the middle of the street?"

She leans out of the doorway to see where I'm pointing.

"Would you happen to remember a family who lived there several years ago? Last name was Pichler. They would have lived there for at least eight years, probably longer. They had a kid named Luca."

She twists her lips, thinking. "Ah, yes," she says after a moment. "I remember the Pichlers. Real nice family, but they had it rough. I've worried about that boy. You know him? How is he?"

I wonder what she means about his family having it rough. This seems like a nice neighborhood, and Luca never complained of a rough childhood in his letters.

"Luca was my pen pal, and we lost track of each other over the years. I was hoping you could tell me about him or his family. I'd love to be able to write to him again."

"Oh, that is just so sweet," Carol says. She purses her lips, her eyes wandering back across the street to the blue house. When she continues, her tone has changed. "Lydia and that husband of hers were always fighting. I don't think he ever hit her, but there were screaming matches in the street that would wake the whole neighborhood. The cops were called a few times, but neither of them was ever arrested. Then Mr. Pichler left one day and never came back. It was probably for the best, but I think the kid took it pretty hard. It was a few years later that Lydia got sick. I can't imagine being a kid and losing both of my parents before I'm even out of school."

Carol says all of this nonchalantly, as if this should have been common knowledge since I was Luca's pen pal. I stare at her, dumbstruck, trying to process what she's saying. I didn't know that Luca's father left him or that his mother got sick. He never mentioned any of this in his letters. But then again, maybe he did in his own roundabout way. I think about the few letters that were harsher than the others, the ones that were so mean that it didn't feel like a game anymore. I don't think I understood the extent of what he was going through at the time. I decide that when I get home, I'm going to reread all of the letters. There has to be something that I missed.

"That had to be tough," Anne says. "So, his mother..."

"Passed away," Carol says.

"What about Luca?" Anne asks. I'm grateful to her for asking these questions, because I'm too caught up in my thoughts about Luca to think of what to ask next. I can't even begin to imagine what he went through. I'm thinking about him in a whole new light now. I had always wondered if he was an angry kid. I wondered why he was always so mean. I never guessed that he had been faced with so much pain and loss at such a young age. I'm sad that I didn't know any better.

I wish I had been able to read between the lines and say something that might have comforted him. But maybe that would have ruined what we had.

I hope that he had someone he could confide in.

"By the time I heard of Lydia's passing, Luca was already gone. I never heard from him again, but I didn't expect to. To him, I was just the old lady who lived down the street." Carol turns to me. "Is that the last time you heard from him too?"

I shake my head, swallowing around a lump in my throat. "He continued to write to me for years after that. He was doing really well when I last heard from him. He was getting married." I force a smile.

Carol's eyes light up. "That's wonderful news. I never stopped worrying about that boy. I'm so glad to hear that he's okay."

"I was hoping that you might know where he lives now, but I'm guessing that you don't. You don't happen to know anyone else in his family, or someone who might know how to contact him?"

She shakes her head. "Unfortunately, I don't. He was an only child, and so were Lydia and Mr. Pichler. As far as I know, the kid didn't have any cousins or uncles or aunts. No one ever came by to visit." She purses her lips, thinking for a moment. "He did have a friend who lived around the corner. They would ride their bikes up and down the street, but I was never quite sure which house the friend came from. I'm sure he's long gone by now too. Young folks these days don't stay in the same house forever."

I look over my shoulder at the street, picturing Luca riding his bicycle with a friend. I wonder if it was one of the boys from the beach photo he had as his profile picture on Facebook. The image is interrupted by Carol's words, still ringing in my head. Luca grew up in a broken home and then lost his mother too. Meanwhile I grew up taking happiness for granted.

"No, they don't," I agree. "If I had stayed in my childhood home, I'd be living in a rundown trailer in Oklahoma."

My family wasn't wealthy, but the thought of losing either of my parents never even crossed my mind. I never had to wonder if my father would come home. It doesn't feel fair that this was Luca's reality.

"You need to find a man who will build you a house like my daddy did for my momma," Carol says.

"Now that's a relationship goal," Anne says with a smile. It's clear that she's unaware of how hard I'm trying to keep it together. I came here looking for answers, but I wasn't expecting the ones I found to make me so emotional.

I clear my throat. "That's probably pretty hard to find these days," I say. Not that I need a man to build me a house. I've worked hard the last several years and saved up to buy my own house without help from anyone except the bank.

"I wish I could help you," Carol says.

"You have," I say, even though I feel like I'm back at square one. At least I can rule out Luca's childhood home as a place to find him.

Chapter Nine

ONE MORE DAY

Luca

I was a senior in high school when my mom was diagnosed with pancreatic cancer. It seemed like it came out of nowhere. I had been talking to a Marine Corps recruiter the day that my mom got the news. She waited until I was home to tell me what the doctor said. It came as a shock to both of us. She was younger than most people with the disease.

"I haven't signed anything yet," I said. "I don't have to join the Marine Corps. I'll stay home and I'll take care of you."

She shook her head. "Don't put your life on hold for me."

That request made no sense to me because I didn't see it as putting my life on hold for her. She was my mother, and she was all that I had. She had stayed strong and taken care of me when my father left. I refused to abandon her now that she needed me to take care of her.

"I'm not leaving until you're better."

She reached across the dining room table and clasped her

hands over mine. When she spoke, her voice was soft but sure. "I'm not going to get better."

"Don't say that. People survive cancer all the time these days. You'll do chemotherapy, won't you?"

"I've discussed my options with the doctor," she said. "I'm getting a second opinion, but Luca, it's not good news. People don't survive pancreatic cancer. Even with chemotherapy, the prognosis isn't good."

My throat tightened, making it difficult to speak. "How long do you have? A year? Two?"

She closed her eyes, and I watched as a couple of tears slipped down her cheeks. "Months, probably. Chemo might make me feel better, and it might help me live a little longer, but the doctor doesn't … the doctor doesn't…" She broke off on a sob. I held her hand tighter. When she began again, her voice was barely audible. "The doctor says that I would be lucky to make it past April."

My mother's second opinion confirmed the first doctor's diagnosis. I was in denial those first couple of weeks after we got the news. She didn't seem like she was sick enough to be dying. I was afraid that if she started chemotherapy, it would change her. I guess I was afraid that her doctors were wrong, and that she was healthy, and chemotherapy would only weaken her. But it wasn't long before the cancer began to show its ugly face.

After I missed several days of school to take care of her, she insisted that I not miss another day. I argued with her about it. I only had so much time left with her, and I didn't want to waste it by spending the better part of the day away from her. The chemotherapy made her feel a little better though, and she became determined to outlive the doctor's prognosis by at least another month. She told me that her only goal was to live long enough to watch me graduate high school. She told me that if I didn't show up to school every day, I would be taking that away from her. I stopped arguing with her after that.

It was hard to write mean letters to Naomi while I was watching my mother get weaker every day. When my father left, I had used my letters to Naomi as a pseudo punching bag. The letters were how I vented the anger he had left me with. But when my mother got sick, when it became clear that she was slowly dying, I didn't feel that same anger. She wasn't choosing to leave me. She was being taken away from me against her will.

When my mother got sick, Naomi's letters became a much-needed distraction.

Dear Naomi,

You're not going to get into any of the colleges you applied for because you're not as smart as you think you are. Your parents and your teachers have been lying to you all these years. You probably aren't even going to graduate. The principal is going to let you get all the way to the stage, and when they announce your name, instead of congratulating you like all the other students, they're going to say that you failed and you need to start high school all over. All four years of it. It's going to be really embarrassing, but not really that surprising to me.

Love,

Luca

When I wasn't at school or acting as chef or chauffer for my mother, I sometimes found myself visiting Naomi's Facebook page. I looked through all of the photos I had seen a hundred times before as well as the new ones I hadn't seen yet. She posted something new almost every day. I wondered if she knew that her private thoughts were available to the whole world. I wondered if she knew that I could read all of these things that she didn't include in her letters. Sometimes what she wrote was funny, sometimes it was an update about what she planned to do that day, and sometimes she vented about something someone had done to hurt her. Between snooping through her Facebook page, and the letters she had been sending to me since fifth grade, I felt like I knew her. I doubted that her friends knew just how dark her sense of humor was.

I felt a little jealous every time she posted a photo of her and some guy. I guess he was her boyfriend because some of her updates were about him. I wondered if she would stop writing to me if she knew how much time I spent looking at her photos and reading the things she wrote on her Facebook page. Sometimes I went to bed imagining that it was me holding her in that photo she posted.

Early one morning before my mother woke up, I typed my father's name in the search bar on Facebook, but I couldn't find a profile for him. I tried calling his old cellphone number, but the call went straight to someone else's voicemail. I knew it would. It's not like this was the first time I had tried his old number.

I didn't miss him. He had made his choice. I threw my phone down on the bed and watched as it bounced off and hit the wall before settling on the floor. It wasn't fair that my father left me to deal with this all on my own. I hated that he was out there somewhere having the time of his life without a care in the world about what my mother and I were dealing with.

I picked up my phone and saw that there was a new crack in the screen. I kicked the side of my bed and cursed. I was angry at my phone, at my father, and in that moment, I was even angry with my mother.

I was angry with myself for even having that last thought. I was angry at the cancer, not at her. And I was angry that I wished my father was here and helping us through it. We didn't need him. I just wished that he would call.

My mother's health had deteriorated further by the end of April. She wasn't supposed to make it to May, but she was holding onto life as tightly as she could. She was adamant about living long enough to see me graduate. When she flipped the calendar to May, we felt like we had reached a milestone. She had surpassed her life expectancy, if only by a day.

And then another day passed, and another, and before we knew it, we were reaching the end of May. She wasn't getting better. There was a hospice nurse in our house most days. It was her job to make sure that my mother was comfortable. Every day was merely another day of survival, another day of wondering if this would be the last.

On the morning of my graduation, she gave me a hug with tears in her eyes. She was so weak that I barely felt her arms around me. It was the first time she had managed to get out of bed in several days.

"We made it," she said. "I'm going to see my baby graduate."

My own tears stung my eyes when she said that. Over the last month, I often found myself wondering if the only thing that was keeping her alive was the goal of making it to this day. Now that we were here, I didn't want to let her go, but I also didn't want her to continue suffering just because I wasn't ready to say goodbye.

"We made it," I repeated.

I drove myself to school that day, thinking about everything that had happened over the last few months. Sometimes it felt like it had only been a few days.

The extension of her life by another month wasn't all that exciting to her doctors. It would have been a different story if she was hopping out of bed every morning and dancing across the living room on her way to make a pot of coffee. She wasn't a medical miracle by any means. Although I cherished every extra day that I got with her, it seemed like everyone else was surprised that she hadn't passed away in her sleep yet.

I caught up with Ben when we were both wearing our caps and gowns after rehearsal. His girlfriend was taking photos with a group of girls – two of whom I had dated sophomore year – so I had him to myself for a few minutes.

"How's your mom?" he asked. This was how most people started conversations with me these days. Sometimes I wished that someone would ask about anything else. I would have been grateful for the distraction. But today it felt good to talk about her.

"She's really happy today," I said. "She's not any better, but she's made it a month longer than the doctors thought she would. She's just glad that she made it long enough to see me graduate high school."

"That's great," he said. "I know how much that means to you both. Are you still joining the Marine Corps or are you putting that on hold?"

"I start boot camp next month."

"You're not going to put it off? What about your mom?"

"She wasn't supposed to make it this long."

"But she did. What if she makes it another month?"

I didn't think she would make it another month, let alone another week, but I knew that I would sound heartless if I said that. I needed to join the military so that I could serve my four years to collect the G.I. bill and go to college after. If I didn't have this plan, I would have nothing. "I'll be right here in San Diego if anything happens."

Ben's girlfriend turned from her group of friends and started calling for him. He waved to her, then turned back to me. "I gotta go." He was about to turn away, but hesitated. "We're having a graduation party at my place tonight. You should come."

"Okay. I'll try."

As much as I missed having a social life outside of school, I doubted that I would make it to that party. My mother's days were limited, and I didn't see myself spending the evening anywhere but by her side after I was finished walking the line.

The graduation ceremony was held at the football stadium. We had a large graduating class, and the stadium was packed. As our names were announced, we went up onto the stage one by one, where we shook the principal's hand and had a photo taken with our diplomas. There was a round of applause and some cheering when my name was called. I scanned the crowd, but I didn't have time to look very hard before I had to return to my seat.

When the ceremony was over, and the other students were throwing their hats up in the air and taking photos and reuniting with their families, I searched the crowd again. I doubted that my mother had the strength to walk, so I looked for a wheelchair. The football field was suddenly so congested that it became all but impossible to find her. I walked the entire length of the seating area twice before I began to worry.

And then I saw her. Not my mother, but the hospice nurse who had been at our house this morning. I glanced around her, knowing that my mother couldn't be too far. It took me longer than it should have to recognize the look on the nurse's face.

"I'm sorry, Luca."

"Where is she? Did she have to go to the hospital?"

The nurse pinched her lips together. "Let's go to the parking lot," she said.

I caught Ben's eye as I followed her away from the crowded field. He maintained eye contact with me until I turned away from him.

"It happened. Didn't it?" My voice sounded flat, like it had come from someone else.

The nurse's eyes were full of tears when she turned back to me. I didn't imagine that going to a high school student's graduation to inform him of his mother's death was a regular part of her job.

"I'm so sorry," she said. "I know how badly she wanted to be here. It's all she talked about today. If it's any comfort, her last words were about how much she loved you, and how she was looking forward to seeing you walk the line after her nap."

"She died in her sleep?"

The nurse nodded. "She wasn't in any pain. I promise."

"I should have been there."

"I know how hard it is to find out this way, but you were right where you were supposed to be. This was where she wanted you. If she could have been here, she would have, but I think that she was happy when she passed away, knowing that you were here."

The numbness that came with the initial shock of the news was fading. I could feel my throat constricting, and my eyes heated with tears. The nurse, sensing that I was about to break down, stepped toward me and wrapped her arms around me in a tight hug. I didn't realize how much I needed that hug until it was happening. I cried into her shoulder, into her hair, until the parking lot began to fill with other students and their families. It didn't occur to me until later that I didn't even know the nurse's name.

Chapter Ten

THE BAD LETTER

Naomi

"I don't think we're supposed to have these on the beach."

Anne looks at the bottle of spiked lemonade in her hand. "If we weren't supposed to have these, then why would they sell them so close to the beach?"

I glance around. We're surrounded by couples lounging on the sand, families playing in the waves, and kids building sandcastles. "No one else is drinking."

Anne shrugs, then takes a sip of her drink. "I'm sure if we weren't supposed to have these, someone would have stopped us after the first two."

"You might have a point." I finish off my bottle, then grab another.

"So," Anne says. "Are you going to tell me about the picture Husky Eyes sent you?"

I shake my head, smiling. "He didn't send me a picture."

"Lame. You should send him one."

"A sexy picture? I don't think so."

"Come on," she says. "You can make it tasteful. Don't you want to make sure he's thinking about you?"

"He's been texting me all day. Pretty sure he's already thinking about me."

Before I can stop her, she reaches over and snatches my phone off my towel.

"Hey! What are you doing?" I reach for my phone but she holds it away from me.

"Just doing what you're too afraid to do." She angles it toward me and snaps a photo. "Perfect."

She shows me the screen. It's an awkward photo of me wearing a bikini and reaching for the phone, a startled look on my face. It's probably the worst photo I've ever seen of myself.

"Should I send this?" she asks, waving the phone just out of my reach.

"No way."

"Are you sure? This will definitely get his mind racing."

"The only thing that will be racing is his body as he runs away from me." I stand up. "Take a better one."

She smiles, her eyes lighting up. She stands up too, directing me to stand in front of the ocean. She takes a few photos, and then gives me my phone. I choose one of the photos, then send it to him, along with a text.

Naomi: *You might have to come to San Diego to take me on that date.*
Husky Eyes: *I can probably be convinced.*
Husky Eyes: *You look beautiful.*

His message sends a rush of warmth over me that has nothing to do with the temperature of the sun. I try to fight the smile I feel creeping across my lips, because I know that Anne is watching me. I sit back down on my towel, then lie back, soaking in the cool California sunshine. It's a lot cooler here than it is back home in Miami. I could lie here for the rest of the day if Anne would let me. The thought makes me remember one of Luca's earliest letters to me. I picture myself as a whale with a crowd of people around me, trying to push me back into the ocean.

"What are you smiling about?" Anne asks, interrupting the memory. "The picture worked, didn't it? I told you he'd like it."

"Yep. I don't know what I would do without you."

She smiles, then lies back on her own towel. "What can I say? I make an excellent wing-woman."

I close my eyes, soaking in the sun and the cool, salty air for a while. This weather is almost enough to get me to move out here.

"We should do this more often," I tell her. "Why did it take us traveling almost three thousand miles to drink together on the beach?"

"Let's do this every Saturday," she says. "No. Scratch that. Let's go every single day."

"I don't know if I can handle that much of you."

She sits up and looks at me. "I don't think you can handle that much sun."

"I could if Miami had weather like this."

"No, really. You're starting to look like a lobster."

"Huh?" I stick my leg up in the air so that I can see it. I groan when I realize she's right. "Oh, come on. I put on sunscreen."

"That was a while ago," she reminds me. "And you waded into the ocean afterward."

"Please tell me it's just my legs."

"Your face is a little pink too, but not as bad."

I reach into my bag and grab the sunscreen. I begin applying it to my burned legs, even though I know the damage is already done.

"You would think a meteorologist would know better than to get sunburned," Anne says.

I throw the bottle of sunscreen at her, but she dodges it. "You would think an assistant would be better at assisting," I say, mocking her tone.

"My bad. I didn't realize putting sunscreen on you was in my job description."

"It is now."

"We should probably get to Luca's apartment soon and then grab dinner if we want to make it back to the airport on time."

"You're right. I think I've roasted enough anyway."

We take a cab to the address that Luca's last letter had come from before he disappeared for two years. The last two letters that I sent to this building were rejected by whoever lives there now. I already know that Luca isn't here, but I have to try anyway. Just like at the blue beach house, when we knock on the apartment door, we learn that the current tenants don't know who he is. By the time we make it to the airport, we've each spent a couple hundred dollars and flown a few thousand miles just to find out that the sand is darker and the air is a little cooler in San Diego.

We make it through airport security without any hiccups, but Anne seems to notice how pale I am this time.

"What's wrong?" she asks. "Are you seriously scared again? You did just fine on the flight here. Why are you scared?"

It's not something I can easily explain, especially while

we're standing so close to the TSA agents. I ignore her, but she doesn't look like she's going to let it go. When we make it to our gate, I open my backpack and pull out the letters from Luca. We left off at the end of junior year, so all we have left are the letters from senior year. I flip through them, knowing that what I'm looking for is at the bottom of the stack.

"Hey!" Anne scolds, grabbing the letters that I'm skipping. "I haven't read these yet."

"You can read them after," I say. I find the letter that I'm looking for and hold it against my chest so that she can't read it until I explain what I wrote first.

"What's that?" she asks.

"The last few letters in here were from the summer after high school before I went to college. I hadn't heard from Luca for about a month after graduation, and when he wrote to me next, he was at basic training for the Marine Corps. We always wrote mean letters to each other, but I didn't really think it through when I wrote to him. It was bad. Really bad."

I take a deep breath, then look at the letter that I'm hiding from Anne. I look back at her. She's watching me, her brow furrowed, waiting for me to continue.

"I told him that I was surprised they let someone like him defend our country, and that I hoped someone's weapon misfires in the middle of a training exercise and his head gets blown off. Then I said that they would probably give the medal of honor to whoever accidentally did it."

"That's dark," Anne says. "But he definitely wrote worse things to you."

She gestures to the letters we read together on the way to San Diego. There are multiple letters where he described in detail how he hoped I would die. My letter was hardly the first death threat either of us sent.

Without another word, I hand her the letter that Luca wrote in response.

Dear Naomi,

I bet you didn't know that every letter you send to me is read by the drill instructors before I'm allowed to read it. They have to make sure that none of us are spies or terrorists. Anyway, they read your letter and questioned me for hours about why you want my head to get blown off. Long story short: the department of homeland security got involved, and you are now on the terrorist watchlist. You will never be able to get a government job, and you will never be able to fly without a full cavity search. So, congratulations on screwing up your whole life with one letter. I bet you didn't see that coming, did you?

Good thing you got into college already, because they probably wouldn't have let you in if they saw this on your record. What are you going to study? My guess is the weather since it seems like that's all you know how to talk about.

Love,

Luca

Anne finishes reading the letter, then frowns at me. "This is why you were scared to fly?"

I nod. I have never told anyone else about this letter. I thought that the fewer people who knew I was being investigated by homeland security, the better.

"You thought TSA was going to make you strip down and check your butthole for weapons?"

I stare at her, watching as her frown lines gradually fade and she bursts out laughing.

"It's not funny."

"Yes, it is," she says.

"No, it's not. You don't know what it's like having to be careful about what I say over the phone, knowing that the government is probably listening. And constantly having to wonder if and when I'm going to be brought in for questioning."

"Wait. You're serious?"

I glare at her.

"You're not on the terrorist watchlist," she says.

I shush her and look around, hoping that we're not drawing too much attention. "You don't know that."

"Naomi." She takes a deep breath like she's gathering her patience. "The station did a full background check on you before we hired you. Something like that would have come up."

"But this letter," I say, holding it up. The corner of her mouth creeps up, and before I can continue what I'm about to say, I realize what's happening. "He was fucking with me. Wasn't he?"

"Just like all the other letters," she says.

I look at the letter again, skimming over it with angry fascination. "Holy shit," I say. I throw the letter to the floor. "All these years of writing to each other and one-upping each other. All these years and I didn't realize that he had already won. It didn't matter how mean I was because I was never going to win. Not after I fell for that stupid shit."

I can tell that Anne is holding back laughter. I roll my eyes. She bends over and picks up the letter, tucking it back into the stack inside the folder.

"It could have happened to anyone," she says. Her tone isn't very reassuring.

"I had a full-blown panic attack when I bought the plane ticket. I've never flown because I was terrified of going to jail just for trying to get on a plane. I've driven thousands of miles just to avoid stepping into an airport. And I nearly passed out several times going through security last night and just now."

"Yep. He won, all right," Anne agrees.

"Thanks."

"But you're going to win the next round."

"How?"

"You're going to defy all the odds and find his address."

"What if this is him winning again?" I ask. "What if his whole plan is to send me on a wild goose chase, flying around the country looking for him, knowing that I won't be able to find him?"

"Oh, you'll win this one," she says. "He doesn't know who he's dealing with."

"We already flew all the way to San Diego and we're not any closer to finding him," I remind her. "What if I can't find him?"

"Then you'll win anyway, because you get to go on an adventure. With me," she adds with a wink. I roll my eyes. "Just because we didn't find him here doesn't mean I'm giving up. We're going to find him, Gnome."

Chapter Eleven

REVENGE ON THE WHALES

It's still dark outside when the plane touches down in Miami. I must have dozed off for a couple of hours because the flight home seems much shorter. Anne is still asleep, so I nudge her shoulder. She jolts awake, then uses her wrist to wipe a drop of drool off the corner of her mouth.

"We landed," I tell her.

We're at the back of the plane again, so we have to wait for everyone else to deboard before it's our turn.

"We should take another trip next weekend," Anne suggests as we make our way to her car. "Where else did Luca live?"

"I'm supposed to go on a date with Jake next weekend," I remind her.

"Who?"

"Jake."

She shoots a weird look in my direction like she doesn't understand who I'm talking about.

"Husky Eyes," I say. She smirks, and I realize that she made me say that just to mess with me. I roll my eyes.

"Maybe you can go out with him during the week," she says. "You don't want to wait too long to write back to Luca."

"He waited two years to write back to me. Besides, I don't want to change my date with Jake again. I'm looking forward to going out with him."

"Maybe there's someplace closer than San Diego," she suggests. "Did Luca ever get stationed in Florida while he was in the military?"

"No, but he was stationed in Georgia for a while."

"Let's fly to Georgia then. Next weekend. You can have your date Friday, then fly out Saturday morning. We'll be back the same day."

"You're serious about this whole adventure thing, aren't you?"

"I clearly have nothing better to do."

"You need to get laid."

She sighs. "You're probably right."

"Maybe I can find out if he has a cute friend I can set you up with."

We reach her car, and she smiles at me over the roof. "See? This is why I keep you around, Gnome."

"Don't call me that," I say, but she's already inside the car with the door closed.

She drives me home with the radio turned up. I'm hungry, but also ready to go to bed by the time she pulls the car up to the curb in front of my building.

"Oh boy," she says. "He runs. And look at that body."

I frown at her, then follow her gaze to the sidewalk ahead of us just in time to see a half-naked man running toward my building. As he passes under a streetlamp, his muscles glisten with sweat under the golden light. It takes me a second to realize that we're both drooling over Jake, although Anne seems to have known it from the beginning.

"Shirtless," she murmurs, as if she's lost the ability to form a complete sentence.

"Oh my..." It seems that I'm at a loss for words too.

"You better go catch up with him," she says, nudging my arm.

"I can't let him see me like this." I'm sure I still have sand in my hair from lying on the beach yesterday.

I watch as he stretches in front of the building, then picks up a shirt that he must have left on the steps when he started his run. He slips it on.

"Take it back off," Anne mumbles as he lets himself in. I wait until he's out of sight before I open the car door.

"See you tomorrow, Anne."

"Later, Gnome."

I don't respond, hoping that if I ignore her enough times, she'll stop using that nickname. I let myself into the building and wave to Joel, who's planted at the security desk as usual. He nods at me, the weathered skin around his eyes wrinkling when he smiles. As I turn, I collide with an unexpected object, knocking me off balance. Before I can hit the ground, my fall is broken by the person I just ran into. It takes me a moment to realize that it's Jake. He smiles down at me, looking amused as he pulls me back up.

"Thanks," I stammer.

His hands are warm on my arms. Despite the warmth, his touch sends goosebumps over my skin. He's so close that I would have to tilt my head all the way up just to see his face. I'm eyelevel with his collarbone. I'm afraid that if I look into his eyes, he'll know that I'm holding my breath, so I find myself staring at his chest instead. I take a moment to appreciate the way his shirt hugs his pectorals. His chest rises and then falls with a deep breath. Time stops for a moment. I can hear his heart beating, or maybe it's my own. It drums in my ears, so loud that in this moment it's the only thing I can hear.

He releases my arms slowly. When he lets go, my skin feels cold, and I wish he was still holding onto me. I tilt my head up to meet his eyes. The way he stares at me makes me wonder if I just said that out loud. I think about running upstairs to put an end to my embarrassment, but something holds me here in the lobby with him.

"Thanks for catching me," I say, trying to laugh it off. I step around him, allowing my arm to brush against his as I head for the mailboxes.

He follows me. I can feel him watching me as I open my mailbox.

"Good trip?"

For a second, I think he's talking about what just happened a minute ago. It takes me a moment to remember that I just came from San Diego and that's what he's asking about. When I look up at him, he has that crooked smile that looks so good on him.

"Yeah. Sorry. I'm not fully awake right now."

He looks at the number on my mailbox, then back at me. "Huh," he says. "I didn't know that you live in the apartment right below me."

"I do?"

He gestures to his own mailbox. It's exactly one floor number above mine. I close my mailbox, then turn to face him, my hand on my hip. I think of all the times the noises upstairs have kept me awake late in the evening or distracted me.

"I have so many questions," I say.

"Like what?"

"Like what the hell do you do up there? Do you have a bowling alley in your living room or something?"

He scoffs. "Yeah, right. Coming from the girl who blasts her music so loud it sounds like it's in my own apartment."

"I only do that to drown out the sound of all that noise you're making up there."

"I can't be that loud."

"Seriously. What do you do up there to make so much noise?"

He shrugs. "I can't think of anything that would disturb you. I've always thought I was a quiet neighbor."

"You can't possibly think you're quiet. On top of the bowling alley, it sounds like you're running laps up there at all hours of the night." I gesture to the front door. "Is running outside not enough?"

"I knew it," he says. "You did see me out there."

"You saw me in the car?"

"I might have noticed you checking me out."

The way he leans against the mailbox and smiles makes me forget what we were just arguing about. I almost forgive him for being so loud, but I decide I can't let him off the hook that easily.

I poke him in the chest. "Quit changing the subject. I want to know what you do upstairs that makes so much noise."

"How about I tell you over breakfast?"

I'm caught off guard by his invitation. My heart speeds up, hammering away in my chest. I want to say yes, but I also want to wash the sand out of my hair and get a few hours of sleep.

"I can't. I just got home. I need to feed my, uh, my plant."

He tilts his head, his smile still teasing the corner of his lips. "Is that the best you can come up with?"

"I barely got any sleep on the plane," I say. "Plus, I was at the beach all day yesterday. I probably smell so bad." I give my armpit a quick whiff to drive home my point, though to my surprise, I find that I don't actually smell that bad.

"I just ran three miles," he says. "If either of us stinks, everyone will assume it's me."

After having just collided with him, I can confirm that he doesn't stink either. I'm quiet for a moment while I try to think of another excuse. My stomach chooses that moment to growl.

He looks down at my stomach, then meets my eyes again. "Hungry?"

"Fine," I say, unable to fight my smile anymore. "But I need to put my things away first."

He waits in the lobby while I run upstairs to put my backpack and my mail in my apartment. I give myself a quick spray of perfume just in case I'm nose-blind to my own smell. When I come back down, he's talking to Joel. He turns and smiles at me as I come out of the stairwell. His eyes wander down my body and back up again as I come near. I hold my breath, my heart racing. I don't know why it feels so good to be looked at like that when a few minutes ago I was cursing his noisy existence. My mind must not be functioning properly. I blame all the sun I got yesterday.

Joel eyes me warily. I wonder if he disapproves of me going out with someone who lives in the building.

"Have you been to the Spanish diner down the street?" Jake asks when I reach him.

"Yeah, it's good. Let's go there."

He holds the door open for me as I pass through. As we walk toward the diner, I notice that he's watching me. I turn my head to see what he's looking at. His eyes are trailing from my shoulders, down my arms to my hands.

"Why are you looking at me like that?" I ask.

He reaches over and grabs my arm, holding it out in front of himself to get a better look. When his hand comes in contact with mine, I feel like an addict getting her fix. I suck in a breath, hoping he can't feel my pulse through my wrist.

"You're pink," he says, examining my arm.

It takes me a second to be able to speak. I clear my throat. "I might have gotten a little too much sun yesterday."

"It's easy to do when the air is cooler. It doesn't feel like you're burning." He lowers my arm, but doesn't let go of my hand. His fingers intertwine with mine, making me forget what we're talking about for a moment. All I can focus on is the touch of his skin on mine. It sends a pulse through my body like I've been hit with a wave of electricity.

"I should have known better," I say, pulling my focus back up to his face. "I'm going to have to pack on the makeup at work to cover this up."

"I disagree. I think pink is a good look for you."

I laugh. "Thanks, but it's not a good look on camera. I don't want to scare my viewers."

"I think you would have to try a lot harder if you wanted to scare people."

We reach the diner. He lets go of my hand to hold the door open for me. I find myself wishing that the doors were automatic, or that I had an excuse to grab his hand again once we're through the doorway. A waitress greets us at the door. I notice that her eyes move over his body, a dazed smile on her face. I don't blame her for checking him out. I look up at him to see his reaction, but his eyes are on me. His hand lands on my back as the waitress leads us to a booth at the back of the restaurant. It's the only thing I can focus on for the few seconds that it takes to reach our table.

We're the only two people here this early. He sits down across from me. The table is small, and his leg bumps mine underneath. Neither of us moves out of the way. He settles his knee against mine. The contact sends a tingle that starts where our knees touch, all the way up to the top of my thigh.

I watch him as he looks over the menu. I've been here enough times that I know what I'm going to order, but I open my menu anyway and pretend to look it over. The waitress comes back to take our order. She asks him what he wants first, and when he asks a question about the menu, she giggles and leans down, putting one hand on his shoulder while she points at the menu with the other. I resist the urge to roll my eyes.

"So," he says after the waitress leaves. "Did you figure out which city has better beaches?"

I sip my coffee while I think about my answer. "It's a toss-up," I decide. "The sand is prettier here in Miami. So is the water. But there's so much seaweed on the beaches here lately, and there wasn't nearly as much in San Diego. It's cooler in San Diego, too, which as you can tell from my sunburn, makes it easier to stay out in the sun longer, but the water was also a lot colder. The waves were better there, so I guess if I was a surfer, I would choose San Diego."

"That's good to know." He stirs a little cream into his coffee and then takes a sip. "I haven't been to any of the beaches here yet."

"Seriously? How long have you lived here?"

He shrugs. "About six months."

"How do you live in Miami for six months and not go to the beach?"

He picks up an unopened creamer cup and stacks it on top

of another. "I spend most of my day in the water," he says as he stacks a third cup on top. "I guess the last thing I want to do when I get home is get back in the water."

I think of the scrubs I've seen him wear a few times, making me wonder what he does for work. I had assumed he was a dentist or a nurse, but now I'm even more confused.

"Why do you spend all day in the water? Are you a water aerobics instructor, or are you just addicted to taking baths?"

He snorts, then clasps his hand over his mouth to keep from spitting out his coffee. "I'm an aquatic veterinarian," he says.

"Aquatic veterinarian? What does that even mean?"

He smiles. He stacks a fourth creamer cup on top of the other three, then looks at me. "What does it sound like?"

"I imagine you do underwater surgery on dogs and cats."

To my surprise, he doesn't seem put off by my dumb jokes. "Close. I majored in marine biology before going to veterinary school. I work at the aquarium."

"Oh. So, like, sea turtles and stuff."

"Yep. Penguins, walruses, dolphins. All kinds of fish, too."

"Now I feel like a jerk for making fun of you."

"I'm not offended," he says. "So. Tell me what it's like to have a career that fuels the small talk of millions of Americans."

"Wow. Okay. I see how it is. Well, your small talk cost me four years at the University of Oklahoma."

"Hey, I never said it wasn't an important job. I take it that's what you actually went to school for, then. You don't just go on camera and recite someone else's weather predictions?"

I shake my head. I pick up a jelly packet and balance it on top of his creamer tower. "I'm at the station by three every morning to get my reports and graphics done in time to go on air."

"That's early." He stacks another jelly packet on top of mine.

"I don't have much of a life considering I'm usually in bed by the time everyone else is eating dinner."

"At least you see more of the day than most people do. You're always at that coffee shop across the street around noon. Is that when you get out of work?"

I nod. "I always see you there too. Do you have weird hours at the aquarium or something?"

"I get a couple hours off for lunch," he says. "I use that time to go home and play with the kittens."

I raise both eyebrows. I'm suddenly a lot more excited than any reasonable person should be. "You have kittens?"

"Two foster kittens." He pulls his phone out, taps on the screen, and then holds it up to show me a photo of his kittens. I lean over the table to get a better look. He leans closer too so that we're looking at the photo together. His face is so close to mine that if I tilted my chin just the right way, I could reach his lips. My eyes land on his mouth. I have to pull my focus back to the photo of the kittens before he realizes that I'm not paying attention.

"They were feral," he continues. "Someone found them on the street and handed them over to the pound. I volunteered to take care of them and get them used to human interaction. They're ready for their new homes now. I'm supposed to take them to an adoption event next weekend."

He looks a little sad when he talks about giving up the kittens.

"I couldn't do it," I say. "I would get attached and keep them."

He shrugs. "It sucks, but someone has to do it. Besides, I get a new foster animal once the kittens are gone."

The waitress appears at the table with our food, knocking over the stack of creamer and jelly as she sets the plates down. She touches his shoulder again and encourages him to let her know if he needs *anything*. I can't help but notice that she doesn't seem to have the same concern for my needs. He responds with a frown and, "Sure," and then we both dig in.

"Did you always know you wanted to be a meteorologist?" he asks after clearing most of his plate.

I take a bite of toast while I think about my answer. "I've always been fascinated by the weather. And I loved watching the weatherman on TV when I was a kid. I probably talked about the weather more than most kids my age at school."

That was something that Luca often made fun of me for in his letters. I had never considered that it was something I could turn into a career until Luca mockingly suggested that's what I was going to study when I got to college. I find it ironic that he was trying to make fun of me, and instead ended up helping me make one of the best decisions of my life.

"I think that's awesome that you always knew what you wanted to do," he says. "I didn't figure it out until I was twenty-two."

"Really? What did you do until then?"

He rips a packet of sugar open and stirs it into his coffee. His blue eyes meet mine for a moment before he returns his attention to his coffee. "I guess you could say I was sort of a police officer."

"Sort of? What does that mean? Were you a security guard?"

He smiles, telling me all I need to know.

"Oh my God. You were a mall cop, weren't you?" I laugh,

because I can't imagine him with a job like that. "Did you ride around on a Segway yelling at kids in the food court?"

"That about sums it up," he says. "It wasn't exactly my dream career."

"Why did you choose marine biology?"

"Other than basically closing my eyes and blindly picking from a list of majors? I've always loved animals. And I loved going to SeaWorld as a kid. I guess it never occurred to me that I could actually work with dolphins every day."

I watch him for a moment, wondering what the catch is. This man can't possibly be this perfect. Fosters kittens, heals sick dolphins, and has a body built like a Greek god? He has to be married, or maybe he has a crazy ex-wife. Or maybe he lost his penis in a terrible accident as a child. Maybe a whale at SeaWorld jumped out of the water and bit it off. But that wouldn't make sense with his current career choice. Unless he chose this path as a twisted long-term plan to get revenge on the whales.

"I guess we both chose our childhood passions," I say. "Why did you come to Miami? It couldn't have been for the beaches."

He smirks. "My family was out here. I wanted to be closer to them."

Ugh. And he's close with his family, too? I want to tell him to stop being so perfect. He's making me look bad, especially since moving to Miami took me far away from my parents and cousins.

"What are your flaws?" I ask before I can stop myself. "Nobody's that perfect. You're either making amends for something, or you're just trying to impress me."

His smile falters. "You want to know what my flaws are?"

I raise an eyebrow.

"Okay." He lowers his voice. "I'll tell you."

I lean a little closer to hear him better. I notice the stubble on his face, and my eyes are drawn to his lips again. I wonder what it would be like to kiss him, how that stubble would feel against my face. When I look at him again, I notice that his eyes are on my mouth too. He meets my eyes, and I feel a rush of warmth come over me. His lips part, and somehow the rest of the world gets a little quieter, and all I can hear is my own heartbeat as I wait to hear what he's going to say. I wonder if he can hear it too.

He continues in a whisper: "I'm told that I'm a very noisy neighbor."

I can't help but laugh, releasing a breath I didn't know I was holding. "You are. And I still want to know how you manage to make so much noise up there."

"I really don't know what you're talking about. Maybe it's the kittens. They like to run around the apartment."

"Two little kittens can't possibly make that much noise."

"You'd be surprised," he says.

"Okay. I'm going to add 'liar' to your list of flaws, because you're obviously trying to hide the fact that you have a bowling alley up there."

I expect him to use that as an opportunity to invite me up to his apartment, but he doesn't. He smirks. "Fine. Believe whatever you want."

The sun is up by the time we finish eating. He grabs the check before I have a chance and pays for our meal at the register. The same waitress cashes us out. I watch him as he signs the receipt. His biceps bulge out of the short sleeves of his T-shirt. His shirt isn't tight, but I can see the shape of his muscles beneath it. My eyes wander up to his and I realize that he's watching me as I check him out. My face flushes. I wonder how long ago he finished signing the receipt.

The waitress hands him a copy of the receipt, then looks at me and winks. I raise an eyebrow, wondering what that was about. I notice him frowning at the receipt as he steps away from the counter. I sneak a glance and see that she wrote her phone number on it. I'm not sure whether it's appropriate to laugh. I hold it in, pretending I don't notice so that I can see what he'll do. Without a word, he wrinkles the receipt into a ball and tosses it into the trash can by the front door.

"Ready to go?" he asks me.

I resist the urge to look back at the waitress to see her reaction. I figure she's had enough embarrassment for one morning. We step outside and head across the street toward our building. As soon as we reach the sidewalk, he says, "Wait. Naomi."

For a moment, I think that he's about to comment on what just happened a minute ago. Instead, he grabs onto my shoulders, steering me away from the edge of the sidewalk so that he's between me and the road.

"There. That's better."

I frown. "Excuse me?"

He points at the road with his thumb as he starts walking again. I stare at the road, then look back at him, confused, before I realize what he's doing. I take a few quick steps to catch up with him. I think it's cute that he's following such an old-fashioned rule where the man blocks the woman from traffic. Even so, I can't help myself.

"What are you protecting me from?" I ask. "Getting splashed by a puddle?" I look at the dry road, then back at him. The corner of his mouth quirks up.

"You never know when a car will veer off the road and onto the sidewalk," he says.

"Oh. I see. And you think you're strong enough to stop a moving vehicle from trampling both of us."

He frowns, thinking about my response. "You don't think I could?"

I shrug, stealing another glance at him. "Maybe. You felt pretty hard when I bumped into you this morning."

He snaps his head in my direction, making me realize what I just said. My face heats. I hope that my sunburn is enough to disguise my blush.

"Oh God. That came out wrong." I slap my hand over my face. "Solid. I meant that your body was solid when I touched you and … none of this is coming out right, is it?"

I peek through my fingers to see that he's laughing at me. He pulls my hand off my face.

"You should stop while you're ahead," he says.

"I don't feel like I'm ahead."

He smirks. "If either one of us should be embarrassed, it's me. You just accused me of…" He glances down at his waist, then looks back up at me.

"Can we just pretend I never said that?"

"Not a chance." He opens the front door of our building and lets me go in ahead of him.

Joel is still sitting at the security desk. He tilts his newspaper down as we come through the door. His brow furrows slightly, but he says nothing as he goes back to reading. I head toward the stairwell, and Jake follows.

We reach the third floor. I hesitate, my hand on the door that opens to the hallway. He still has one more floor to climb, but he stops next to me. He looks at the staircase that continues up to the fourth floor, then returns his attention to me. He leans against the door so that I can't open it. I keep my hand on the doorknob. The stairwell somehow feels smaller when he's standing right in front of me. I'm not sure how he managed to step closer without me noticing. Maybe it's because I can't take my eyes off his lips.

He looks indecisive, like he's waiting for something, and I realize that I think I know what it is. He's standing close enough that all I have to do is raise up on my toes to reach him. I hold the back of his neck, pulling his face just a little bit closer to mine, and then our lips are together. His mouth is warm. I feel weightless, and like my body is too much for my legs to hold up at the same time. His hands land on my back, trailing down to my waist. He steps in closer until I can feel the heat from his body, and then he's holding me against him, our bodies pressed together, like he somehow knows that I'm afraid I might fall. His heart beats against my chest. I wonder if he can feel mine too.

Our lips separate for a moment so that I can catch my breath, and even then, he doesn't stop kissing me. His lips make a trail across my cheek, down to my jawbone. His stubble scratches my face, and I find myself imagining how it would feel on other parts of my body. I turn my head, searching for his lips, and then they're on mine again. I pull at his lower lip with my teeth. He tightens his hold around me.

I don't want to let go of him. I could live right here, wrapped up in his arms, and probably die happily. I forget that we're standing in the stairwell until I hear a door opening above us and then footsteps coming down the stairs. He separates his lips from mine and takes a step back. I catch myself against the wall, because I'm still not sure if my legs can support me. He has this way of making gravity feel all wrong.

He watches me, his chest rising and falling heavily, neither of us turning to look at the neighbor who passes us on their way down to the lobby.

"You probably want to go catch up on sleep after that plane ride," he says, his voice husky.

I find myself a little disappointed that he's not inviting himself into my apartment or trying to get me to go upstairs with him. He's right, though. I need to recover from my trip to San Diego.

"Yeah," I agree. "You probably need to go make a bunch of noise upstairs."

He smiles. "I'll try to keep it down for you."

He leans down and gives me one more kiss on the lips. I open the door and head toward my apartment. I can hear him taking the stairs up to the fourth floor.

When Anne first dropped me off, I imagined that I would fall asleep as soon as my head hit the pillow, but now my mind is too busy for sleep to come easily. I keep thinking about his eyes, his crooked smile, the way his hands caressed my waist. I replay our breakfast date in my mind, the things that he said, and I feel a smile creeping across my lips.

I close my eyes and try to quiet my brain, but the harder I try, the more I think about him. I focus on the sounds in my apartment – the buzzing of the refrigerator in the next room, the humming of the air conditioner. I can't stop thinking about the way Jake's lips felt against mine, and how I so badly wished that he had invited me up to his apartment, or that I had the courage to invite him in here.

It's been a while since I've been with anyone, and I'm not used to being the one who has to ask for it. Somehow that makes me want him more. I slip my hand beneath my sheets, making my way into my shorts and between my legs. I take a deep breath, my eyes still closed, and I imagine that he's in the room with me and he's the one touching me like this.

I dip my fingertips in, feeling how wet I already am just from that kiss in the stairwell. I can still feel where his hands touched my waist, but now they're moving lower, trailing down my hips and cupping my ass, his hand sliding between my legs and – *ooh*.

I spread my legs a little wider for him, imagining that his head is down there and he's going down on me. I let out a little moan. I arch my back, increasing the pressure. I have this image of him sprawled out over the end of my bed, doing things to my body that would make me blush to admit out loud.

My heart rate picks up as I climb higher. I take a deep breath and close my eyes tighter, trying to hold onto this fantasy. I picture him sitting on the edge of my bed, and I'm on his lap, straddling him. I look down as I unzip his pants, and just as I'm about to slide him into me, I look back up at his face. He's not Jake anymore, but Luca, or at least what I imagine he might look like. I try to change the image in my head, but it's too late. My clit begins to pulsate and I release my breath, riding my climax all the way to the top and back down slowly.

I lie there, breathing heavily as I come back down. My whole body feels good even though my mind is conflicted.

It's been a while since I've allowed Luca to slip into my thoughts like this. I'm not sure what to do about it. I stare up at my ceiling, feeling oddly guilty about the man I kissed in the stairwell not long ago.

I listen for any noises coming from upstairs. It's quiet. He kept his promise.

Chapter Twelve

THE DELI MEAT DILEMMA

I'm working on my graphics when a cup of coffee appears next to me. I look up at Anne, then reach for the cup and take a sip. She grabs a chair and sits down.

"Careful," I warn her. "Patty-boy doesn't like seeing us mingle, remember?"

"Patty-boy?" She raises an eyebrow. "I saw him carry his phone into the bathroom, and I'm pretty sure he was playing a game on it. We should be good for at least ten minutes."

"I have work to do."

"I thought maybe we could plan our trip to Georgia. Did you talk to Husky Eyes about having your date Friday night so that we can go on Saturday?"

The mention of Jake brings a smile to my face as I think of our breakfast date yesterday morning. Then my face pinkens as I remember the way my thoughts wandered afterward.

"What?" Anne prods, watching my change in facial expression.

"Nothing. I'm busy. We can plan the trip later."

"As soon as I mentioned Husky Eyes, you got this goofy smile on your face. You talked to him, didn't you?"

I smile and turn back to my graphics. "I don't know. Maybe."

Anne groans. "Don't leave me hanging." She drums her hands on the desk. "Spill."

I shrug, taking another sip of my coffee. "It's boring. You wouldn't want to hear about it."

Anne leans in closer to me, tightening her fists on top of the desk. "Don't do this to me, Gnome. Tell me what happened."

I let out a long sigh, fighting a smile while I roll my eyes. "He saw me when you dropped me off yesterday. We got breakfast."

Anne's eyes widen and she squeals. "I knew it!" Then she lowers her voice to a whisper. "Did you have sex with him?"

My face starts to heat at the mere suggestion. Seeing my blush, Anne gets even more excited.

"You did, didn't you?"

"No!" I say, shushing her, because she's being loud now, and I'm worried that Patrick will walk in at any second.

"Tell me everything."

I purse my lips, deciding how much I want to tell her. "We might have made out in the stairwell after breakfast."

Anne squeals again. "Did you move the party from the stairwell to the bedroom?" She wiggles her eyebrows.

"Unfortunately, no. I was so close to inviting him into my apartment when he told me to go inside and get some sleep." I mock pout, pretending to be sad. "I don't think he likes me."

"You're right. He doesn't. Taking you out to breakfast and then making out with you is a huge red flag. He should have tried harder to get your pants off."

I laugh. "We shouldn't talk about this at work. Someone might hear us."

"I've heard much worse from the anchors," she says.

I'm dying for this conversation to be over because I'm afraid that Anne will keep pushing to know more. I wouldn't put it past her to guess exactly what was on my mind when I had my hand between my legs yesterday. She would probably say it as a joke and then my face would give me away. I would never hear the end of it.

"I think I just heard the toilet flush in the men's room," I say. "You better get back to work."

"You're lying," she says. "I would have heard it too."

"I have work to do, Anette."

"Speaking of work, guess what I saw last night."

"What?" I ask, glad that the conversation seems to be steering away from my love life.

She pulls her phone out of her pocket and shows me her screen. I recognize the dating app she uses all the time. She scrolls through a few photos of single men, then stops on a familiar face.

I gasp. "Is that…?"

"Patrick," she finishes for me. Her lips are contorted in an expression I can only describe as a grimace. "Do you think this means he saw my photo too?"

"He's probably looking at your photo right now. On the toilet."

"Ugh. Don't say that!"

"I bet that's why he takes so long in there," I say. Anne frowns, and then her eyes widen. "He probably sits in there swiping right, and all those poor girls he's matching with have no idea that he was pooping while he did it."

"Jesus, Naomi. I thought you were going in a completely

different direction with that. Either way, gross. I don't want to think about that."

I hear the toilet flushing. We both turn to look in the direction of the bathroom. Anne rolls her eyes at me, then saunters off. I turn back to my desk to continue preparing my weather report, and then I do my first on-air appearance of the morning. Anne is busy with her own work, so I don't see her again until she makes her rounds handing out the mail. By the time I'm finished with my last appearance, Anne is waiting at my desk with an unopened envelope in her hand. I can tell by the look on her face that it's another letter from Luca.

"He sent another one already?"

"He's not waiting for you to write back because he knows you can't." She hands the envelope to me when I reach her. "Open it."

I rip the envelope open, bracing myself for whatever his letter contains today.

Dear Naomi,

I want to play a little game. It's probably killing you that you can't write back to me, right? I can just imagine how badly you want to. I'll make you a deal though. I want you to say the word 'bologna' in your 5AM weather report. If you can do that, I'll give you a hint about where I am now. Maybe I'll even include my return address on the next letter. Maybe.

Love,

Luca

Anne reads the letter over my shoulder. "What the hell is bologna?" she asks, pronouncing the word incorrectly.

"It's a type of deli meat, and it's pronounced like baloney.

Didn't you ever see the Oscar Mayer commercials growing up?"

She shrugs. "My parents were vegetarians and I didn't have a TV for most of my childhood. My family was all about exploring the great outdoors." She rolls her eyes.

I start singing the jingle from the commercials, but she shushes me as if this is more embarrassing than talking about sex at work.

"You're not going to do it, are you?" she asks, returning her attention to the letter.

I think about it for a moment. If he gives me his return address, I won't have to spend hundreds of dollars traveling to all the places his past letters came from just to find clues about where he might be now. If I could just write back to him, maybe I could get him out of my head. "Why not? It would sure make things easier."

She frowns. "How are you going to fit bologna into your report?"

"I'm sure I can find a way."

"This is ridiculous," she says. "If you do what he says, you'll just be letting him win."

"He's already winning."

"Not if we go to Georgia this weekend and find someone who knows him."

"And what if no one knows him?"

"Then we keep looking. Don't even entertain him. He probably just wants you to say it so that he can make sure you're getting his letters. Let him keep wondering."

"You're probably right." With a sigh, I read over the letter again, then stuff it in my purse. "Let's go get lunch."

We grab lunch at a Greek restaurant, and then we plan the logistics of our trip to Georgia. We won't need a hotel, because we're flying there and back the same day. We shouldn't need more than a few hours to visit Luca's old address and interview his neighbors.

"This is so much fun," Anne says as we use our phones to buy our plane tickets. "Luca's going to be waiting all week for you to say bologna on national television. Meanwhile he has no idea that we're heading to Georgia to track him down."

"It's a little bit weird that you're so obsessed with tracking him down."

"Says the girl who's upset that she didn't get to sleep with a guy she barely knows."

"When you say it like that, I sound pretty pathetic."

"You are."

I press my hand against my chest. "Wow. I can't believe I'm friends with you."

"Wait. We're friends? I thought we were just coworkers."

I throw my napkin at her. "I don't have to take you on these trips with me, you know."

"Too late. Plane tickets are already bought," she says. "I'll be picking you up bright and early Saturday morning. And don't you dare say bologna on national television."

"I promise I won't."

We go our separate ways after leaving the restaurant. I park my car in the parking garage next to my building, and then I walk around to the front. I spot Caterpillar Kid sitting on the sidewalk, using crayons to color the pages of a coloring book. I look around, searching for a responsible adult. Once again, it appears this kid is alone.

I kneel down to check out the artwork. Caterpillar Kid smiles up at me. It turns out my nickname is spot-on, because the kid is coloring in a book full of images of caterpillars.

"What kind of caterpillar is that?" I ask.

"This is a monarch caterpillar."

"Is it going to turn into a moth?"

She laughs, making me feel dumb. "No. It's a *monarch* caterpillar. It's going to turn into a monarch butterfly."

"You know a lot about caterpillars."

"I'm going to be an entomologist when I grow up," she says.

"Wow. You're a lot smarter than I was at your age." I realize after I say it that I'm not exactly sure how old she is. I don't think I could say a big word like that when I was in the age-range I assume this kid is in.

"Don't feel bad," she says. "You know a lot about the weather, and you're on TV." She stops coloring for a moment to look up at me. "Do you think I could be on TV one day?"

"Maybe if you work really hard studying your bugs, you'll get your own TV show where you get to teach other people about them."

She smiles wider, exposing a couple of missing teeth. "Would you watch it?"

"Of course I would." I watch as the kid returns to coloring. "Where's your mom? Does she know that you're out here all by yourself?"

"I'm not all by myself," she says. "He's watching me."

The way she says it makes me feel unsettled. I check over my shoulder, wondering if there's someone I missed, or if the kid has an imaginary friend. I've always been creeped out by children who have imaginary friends. Seeing no one, I force myself to ask: "Who is watching you?"

She uses a crayon to point through one of the front windows of the building. I spot Joel sitting behind the security desk. He waves his fingers at me. Okay. I feel better now.

I straighten up. "I guess if you're fine out here, I'm going to go upstairs. Don't talk to strangers, okay?"

I head inside.

"Playing babysitter, huh?" I say to Joel.

He shrugs, reaching his hand into a large jar of pickles on his desk. "Might as well. Not like I have anything better to do."

I can't help but think that's probably true. The man is at the security desk day and night, it seems. I feel a little bad for him, but I imagine he makes a lot of money with all the overtime he works.

When I get to my apartment, I can hear the usual loud noises coming from the apartment above mine. Now that I know who it is, I listen more carefully. It sounds like something heavy is rolling across the floor, followed by several running footsteps. I decide that these sounds can't possibly be from two kittens. He has to be messing with me or something.

I head to my speaker and turn on some music. A minute later, my phone buzzes.

Husky Eyes: *Can you turn the volume up? I'm having a little trouble figuring out what song is playing.*
Naomi: *There you go. Is that better?*
Husky Eyes: *Much better. The kittens love Britney Spears.*

I snort out a laugh.

Naomi: *This isn't Britney Spears.*
Husky Eyes: *Seriously?*
Naomi: *It's Shakira.*
Husky Eyes: *Oh. Well, the kittens love Shakira.*

There's some more thumping on the ceiling that I can hear

even over the music. I listen for a moment, noticing that it seems to be moving along to the beat.

Naomi: *Is that you dancing up there, or do the kittens just have excellent rhythm?*

The thumping stops almost as soon as I send the message. Then my phone buzzes again.

Husky Eyes: *You can hear that?*
Naomi: *Yes.*
Husky Eyes: *That was definitely the kittens.*

I find myself smiling at my phone. I turn down the music, then lie down on my couch with my phone, feeling like I'm sixteen again.

Naomi: *What are you doing? Do you have time to come downstairs?*
Husky Eyes: *I have to head back to work.*
Naomi: *Oh ok. Another time?*

I stare at my phone, watching as a bubble with three dots pops up, indicating that he's typing a message. The bubble disappears for a moment, and then reappears. I hold my breath. It's quiet upstairs. I wonder if he already left.

I let my screen go dark. I get up and walk to the kitchen for a glass of water, leaving my phone on the couch. When I hear it buzz from across the room, I skip back over to see what it says.

Husky Eyes: *Come to the aquarium.*

Chapter Thirteen

A LITTLE FISHY

I send a text to let Jake know that I'm here, but as I step through the front doors of the aquarium, I realize that I didn't need to send it. He's already waiting for me, leaning against a wall in the grand entryway. Visitors of all ages are scattered between us, looking at pamphlets and choosing which animals to see first.

His eyes drop to his phone as my message makes it to him. The corner of his mouth quirks up, and then his eyes raise up from his phone, and when they meet mine, his smile grows wider.

He steps toward me, not seeming to care about the crowd of people in the way. Somehow, he dodges children and couples without taking his eyes off me. We reach each other in the middle. My heart drums inside my chest. He leans down like he's going to kiss me, but at the last second, he seems to remember that he's at work and we're surrounded by children. He redirects, aiming for my forehead, but his lips land on my eyebrow instead.

"Wow. I don't think I've ever been greeted with an eyebrow kiss before," I tease him.

He smiles, then kisses my other eyebrow. "Just to even things out," he says.

He takes my hand, leading me past the ticket line.

"Are we sneaking in?" I ask as he punches in a code to let us through a door labeled for authorized personnel only.

He shushes me. "Don't tell anyone. I know a guy."

He leads us down a hallway. "I'm not going to get you fired, am I?" I ask.

"Probably not." We reach another door. He opens it, and guides me through with his hand on my lower back. We've made it past the ticket line and bag check.

"What do you want to see first?" he asks.

I turn around, taking in our surroundings. There are tanks built into most of the walls, filled with colorful fish, coral, and aquatic plants. The overhead lights are turned down low so that the tanks are illuminated, casting a glow on the hallways and providing light for the darker parts of the aquarium.

"Do you have otters?"

"Of course." He takes my hand again. We head down a curved corridor that's lined on both sides with glass walls. I slow down to look at the different species of fish, some swimming around in schools and seemingly unaware of their audience. Others swim up to the edge to watch us curiously, while others scurry away and hide as soon as they see us.

We reach the river otter enclosure. It's set up differently from the fish tanks. There are dry surfaces where the otters can come up to take a break from swimming. Two otters float on their backs on the surface of the water. A third otter swims around underwater, entertaining the children watching him from the other side of the glass. We have to head down a set of stairs and loop around to see underwater.

"Just three otters?" I ask. It seems like a large enclosure for only three animals.

"The otters are part of our rehabilitation program. The young one you see swimming around only came to us a couple of months ago. He was found in someone's backyard and his mother couldn't be located so he was assumed to be orphaned. The people who found him kept him as a pet for a few months before turning him over to us, so he probably won't be eligible for release."

"Do you usually release animals back into the wild?"

"That's the goal, but it doesn't always work out that way. We have to keep the safety of the animal in mind. If the otter becomes too tame, like the three you see in this exhibit, they can't usually be released."

The idea that none of these otters will be able to swim in a real river again makes me sad. "So none of these otters will be able to go back to the wild?"

"Not these three. We have several more in another enclosure that isn't accessible to guests. The otters we have there aren't accustomed to humans, and we need to keep it that way so that they can be released."

I watch him while he talks about the animals. He focuses on the enclosure, watching the young otter swim playfully, before his blue eyes rise to meet mine. I can see the reflection of the otter dancing in his eyes.

"What do you want to see next?" he asks.

"What do you recommend?"

He takes me to see an octopus, and after that we see the stingrays, which are popular with the children. Another small crowd is gathered around the jellyfish exhibit. We watch for a minute, listening as a tour guide explains how a jellyfish sting should be treated.

I walk alongside the tank, watching the creatures inside. I'm mesmerized by the way they move, and how such a strange bloblike animal can not only survive, but also cause so much pain. The tank wraps around a curved hallway that takes me to a less populated area of the aquarium. It takes me a minute to notice that Jake isn't beside me anymore. I turn around and see him watching me from a few feet behind. His hands are tucked into his pockets and his head is tilted at a slight angle. His lips part like he's going to say something. I watch him, waiting, but then his mouth closes again. His brow wrinkles for just a second, and then he pulls his hands out of his pockets and steps closer to me until he's right next to me.

"What's up?" I ask.

He shakes his head, reaching one hand up to rub the back of his neck. I wait another moment, thinking he might still say whatever is on his mind, when my eyes land on the sign for the next tank.

"Salmon?" I say, reading the name of the species. "I didn't know you had food here."

He snorts, his lip curling up in a half smile. He jabs me with his elbow. "Very funny."

"Oh no. Don't tell me you're against eating seafood."

He cringes, making me worry that I crossed a line. "I'm not a huge fan of seafood, but I promise it's not because of my job."

I swipe my hand over my forehead. "Phew. I was afraid that I offended you for a second. I guess that's kind of like asking a regular veterinarian if they eat dogs and cats."

He laughs, and just like that, I've almost forgotten that I was waiting for him to say something before I interrupted. "I don't think it's the same at all," he says. "I'm sure livestock veterinarians still eat burgers."

I shake my head. "I don't think I could do it. I couldn't spend all day fixing and healing those animals just to go home and eat them."

He leans against the tank, crossing his arms and watching me. "Good thing you're a meteorologist and not a veterinarian, then," he says.

"You're right. I can't go home and eat a hurricane."

He smiles and pulls away from the tank, taking a step toward me. "You're really something else, you know that, Naomi?"

He's so close that I have to crane my neck up to see him. When I do, he tilts his chin down, and a second later, his lips are on mine. He cups his hands around the sides of my face before sliding his fingers into my hair. My heart speeds up. I stand on my toes to reach him better.

For a moment, I forget that we're in a public place where anyone could walk around the corner and see us. It feels like we're all alone, just us and the occasional splash of water in the tanks and the humming and bubbling of filters. There's something about the way his fingers comb through my hair that makes me feel like I'm melting. I'm taken back to that moment in the stairwell yesterday when it was just the two of us. If I could go back, I would try harder to get him to come inside with me. Maybe then my thoughts wouldn't have strayed to Luca when I should have only been thinking about Jake. I clutch the back of his shirt, pulling him closer to me, which is a mistake, because now that his body is flush with mine, I'm not sure I can let go.

The taste of his lips on mine is something that I want to savor. I've been craving the feel of him, the way his lips fit perfectly against mine, since he let go of me yesterday morning.

He deepens the kiss, tasting me with a flick of his tongue. Before I know it, I'm backed against the wall of the salmon tank. I slide my hands under his shirt, feeling the smooth skin of his back, before snaking them around his ribcage to feel his abdomen. He lets out a startled grunt. I let go, but he catches my hand, putting it back on him.

"That tickled," he scolds against my lips.

"You mean this?" I slide my hand back over his ribcage and he jolts again.

"Yes, that." This time, he grabs my hand and pulls it away from him.

"It was brave of you to trust me enough to tell me that you're ticklish," I warn him.

"Are you?"

"Ticklish? Not at all."

He watches me for a second, eyes narrowed, then reaches both hands over and digs his fingers into my ribcage. I shriek and try to run away, but he wraps his arms around me, locking me into a hug. I stop fighting once I realize he's not trying to tickle me anymore. I relax into his embrace.

"Okay, so we've established that you're a liar," he says.

"How about we make a truce?" I offer. "I won't tickle you if you don't tickle me."

"I think I can agree to that." He pulls back just enough to plant another kiss on my lips.

The effect he has on me is dizzying. I can't let him get away with just one kiss, so I catch his lips just as he's pulling back again. When I pull away, he dives back in for another, and then it's my turn again, and each new kiss is longer and sweeter than the last.

His touch sends a pulse through my body. I find myself calculating how far it is from here to my car, and wondering if I can get him all the way there without undressing him first.

"Jesus, Naomi," he whispers against my lips. "I can't get enough of you."

My heart is beating so hard that I can feel it vibrating in my ears.

"Oh good," I say, catching my breath. "I was afraid after that eyebrow kiss that you were trying to put me in the friendzone or something."

I don't say it out loud, but I also think about the way he looked at me by the salmon tank, when he had me thinking something might be wrong. I must have misinterpreted the look on his face.

"Not in a million years," he says. "But we should probably calm down before I get fired."

"Right. And before I get arrested."

He raises an eyebrow, making me realize maybe I was the only one thinking about undressing in the middle of the aquarium. "Why would you—"

"Do you have penguins here?" I interrupt. "Let's go see the penguins."

Chapter Fourteen

INAPPROPRIATE HALLWAY BEHAVIOR

The closer we get to the weekend, the more excited Anne is about our trip on Saturday. I feel like she's more excited than I am, which is weird, and I keep telling her that. I haven't received another letter from Luca. I also haven't said 'bologna' on air like he asked me to do. By Friday, I'm starting to wonder if I should have just said the word. After receiving fairly frequent letters from him over the previous weeks, I'm a little disappointed that he hasn't sent anything else. Maybe Anne's reasoning for not doing what he said backfired on me. He probably thinks I'm not receiving his letters now, and he isn't going to waste any more time sending them.

"Have you talked to Husky Eyes again?" Anne asks at the café after work.

I smile, thinking about my spontaneous trip to the aquarium earlier this week. After making out with Jake in front of an audience of salmon, we spent the next half hour looking at penguins and seals and walruses. I don't think I've ever had such a good time at an aquarium.

"We've been texting," I tell her. I look over my shoulder at the front door, hoping to see him come in. I want to catch him before Anne and I take off for Georgia, but so far, our schedules have been conflicting. I figure the café at lunchtime is the best time to run into him.

"You're going to hurt your neck twisting it around like that," Anne says. "We don't need you wearing a neck brace during your weather report. Besides, I'm facing the front door. Don't you think I would tell you if he came in?"

I turn back around, smiling. "You're always looking out for me. What would I do without you?"

"I really don't know," she says, blowing a puff of air through her lips. "If it weren't for me, you would have said 'bologna' in the middle of a weather report."

"I considered it," I say. "I thought about doing it this morning." I clear my throat, changing into my on-air voice: "It's hot enough to fry bologna on the sidewalk today."

"That's what you were going to say?"

I nod. "I haven't heard from him all week."

"You'll hear from him again," she says. "Do you really think that's the end of it?"

"Probably."

She rolls her eyes. "You give up way too easily."

After lunch, I head back to my apartment. I say hi to Joel, then grab my mail on the way up. It's quiet upstairs when I get inside. I toss the mail onto my kitchen counter without looking at it, then head to the closet where I keep the box of Luca's letters. I flip through the pages, pulling out the ones I want Anne to read on our flight tomorrow. I sift through the stack until I find the letters that he wrote to me while he was stationed in Georgia. We were in our early twenties. It was my last year at the University of Oklahoma, and his last year in the military. He had made the mistake of telling me once that he had joined the military so that he could go to college for free after his four years were up. I didn't let him live it down, calling him a phony and telling him that he wasn't a real hero since he never went overseas. I'm sure he didn't like my jokes, but then again, he never did.

Before I know it, I've spent a couple of hours sitting on the floor and reading old letters. I have them scattered around me, grouped by different eras. There are the junior high letters, the high school and the college letters, and then there are the letters we wrote when my career was just starting and Luca was out of the military and going to college. I notice that his handwriting evolved from the first letter he sent. His first letter was hard to decipher, but after that, his handwriting gradually became neater and easier to read.

Dear Naomi,

Of all the people I've ever met, the ones in Georgia are the nicest. Anywhere else, when I'm walking into a store at the same time as someone else, the closest thing I get to a greeting is an impatient grunt as they're forced by society's expectations to hold the door open for me. But it's not like that in Georgia. Out here, it's always a friendly smile and a happy greeting, and sometimes they run ahead just to hold the door open. It's like everyone you meet in Georgia is a friend by default.

I would invite you to come see for yourself, but I imagine even the friendly folks in Georgia have standards, and they'd know better than to smile at someone like you. In fact, you'd probably put the whole state in a bad mood, and no one out here would ever smile again.

Love,

Luca

Dear Luca,

I find it a little hard to believe that anyone would be so polite to you. You must be really good at faking your personality. Besides, you won't know friendly until you've been to Oklahoma. The people out here are nicer than anyone else on earth.

Love,

Naomi

Dear Naomi,

Is that an invitation to come to Oklahoma? Because I kind of feel like it's an invitation. Regardless, the people in Oklahoma are only nice to each other because they're afraid of being shunned at the next family reunion. And I'm not really sure how you would know that they're nicer than anyone else on earth when you've never been out of the state. I've been all over the country, and I can guarantee you, the people in Georgia are the nicest.

Love,

Luca

Dear Luca,

Why would I have a reason to leave Oklahoma when everyone is so nice here? You've never been to my state, so I don't think you can make that guarantee. I guess we'll just have to agree to disagree.

Love,

Naomi

Dear Naomi,

I refuse to agree to disagree. In fact, I plan to argue with you about this until you at least leave your state. Maybe then I'll agree that you have a valid argument. Next month, I'm going to Dallas for a few weeks, so I won't be able to write for a little bit. You're at the

University of Oklahoma, right? I think Dallas is only three hours away.

    Love,

    Luca

I stare at his letter, trying to remember what I wrote back. I can't figure out what was going through my head when I got that letter, because it's not until now, years later, that I realize he was trying to open the door to us meeting while he was in Texas. I didn't receive another letter from him until he was back in Georgia, and by then, the conversation had taken a different route.

Surrounded by his letters, I imagine how things might have turned out differently if I had suggested he come visit me, or if I had taken the plunge and went to Dallas for the weekend. I wonder if we would have gotten along in real life. Maybe it would have been awkward, and even though we had been writing to each other for years, we would have found that we had nothing to say to each other when we weren't hiding behind a piece of paper and a pen.

Or maybe it would have been like I sometimes imagined it being. We might have said mean things to each other like we did in our letters, but I would know that he didn't really mean it. There were times when I thought that meeting up with him would ruin what we shared with our letters. During the two years that I didn't hear from him, the idea that what we had might change stopped mattering. If what we had was coming to an end regardless, then maybe meeting him in person could have saved it. Maybe it would have made it better.

There's a knot in my throat as I think about what might have been. I feel silly for mourning something that never existed, but reading these letters again reminds me that it *could have* existed, and my reluctance for change was the only thing standing in the way.

I gather up all of the Georgia letters that I set aside, and slide them back into the box. It doesn't feel right to show these to Anne anymore.

My phone buzzes with a notification. A food order I forgot I placed was just dropped off at the security desk downstairs. I slip on my shoes and jog downstairs to get it. As I'm coming out of the stairwell, a family catches my eye outside the window. I have to do a double-take. No, not a family. It's Caterpillar Kid and a woman who I assume must be her mother. Next to her is Jake. I stop and watch them for a minute. Caterpillar Kid is holding some kind of bug and showing it to Jake. I'm sure it's another fuzzy caterpillar but from this distance I can't see what it is. Jake is holding a plastic bag in one hand. The kid hands the bug to him and he takes it in his other hand and laughs. The sound of their voices and laughter is muffled through the window, but it still makes me smile. He says something that makes the kid laugh too. He turns and shows the bug to the woman. She backs away a step, squealing. He tells her something that I can't hear from inside the building and then she laughs.

It strikes me how the three of them look like they could be a family, standing out there and laughing together. I know I shouldn't feel jealous, but I do. I watch them for another minute. I wonder if he's ever invited this woman out to dinner or taken her on a spontaneous breakfast date. I wonder if she's been to the aquarium. She's pretty. I wouldn't blame him. But he's not focusing on her. He's talking to the kid, and every once in a while, the two of them exchange a few words. She smiles at him and moves her hair away from her eyes. I'm sure she has a huge crush on him. Maybe they're not dating, but one thing is for sure: this guy could have any woman he wants.

He finally turns away from them and heads for the front door. Realizing that I'm about to be caught spying on him, I panic. I hit the button to open the elevator, then quickly duck inside and hit the 'close doors' button a few times until it cooperates. I'm lucky that Joel isn't at his desk to witness me embarrassing myself. I wait, holding my breath, and then I realize my mistake. He's not afraid to take the elevator like I am. I also haven't hit the button for my floor, so the elevator is just sitting here on the first floor, waiting for the next person to open the door. Just as that realization dawns on me, the doors slide open. Jake's eyebrows shoot up when he sees me.

Then he smiles. "Look at you riding the elevator."

Okay, I guess he doesn't suspect me of spying on him. I need to get out of here, but he's blocking my path. I pull the collar of my shirt away from my neck. It feels like it's choking me. "Just trying to conquer my fears."

He steps in next to me and hits the button for his floor. I'm too panicked to appreciate how close he's standing to me, or how good he smells. I look down at the bag he's holding. It's his own bag of takeout, which reminds me about mine. As the doors start to close, I stick my hand out to stop them. "Actually, I'm getting off. My food was just delivered."

I step out of the elevator and head for the security desk where my bag of food is waiting for me. When I turn back around, I see that he's holding the doors open for me. I think about getting back in, but I just can't bring myself to do it. I gesture to the stairwell. "I'm heading this way."

He rolls his eyes at me, a smile teasing the corner of his mouth. "I'll race you up there."

He lets go of the elevator door, and it closes, leaving me

alone in the lobby. I take in a deep breath, release it, then head for the stairs. I scold myself on the way up to my floor. I should have just taken the elevator and conquered my fear like I said I was doing. It wouldn't have been so bad if I got trapped in there with him again. Plus, we both have takeout, so it's not like we would have gone hungry while we waited for the fire department to come rescue us.

The smell of my food drifts up to my nose, making my stomach growl. The elevator opens just as I come out of the stairwell.

"Looks like it's a tie," he says.

"I gave you an advantage. I took the stairs very slowly."

"Uh-huh. Sure." He gestures to my bag. "Eating alone?"

I smile. "Want to join me?" I don't want him to see the mess I left in my living room, so I lower myself to the floor. I pull the plastic box of food out of the paper bag and set it in front of me. "Picnic?"

The side of his mouth quirks up a little higher.

"My place is a mess," I explain. "I'm packing for another trip with Anne. I can't have you see my living room in the state that it's in."

"I wouldn't mind," he says. He lowers himself to the floor so that he's sitting across from me. He opens his own takeout container. I look over at his food. He has Chinese. It smells so good that it makes me regret my own choice of Italian.

"I was surprised I didn't see you at the café today," I tell him.

"You were there?"

I nod.

"Of course," he says. "The one day that I skip lunch."

"Why did you skip lunch?"

"I had to perform an emergency surgery on a walrus," he says.

"A walrus? Really? Poor thing. What happened?"

"His flipper was injured in an accident at a zoo. The zoo didn't have adequate vet staff or enough money to pay for his care, so they signed him over to us. He'll be fine, though. He's doing better already."

"Wow. You're a real hero to the walrus community."

"Thank you. Maybe you can come by the aquarium again and see him."

I smile. "I'd like that."

"Where are you going with Anne?"

I'm caught off guard by the abrupt change in subject. My mouth is full of pasta, so I take a minute to answer. "We're flying out to Georgia."

He frowns. "Really? Why Georgia? Don't tell me you're trying to compare their beaches too." His tone doesn't sound quite as teasing as I expect. I can't quite put my finger on it. He almost seems annoyed. I shrug it off, reminding myself that he must have had a stressful day with the walrus.

"We won't be anywhere near the beach." I consider explaining the reason for the trip, but I can't find the right words. "It's just a girls' trip. Anne has always wanted to go to Albany."

"Albany's not really all that special." His tone is still flat and unamused.

"You've been there?"

He shrugs. "I've heard."

"I guess Anne and I will just have to see for ourselves. What are you doing tomorrow?"

"I have to take the kittens to the adoption event," he says.

"I was going to invite you, but it sounds like you'll be having more fun than I am."

"Oh. I'm sorry." I guess it makes sense now why he's behaving the way that he is.

"It's okay. I just figured if you weren't doing anything else, maybe you'd want to come."

I twirl my fork on my plate, picking up a string of pasta. "Are you sad to see them go?"

He nods. "A little. I'm happy that they'll get a new home."

The elevator opens and one of my neighbors steps out. She does a double-take when she sees us sitting on the floor. She heaves an exaggerated sigh, shakes her head, then lets herself into her apartment without a word. I look back at Jake in time to catch a funny look on his face. I almost snort out the food in my mouth.

"You'd think she's never seen two people having a picnic in the hallway," he says. There's a glint in his eye that tells me his bad mood is coming to an end, or at the very least, he's trying to move past it.

"Do you think she'll call Joel to kick us out? I don't remember seeing anything about eating in the hallway in my lease agreement."

He laughs. "I think we'll be okay." He takes another bite of food, then asks, "How early do you have to be up tomorrow?"

"Anne is picking me up at four, which sounds early, but for me it means I get to sleep in a little."

"I'm usually up at four to go for a run. Maybe I'll see you on your way out?"

I don't know why I forgot that he was up early and coming home from a run when Anne and I got back from San Diego last weekend. I guess I'm not the only early bird in the building. I wonder if this means I'll get to see him shirtless again. I look at his chest, peeling his shirt off with my mind and trying to remember what he looks like underneath. The image I get is of his body tinted gold under the streetlight, like a statue. The lighting is all wrong for this hallway.

When I move my gaze up to his eyes, I realize that he's watching me. My face flushes. I wonder if he's aware of the thoughts going through my mind about his perfect body. Then I remember that he's waiting for an answer.

"Yeah, sure."

"I still want to take you out for dinner," he says. "When will you be back in town?"

His question makes my heart skip. "It's just a day trip. We'll be back tomorrow night."

"Perfect. I'll take you out on Sunday then. Don't make any plans."

"It's a date," I tell him.

Chapter Fifteen

PENNY PICKLES

I n the morning, I get up and start a pot of coffee, then head back to my room to get dressed. Since it's just a day trip, I don't have to bring anything other than my purse. I know that Anne will be disappointed that I'm not bringing any letters, but after reading through them last night, I don't feel right about that anymore. There was a change in tone from high school to adulthood that I don't think I fully grasped until I reread the letters. Maybe I wanted to believe that we were only ever mean to each other, but now I feel like there was something more, and it should stay between us.

I'm almost done getting ready when I get a text from Anne. She's on her way, and she's bringing me a cup of coffee. We're not even at work, yet she's still supplying me with more caffeine than I need.

At four, there's a light tap at my front door. I gather my purse, check my hair in the mirror, and then open the door. Jake is waiting for me. He's wearing a T-shirt and running shorts similar to what he was wearing last weekend when we went out for breakfast. His eyelids look heavy like he just rolled out of bed, and his messy hair confirms it. It takes a lot of willpower to stop myself from reaching my hand up to comb my fingers through his hair.

"I thought maybe I missed you," he says.

"Nope. Anne will be here any second. I was just about to head downstairs."

I lock my apartment door, and then we head for the stairwell. He takes the stairs faster than I do, but I don't mind because it gives me a moment to appreciate the way his back muscles fill out his shirt. And his shorts... I'm starting to think it's been way too long since I've been laid. As the thought crosses my mind, I realize that sounds like something Anne would tell me. She must be rubbing off on me.

We make it to the front door, and he holds it open for me. His hand grazes my lower back as I pass through the doorway. The contact surprises me, but I don't mind it. He closes the door and stands next to me. Anne isn't here yet, so we have some time. It's different being out here at this time of the morning when I'm not in a rush to get somewhere. The sky is still dark and the city is quiet. The usual hum of traffic is replaced by only the occasional passing car.

"Do you normally run without a shirt on?" I ask, breaking the silence.

My question catches him off guard. He frowns, then breaks into a smile. "Usually, yeah. It's too hot for a shirt."

"Oh, that's why."

He raises an eyebrow. "What did you think?"

"I thought maybe it was part of your mating dance." I wiggle my arms and body in a poor imitation of a male bird seducing a female.

He laughs, grabbing onto my arms to stop me from embarrassing myself. "Yeah. You caught me," he teases. "I'm just out here running around shirtless, hoping some girl will follow me home."

"Does it work?"

His eyes glance over me, a smile tugging at the corner of his lips. "Well, last week the girl I had my eyes on ran right into me." His gaze darts back to the front door of our building before returning to me. "Right there in that lobby."

I shrug, pretending to not know what he's talking about. "I hope you got her number."

Before he can respond, Anne's car pulls up to the curb. I can't see her through the dark windows, but I know that she's watching us.

"That's her." I turn to say goodbye to him. He's a lot closer to me than he was a minute ago, making me have to crane my neck just to look him in the eye. As I do, he takes my face in his hands and his lips meet mine. It's my turn to be caught off guard. This isn't just a peck on the lips. His mouth lingers on mine, and it feels like a promise is being made. A promise of what, I'm not sure, but I'm willing to accept it. I forget that we're standing in front of our building and that we have an audience of one watching from the car. He deepens the kiss, parting my lips with a flick of his tongue. His hands fall from my face to my back, pulling my body against his. With our bodies together, our hearts beat at the same rate, and I feel like I'm melting into him. My hands land on his sides. I clutch fistfuls of his shirt without thinking about it. It takes everything in my power not to jump up and wrap my arms and legs around him.

I force myself to pull away because I know that if I don't, I'll end up missing my flight. His chest is rising and falling rapidly with each breath he takes. There's something different about his blue eyes. His icy stare has been replaced with the hot blue of a flame.

"I should go before Anne starts honking and makes a scene."

"I'll see you tomorrow," he says. His voice is a soft, deep rumble that makes me wish I didn't have to wait until tomorrow to see him again. I want to give him one last peck on the lips, but I'm afraid that if I do, I won't make it to the airport. I can feel his eyes on my back as I get into Anne's car. She's staring at me, her mouth and eyes wider than I've ever seen them.

"You couldn't have, like, texted me an update on the Husky Eyes situation? What the hell, Gnome?"

She steps on the gas pedal, taking us down the street a little too fast. I pat my seatbelt, making sure it's tight enough.

"I already told you about the aquarium," I remind her. "Am I supposed to update you every time he kisses me?"

"You could have told me you started sleeping with him."

I laugh. "I haven't."

She groans. "Seriously? Why are you making the poor guy wait?"

I think about that for a moment. "I'm not making him wait. He just hasn't tried to take my clothes off yet. He's kind of a gentleman." I smile. "I like it."

"What happened to just having a little fun with him until you move out of the building?"

I shrug. "I'm not so sure that's all I want now."

We reach the airport. When we go through the security checkpoint, I feel silly for having been so scared to do this last weekend. I still can't believe that Luca convinced me I was on the terrorist watchlist.

"Did you bring us any reading material?" Anne asks once we're sitting on the plane.

"Sorry. I forgot."

"Seriously?"

"I was going to bring the letters he sent while he was stationed in Georgia, but ... I just forgot them."

"Ugh. You suck."

"It's not a long flight. You'll survive."

"I don't think I will."

She reaches into the pocket on the back of the seat in front of her and pulls out a magazine. She flips through a few pages, then sighs and stuffs it back into the pocket.

"What's the game plan?" she asks. "Same thing we did in San Diego?"

"We'll ring every doorbell on his street until we get an answer."

"Uh, Naomi? I think we have a problem."

We've been on the road for about fifteen minutes after picking up a rental car in Albany. Anne's announcement makes me snap my attention to the road ahead of us, and then to the directions on the GPS screen. I don't need to ask to know what the problem is. There's a gate up ahead where men in military uniforms are stopping cars and checking IDs before letting people in. It looks like this is the only way to get to the address from Luca's Georgia letters.

"What do we do?" Anne asks.

"I don't know. Just drive up to the gate and ask."

"You want me to drive up there?" Her voice is high-pitched, like I just asked her to drive off a cliff.

"It's a Marine base, Anne. They're not going to arrest you for asking for directions."

Anne tightens her knuckles on the steering wheel, then rolls down the window and drives us to the gate. One of the men steps up to the window.

"Hi," Anne says. "Do we need a military ID to get on base?"

"Do you have a visitor's pass?" the man asks.

"No. How do I get one?"

"You need to make an appointment with the visitor center to get approved for a pass. Are you here to see a family member?"

"Not exactly."

I lean over Anne so that I can see the man through the window. "We're looking for an old friend. I didn't realize that his address was on this base. We just wanted to find out if any of his neighbors still know him."

The man glances at the line of cars behind us, then eyes me impatiently. "Who are you looking for?"

"Luca Pichler. Do you know him?"

He scratches his head. "Can't say I do." He looks at the line behind us again, then calls to one of the other men. "Hey, Gibson. You know anyone named Luca Pichler?"

The man he addresses as Gibson shakes his head, but it's clear he caught the attention of an older marine standing nearby. "Pickles?" the marine says.

"You know him, Gunny?"

"I know Pickles." The man addressed as Gunny steps up to the car. "You ladies friends with Pickles?"

He has the heaviest southern accent I've ever heard. Anne glances at me, her brow furrowed. I nod. "Uh, yeah. Luca Pichler? Can I ask you about him?"

He points to a small lot and says, "Go ahead and pull up there. I'll meet you over there."

Anne drives into the lot, and a moment later, the marine is next to the car. We both step out, and he offers his hand to each of us. "Maxwell," he introduces himself.

"I'm Naomi. This is Anne," I say. "This is probably going to sound a little weird, but we're trying to track down Luca. I used to be, uh, friends with him, but I lost contact with him a while back."

"Pickles ain't here anymore," Maxwell says. "He got out after his four years were up. Last I heard, he moved down to Texas with Hayes."

"Hayes?"

"Penny Hayes," Maxwell says. "Though I guess she's Penelope Pichler by now. That chick always wanted that double-P name. Wanted to be Penny Pickles."

I'm suddenly aware of my own heartbeat. It feels heavy. I'm afraid that at any moment, this guy will decide he's said enough and won't give us any more information, but right now he seems like an open book. I decide to push my luck.

"You kept in touch with them?"

"Oh, yeah. Got an invite to their wedding, but I couldn't go. I'm friends with him on Facebook. You try to find him on there?"

"I tried, but I couldn't find him. Do you mind showing me?"

He pulls his phone out of his pocket and taps the screen a few times. He frowns. "Oh," he says. "Looks like I don't have him on here anymore."

"He must have deactivated his account." Because he doesn't want me to find him just yet, but I don't say that.

"When did he get married? Last time I talked to him, he told me that he got engaged."

He blows a puff of air through his lips. "Gee, probably 'bout a year ago. I would've been there if I hadn't been deployed at the time."

"You knew Penny too, then? Did she live here with him?"

He frowns. "Nah. We served with Hayes. They were one of those on-again-off-again things. I didn't even know they were back together until I got the wedding invitation."

"So, they live in Texas now. Any chance you know where?"

He shrugs. "Dallas, I think."

I look at Anne. She has her lips clamped together, but I can tell that she's trying to hide her smile. This is more than what we could have hoped to find out from this trip.

"Thank you," I say, turning back to Maxwell. "This is really helpful."

"No problem," he says. "You can just turn around up there and head on out."

We get back in the car. Anne drives us down the street and stops the car in a strip mall parking lot. "Did Luca ever write to you from Texas?" she asks.

"No," I say, trying to remember what I read in the letters last night. "He went to Dallas once, but he never had an address there. He must have moved there after my last letter to him."

"This is big," she says. "Did you know his wife's name before? Look her up in that database."

I open my phone and log in to PeopleFinder, where I searched for Luca before. I type in 'Penelope Pichler' and wait for the results to load. Nothing looks promising. Maybe she didn't change her name. Or maybe they never got married. I'm not sure why I'm hoping for the latter. I type in 'Penelope

Hayes' and this time, the website loads an address in Dallas, Texas.

"Found her," I say. My heart is pounding. I can hear it thrumming in my ears. I can't believe I might have just found Luca.

"That's his address," Anne says, looking over my shoulder. "It's got to be. Holy shit, Gnome, we did it."

"What now?"

"What do you mean? Now you can write back and surprise the hell out of him."

"But what if he doesn't live there anymore?" I think of the letters that I sent two years ago that were returned. I don't know if I can handle that happening again.

"You heard that marine guy. He lives with her in Texas."

"We can't know for sure. His name isn't listed on here."

"They're married. Of course he lives with her."

I find it hard to believe that they're still married, especially since her last name is Hayes, when according to Maxwell, she really wanted to take Luca's last name. I also just don't want Luca to be married. I can't explain why I feel that way.

"Maybe we should check first," I say.

"Check? How?"

With shaky hands, I dial the phone number listed for Penelope Hayes. It rings a few times, and then goes to voicemail, but it's clear this is an outdated number because the voice recording is of a man who calls himself Bruce. I hang up and stare at my phone for a second before I turn to look at Anne.

"We need to fly out to Dallas."

"Are you crazy? And what then? Just show up on his doorstep? I thought you were afraid of getting pepper sprayed."

"I just... I don't know. I have a gut feeling that we're not done yet."

"Just because it was easy doesn't mean it has to be wrong," Anne says. "Take this as a win. Write to him."

I shake my head. "I can't. I need to know. I'm not sending another letter just to have it returned."

Chapter Sixteen

COME HIDE AWAY

Luca

I t was probably pretty pathetic that I couldn't get Naomi Light out of my head. During my time in the Marine Corps, I only dated a handful of girls. None of them were serious relationships. I never gave them the chance to be. I was too hung up on some girl I had never met. I didn't even know her, yet I held her up on a pedestal, and none of the other girls I dated came close to beating her.

When Penny came along, I didn't think our relationship would amount to much more than any of the others did. I guess I didn't realize just how much she liked me. She knew that I was emotionally unavailable, but she didn't know why. The sex was good, but I guess eventually it wasn't enough. She broke up with me a few times, always crying and asking why I couldn't just act like I cared. Then a few months later, she would be back, apologizing and telling me that she was fine with just having a physical relationship. The cycle repeated itself several times, even when we were both out of the military.

She followed me back to San Diego. That was when our on-again-off-again relationship became more on than off. We went to the same college and eventually we ended up living together. I met her family and they took me in as one of their own. I had been on my own for so long that it felt good to have people who cared about me. Her parents treated me like their son. Her sisters treated me like a brother. It felt like I was part of a family again.

Everything was fine for a while. I wasn't the best boyfriend to her, but she stuck around. She didn't know about my letters to Naomi. I was pretty good at keeping secrets, at least for a little while. Sometimes she would complain and nag me, but for the most part we learned to get along.

And then one day, out of the blue, she started planning our wedding. I hadn't even proposed to her, but suddenly she was wearing a big diamond ring and showing it off to all of her friends. I had no idea where that damn ring came from until I saw my credit card bill.

I thought about confronting her. I considered making her return the ring and telling her to move out. It honestly scared the hell out of me that she was doing this. It also scared me to put an end to it. I wondered if this was the best I was going to get. I had a beautiful woman who wanted to be my wife. The sex was still good, and for the most part we got along. Sometimes I wondered if the only reason our relationship was flawed was because I was afraid to commit to her. Maybe this was the push I needed.

Things were going nowhere with Naomi. I had held onto that fantasy for long enough. She had made it clear several times that she didn't want to meet me. She liked writing mean letters, but she didn't want me, and I was wasting my time believing that one day she would. I had never told her much about my relationships before, but I decided to tell her about Penny.

Dear Naomi,

I think I might be engaged. My girlfriend bought herself a ring with my credit card and now she's planning our wedding. I'm not really sure how this happened since I never proposed to her. What do you think I should do? Can I come hide away with you, or should I man up and marry her?

Love,

Luca

I guess I hoped that Naomi would know the answer. She'd either tell me to leave Penny or she'd tell me that I was being stupid and to just marry her because I deserved a life of misery. I never expected that she just wouldn't write back. I waited for weeks, then months, without hearing from her. The longer I waited, the closer we got to the wedding date Penny had planned for us. Six months went by, and it was too late to argue that we weren't really engaged. She had already booked our wedding venue, hired a minister, and found her dream wedding dress.

She also found a house for us to live in together in Texas. She wanted to be close to her family, and since I didn't know anyone in San Diego except Ben, it made sense that we move to Texas. Her father paid the down payment on the house for us, and then we were packing boxes and furniture into a moving truck.

By the time we made it to Dallas, it had been six months since I had sent that letter to Naomi. I didn't expect her to write back at this point, but I didn't want to lose contact with her. I sent a new letter to tell her that I was going through with the wedding so that she would have my new address.

I knew that she had never promised me anything, and never gave me anything other than rude, disturbing, or funny letters, but it hurt that I hadn't heard back from her yet.

We were in the new house for a month when all hell broke loose. Penny had been exploring all the closets in the house. When I asked what she was doing, she told me that she was looking for a place to hide her wedding dress. That's how she found my box of letters. I was sitting in the living room when she came storming in with my box. Next thing I knew, I was sitting in a pile of hundreds of letters.

"What the hell is this?" she screamed.

"What does it look like? They're letters."

"From Naomi," she said, pronouncing the name like it was poison. "Why do you have these?"

"She was my pen pal in elementary school," I said. "Relax."

Apparently, 'relax' was the wrong word to say, because it made her scream until I felt like my ear drums were going to burst.

"What the fuck, Penny?"

"These letters are from this year, Luca. How are you going to tell me that these are from elementary school? Why have you never told me about her before?"

"There's nothing to tell," I said. "Did you even read these letters?"

"You're cheating on me with her."

"Okay. You definitely didn't read the letters then."

She picked up a couple of letters and read only the closing. "Love, Naomi. *Love*, Naomi. Love, love, love!"

"So, what?"

"So, you'll say that to her, but I have to practically beg you to say it to me."

"I'd like to point out that she was the one who wrote 'love'. Not me."

"Oh yeah? Then what's this?" She pulled another letter out of her pocket and threw it at me. I picked it up and looked at it, confused. It took me a moment to process that this was the last letter I had sent to Naomi – the one I had mailed out a month ago with my new address. Penny must have intercepted it. "Love, Luca," she read aloud. "How can you say that to her, but not to me?"

I wanted to argue that it was just the way we had always closed our letters, but that didn't seem quite as important anymore.

"How long have you had that letter?" I asked.

She looked down at the letter in her hand, then back up at me. Something flashed in her eyes. I had never seen her look so angry. "That's not really the point here, Luca." She enunciated each word carefully, waving the letter like someone might wield a knife. "I guess we have the post office to thank for kicking this back today. You shouldn't even be writing to her in the first place. We're getting married in two months, for crying out loud."

"I never agreed to marry you," I said.

"Are you kidding me?" She held up her hand, shoving her ring finger in my face. "What about this?"

"You bought that for yourself," I said.

"We've been planning this wedding for months," she said. "The venue is already paid for. I have my dress. You can't just back out now."

"If you would just calm down, we could talk about—"

"It's because of her, isn't it? That's why you don't want to marry me all of a sudden."

"Her? I haven't heard from her in months."

"Stop lying to me. I thought I had put an end to this months ago, but it's obvious now that you never stopped writing to her. Where are you keeping the rest of the letters?"

"I'm not lying to you. And what do you mean, you put an end to it?"

"You're full of shit. I saw what she wrote to you about our wedding. That's why you're trying to back out now."

I had a sinking feeling in my chest. I thought about the letter that I sent to Naomi – the one she never answered. "What are you talking about?"

"You told her that we were getting married."

"I did. She never wrote back."

Penny smiled just then, but it wasn't a happy or even a friendly smile. It was demonic. It was creepy as hell. She pulled another letter out of her back pocket. I stood up, dropping the other letters to the floor, and took it from her. It was a letter from Naomi that I had never seen before. It was dated seven months ago, only a few days after I told her about the engagement.

Dear Luca,

I think you should dump that poor girl before she makes the mistake of marrying you and realizes what a true scumbag you are. Come hide away with me if you need to. You know where I live.

Love,

Naomi

"Come hide away with me," Penny recited through gritted teeth. She continued to berate me for having the letters, but I wasn't listening to her anymore. I was angry as hell, and all I could see was red.

"You hid this from me?" I asked.

"I should have burned it," she said. "I should have burned all of them. In fact." She turned out of the room, headed for the kitchen. I followed. She opened a couple of drawers and then, finding a candle lighter, she smiled even wider and held it up. "Time to say goodbye to Naomi."

I snatched the lighter from her hand before she could do something stupid with it. I threw it to the floor and smashed it with my shoe. Then I stormed back into the living room and began to pick up all of the letters she had dropped onto the couch and the floor around it. I shoved them all back into the box, not caring that they weren't in order anymore. I could fix that later. I just needed to get out of here. I needed to get away from her.

"The wedding's off, Penny."

"You can't just call it off," she said. "You owe me for half of everything."

"I never agreed to marry you. You made all of these plans without my consent."

She scoffed. "Right. Like you didn't know we were getting married. I guess it was just convenient for you to live in this house for free, right? Meanwhile you let me keep thinking we had a future together. You're sick, Luca."

I finished gathering up all the letters, then straightened to face her. Her eyes were red, her cheeks streaked with tears. Even though I was angry with her, and nothing about this engagement was my idea, I knew that I couldn't leave her without a proper goodbye and an explanation. I didn't want to be like my father. I took a deep breath to calm myself down, and then I held out my right hand, offering it to her. She took it hesitantly with her left.

"I'm sorry I didn't tell you sooner that I didn't want to get married. I was caught off guard when you started planning our wedding. If I'm being honest, I went along with it because I didn't know what else to do. This is what people do when they reach a certain point in their relationship, right? Get married, start a family. I thought that I was just afraid to make that commitment. That you were just giving me the push I needed to do what was expected of me. What society expected of me. I'm sorry that I didn't realize that I was making a mistake. It wasn't only my life that was affected by my lack of action. Yours was too. It was never my intention to hurt you. I just think that the person I marry should be someone I'm in love with. And I'm sorry that's not you."

With her left hand in mine, I slid the ring off her finger. She cried out in shock. I stuffed the ring into my pocket, then picked up the box of letters.

"I'm going to pack now," I said. "I'm taking my car, my clothes and my letters. You can keep everything else."

Chapter Seventeen

THE HOMEWRECKER

Naomi

"I can't believe you talked me into flying to Dallas."

Anne and I are standing in front of a house that would probably cost a couple million in Miami. It's a beautiful property, and definitely an upgrade from the small blue beach house Luca started out in. The house stands proudly in a cookie-cutter neighborhood where all the other houses are equally as magnificent and with meticulously trimmed lawns.

Now that we're here, I'm afraid to go up to the door. I guess I'm afraid that Luca will open it, and then I'll know that he's still married.

"Come on," Anne says. She grabs me by the arm and pulls me across the lawn to the front door. Before I have a chance to back out, she hits the doorbell.

A moment later, a woman opens the front door. She's about our age, and has dark eyes and black hair. She smiles. "Hi. Can I help you?"

Anne elbows me in the ribs.

"You must be Penelope," I say.

She maintains her smile. "I am. Can I help you?" she repeats.

"We're trying to find Luca Pichler. Is he around?"

As soon as I mention his name, Penelope drops the smile. "Are you kidding? You're looking for Luca?"

"I was told that he lives here. Aren't you his wife?"

She makes a show of rolling her eyes, then the smile returns to her face, and she giggles. "Why don't you come on in?" she offers. "I'll make you a cup of tea."

I exchange a glance with Anne. She gives a small nod. We both know that if we want answers, we'll have to play along. We step into a grand foyer. A staircase with mahogany railing wraps around one side of the marble-floored room. A glass chandelier hangs above us. I wouldn't want to be standing here in the event of an earthquake.

We follow Penelope through the next room into the kitchen. Each room is more elegant than the last. She pours us each a glass of iced tea. I'm a little afraid to drink mine, but Anne sips hers and she seems fine. There's something about Penelope that puts me on edge. I can't quite place it.

"Luca!" she calls out, startling me. Then, louder, "Luca! You have visitors. Luca!"

My skin goes cold, yet I'm sweating like I'm in a sauna. I was so convinced that Luca wouldn't be here that I hadn't stopped to think about what I would do if he was. I can't imagine what he'll think when he comes downstairs and finds me in his kitchen with his wife.

We all wait for a long moment. The house is quiet. I find it surprising that even in a house as large as this, he wouldn't have heard Penelope. I expect her to shout his name again, but she doesn't. Instead, she turns to face me and Anne with that crazed looking smile back on her face.

"Oh, that's right. Luca doesn't live here anymore," Penelope says. She rolls her eyes again and laughs.

Anne raises an eyebrow. She pulls her glass away from her lips, eyeing it like she's only now realizing that this woman might be insane enough to poison two complete strangers.

"That cheating bastard only lived here for a month before I kicked him out," Penelope continues. "Who are you, anyway, and what do you want with him?"

I look at Anne. I regret coming inside. Based on the look on her face, I can tell she feels the same. I turn back to Penelope. I'm trying to think of how to explain who I am and why I'm looking for her ex-husband. Or ex-fiancé. I'm not really sure at what point they broke up. Before I can tell her my name, Anne places her hand on my shoulder, stopping me.

"We're bounty hunters," Anne says. "Mr. Pichler committed a crime and then dropped off the grid. We're trying to trace his steps."

I'm impressed by how quickly she came up with that. Penelope smiles like she enjoys knowing that Luca is going to be arrested. Then she shrugs. "You'd probably have better luck in San Diego. Last I heard, he was staying with Ben Toole. Or better yet, look for Naomi Light. That's the bitch he was cheating on me with."

I freeze. For a moment, I think that she knows who I am, and she's testing me. But she's not making eye contact with me, and I realize that she's genuinely upset by what she thinks Luca did. I manage to maintain my composure.

"Wow," I say. "He sounds like a real piece of shit."

"He is," she agrees. "So, what did he do that you're after him for? I always knew he would get himself into trouble."

I'm about to make up a crime when Anne says, "We're not at liberty to discuss that. It's our job to catch him, and talking about his crimes could compromise the investigation."

"Right. Of course," Penelope says. "I'm sure he'll get what he deserves."

She looks me over, and then her gaze wanders to Anne. It feels a little like she's sizing us up. She raises an eyebrow. "You don't look like bounty hunters."

"Bounty hunters come in all shapes and sizes," Anne replies. "She's really good at tracking them down, and I'm the muscle."

I turn to look at Anne. She and I are the same size. I doubt that anyone would look at either of us and think we could take down a grown man. When I look back at Penelope, I can tell that she's thinking the same thing. Her eyes narrow, moving from me to Anne and back to me again.

"I've had my black belt since I was seventeen," Anne supplies. "I'm stronger than I look."

"We should probably get going," I say. I'm itching to get out of this place before Penelope realizes who I am and locks me in her basement. "Thank you for the tea."

Penelope looks at my full glass. She smiles, but it doesn't reach her eyes. "Sure."

As we reach the front door, she hands us each a business card. "Call me when you find him," she says. "He owes my father a hundred grand for the wedding we had to cancel."

"Will do," I say, taking the business card.

I don't know why it's such a relief to know that they never went through with the wedding. I'm glad that Luca didn't have to go through a long, drawn-out divorce with this woman. Still, I wonder what he saw in her in the first place and how he came so close to marrying her. I was only with her for a few minutes and I'm already terrified of her.

Anne holds my arm as we hurry back across the lawn to the rental car. Neither of us says a word until we're safely inside the car.

"Okay. That was crazy," Anne says.

"You're telling me. Can you imagine if I had assumed that he was still there and tried sending a letter? She'd probably hunt me down and kill me in my sleep."

"She thinks that Luca cheated on her with you. Did you guys write sexy letters to each other or something? Is that why you didn't bring any more letters for me to read?"

"No. Never. We were always mean to each other."

I think about the letter he wrote when he lived in Georgia before he went to Dallas. I wonder if he was with Penelope at the time, or if Dallas was where he met her. If I tell Anne about it now, she'll never believe that I left the letters at home by accident. I wonder if Penelope knew that he wanted to meet me. Maybe she had seen some of the letters and just assumed it was me when he came home smelling like another woman. Or maybe he told her about me. I find that hard to imagine.

"We have to find Ben Toole," I say.

"She said he went back to San Diego."

I pull out my phone and look up Ben Toole in PeopleFinder. His name pops up along with his city, but all the other information about him has been redacted. I wonder if he and Luca are in on this together.

"No address or phone number," I say. "He must have had it removed."

Anne leans over my shoulder to look. "I guess we have to go back to San Diego next weekend."

I don't know where we would even start with such

minimal information about Ben Toole. I know less about him than I do about Luca, and San Diego was already a dead-end once. There has to be a better way to find someone.

I look at the clock on the dashboard. It's getting late. As much as I want to find Luca, this day has been exhausting, and I just want to go home. If we want to make it back to Miami by the morning, we need to get to the airport now.

"Yeah. Next weekend," I say with a sigh.

Chapter Eighteen

THE FIRST DATE RULE

It's midafternoon on Sunday when Jake knocks at my door. I'm not expecting him until later, but here he is, leaning against my door frame.

"You're early," I tell him.

"Am I?" He checks his wrist even though he's not wearing a watch. He frowns, making a show of pretending to be surprised by the time. "I wanted to catch you before you ate dinner in case you forgot that you're going out with me. Did I make it in time?"

"It's only three. I haven't eaten yet."

"I thought we could go in an hour."

"Isn't four a little early for dinner?"

"You said that you're in bed by the time most people are eating dinner, so I figured that means you eat earlier than everyone else."

I feel a smile creeping across my lips. Who knew this guy was so thoughtful? I haven't been on many dates since starting my early morning hours at the news station, but the few guys that I have gone out with didn't seem to think there was anything wrong with taking me out at eight o'clock at night.

"Where are we eating?" I ask.

"I made reservations at that Japanese place down by the beach."

I raise an eyebrow. "Really? I've never been there. I've heard it's really nice." And expensive.

"I hope so. I want our first date to be special."

"First date?" I snort. "More like third. Or even fourth."

The corner of his mouth quirks up. "We haven't been on a date yet."

I frown, fighting a smile. "What was last Sunday then?"

"That was just breakfast. It wasn't a date."

"It was a breakfast date."

"It was breakfast."

"It would have just been breakfast if you hadn't insisted on paying for me."

"Don't tell me you thought the hallway was a date, too. Wait, if that's the second date, then when was our third?" It's clear that he's amused by this.

"It was a picnic date." I poke him in the chest. "And it was our third. The second was the aquarium."

He grabs my hand, pulling it off his chest, but doesn't let go. "Okay. How was *that* a date? You visited me at work and I didn't even buy you anything."

"It became a date when we made out under the romantic glow of the salmon tank. And why does a date have to involve money?"

"Naomi. We haven't been on a date yet."

"Well, we've done a lot of kissing for two people who have never been on a date."

His gaze drops to my lips, then trails up slowly to meet my

eyes again. "That doesn't usually happen. I never kiss a girl until after the first date. Maybe even the second."

I find that a little hard to believe. My gaze wanders up to his mouth. He shaved recently. I thought he looked good with the stubble on his face last week, but he has the type of face that looks just as good whether it's scruffy or clean-shaven.

"So," I say.

"So," he repeats. He's still holding my hand. His fingers intertwine with mine.

I clear my throat, moving my fingers against his. "Have you ever kissed someone right before a first date?"

"I can't say I have."

"Oh. I guess we'll just have to wait until—"

He steps through my doorway, cutting me off, and before I know what's happening, his lips are on mine, and my back is against the wall. His tongue slides against mine and a noise escapes me. I'm not sure if it's a gasp or a moan. Maybe a little of both. I feel his hands on my hips, holding me closer to his body. My hands are in his hair, pulling his face closer, keeping his lips locked against mine.

Our last kiss was just a taste that left me wanting more, but I didn't know what I was in for. Of all the kisses I've ever had, this one is by far the best. His mouth fits with mine like we've been doing this for years. He already knows what I like. It's sensual, but it's not only fueled by lust. This is something else. This is something that I want to hold onto.

He lowers his hands to my ass and lifts me up so that my legs are wrapped around his waist. It's almost too much to handle, having him this close to me, our waists pressed together. He pushes against me and I can feel him, all of him. I grind my hips against his, begging him for just a little bit more.

It doesn't feel like there's anything that can stop us from taking this to the next level.

"Can we skip dinner?" I breathe, my hands now clutching the front of his shirt. "We can just stay right here."

He smiles, driving me a little bit crazy. "As much as I love the sound of that, I made a reservation for us."

"Oh. Right. What time is the reservation?"

"Four."

It's not until he says the time that I remember he already told me. His kiss seems to have given me short term memory loss.

"I can give you some time to get ready."

"I don't need that much time." I tilt my chin back up. His lips meet mine in the middle. There's this heat where our bodies connect, a bulge that tells me that he wants this as badly as I do. I move against him, but our clothes are in the way. I've never been more annoyed with clothes in my life. I want to strip them off, remove all of these barriers between us.

"Do you have a rule against having sex before a first date?" I ask.

He exhales slowly, like he's trying to show restraint. For a moment, I think that he's going to back away from me again, but he doesn't. "When it comes to you, I don't have any rules."

"That's good to know." I pull on his lip with my teeth. He growls, then gives me a teasing peck on the lips. I return the kiss, and then he locks his lips with mine again, pushing my lips open with his so he can taste me. I forget that I'm being held against the wall. I feel weightless, like I'm floating and the only thing I'm aware of is the feel of his lips against mine, the taste of his mouth. It's the kind of kiss that can make a girl forget what her own name is, if only for a second.

"Do you want to?" I ask, reminding him of my question.

"You are very hard to say no to."

"Do you want to say no to me?"

"No. That's the problem."

"Am I moving too fast?" I lower my hands between us and play with his zipper over his distended fly.

He inhales sharply, pushing his waist against mine again, and for a moment, I think that this is going to happen. Before I can undo his fly, a voice from the hallway startles us.

"You know, there are children who live in this building."

He lets go of me, and my legs slide down his body until I'm standing on my own again. We both turn to my door – which I forgot we left open – and see the same woman who scoffed at us when we were eating in the hallway the other day.

My face heats. I'm sure my skin is bright red. I reach over and close the door, but I know the mood has already been killed.

"Maybe we should wait," he says.

My gaze drops to his jeans, where his body seems to be protesting his words. "Right."

"It's not that I don't want to. I do. Believe me."

"You don't have to explain," I assure him.

We stand in my hallway, facing each other. His chest rises and falls with each new breath. A smile teases his lips.

"You might want to fix your hair before we leave," he says.

I snort out a laugh, the tension broken. I reach up and feel my hair, then look him over. His hair is sticking up where I was holding onto it. "You too," I say.

The side of his mouth quirks up, and then he leans down and kisses me. "Get ready," he says. "I'll be right back."

I haven't been to a hibachi restaurant in years. Not since I left Oklahoma. His hand lands on my lower back as we approach the building. His touch is warm. He keeps his hand there even as we come through the doors. The hostess looks up from her stand.

"We have a reservation under the name—"

"Naomi Light!" the waitress says, interrupting him when she recognizes me. "The weathergirl! I watch you on the news every morning." Her whole face lights up like I'm a celebrity or something.

I laugh awkwardly.

"When I saw your name on the reservation list, I thought it had to be a joke," she continues. She grabs a couple of menus. "You can come right this way."

Once we're seated, I lean in and whisper, "Did you use my name for the reservation?"

He shrugs. "I gave them both of our names. I guess yours is the only one she recognized."

The chef arrives at our table and begins preparing our food. He makes a show out of it, playing with fire and juggling eggs. Jake orders steak and I get chicken and shrimp. Once our food is served and the chef leaves, I turn to look at him.

"I forgot to ask how the adoption event went. Did the kittens get a new home?"

He shakes his head. "No one wanted them. Looks like I get to keep them for another week."

"Really? I'm surprised. Who wouldn't want to adopt a couple of kittens that know how to bowl?"

He shrugs. "There's another adoption event this weekend. No one adopted them because I want them to go together, and not many people want to adopt two cats at the same time. But they're bonded, and I'd hate to separate them."

We both spend a few minutes eating and enjoying our food. I'm about to pop a shrimp into my mouth when I notice him watching me.

"I'm so sorry," I say, dropping the shrimp back down on my plate. "Should I cover my face with a napkin while I eat these?"

He laughs. "I told you I'm not offended by seafood. Now if you were eating dolphin on the other hand..."

I frown. "Do people actually do that?"

"In some parts of the world," he says with a shrug.

"Want to try one?" I pick the shrimp back up with my fork and hold it out to him. He cringes, shaking his head. I roll my eyes. "I thought you weren't offended by seafood."

"Seafood in general, no. But shrimp? They're basically sea crickets. No thank you."

I turn my fork to look at the shrimp, then I drop it back onto my plate. "Now I can't eat it. Thanks a lot."

He laughs. "I'm sorry."

"Sorry doesn't cut it," I say, crossing my arms over my chest. "You just ruined my dinner."

He reaches over and picks up my fork, carrying the shrimp back up to my mouth. "Come on. Just eat it. I'm sure crickets aren't that bad for you."

I push away the fork. "You're not helping." I try to look mad, but it's hard to suppress my laugh when he presses the shrimp against my lips.

"In some parts of the world, crickets are a delicacy," he says.

"That's very reassuring." I snatch the fork out of his hand and eat the shrimp, trying not to compare it to a bug while I chew.

"I can't believe you just ate that."

I throw my napkin at him. "I'm never eating dinner with you again."

He laughs. "We'll see about that."

I roll my eyes, still fighting a smile. "Tell me about your family," I say. "How many siblings do you have?"

"Three," he says. "Twin sisters and a brother."

"Oh, wow. Twins? I always wanted a twin sister. Did they ever wear the same outfit and trick you or your parents while you were growing up?"

He smirks. "Sometimes. They're identical, but if you really know them, you can spot their differences easily."

"I am so jealous that you grew up with a big family. I'm guessing you're pretty close with your family?"

He takes a moment to chew his food before responding. "I guess you could say that. I see my dad every day. I get together with my brother and sisters a couple times a month. We have a family dinner once a month. It gets pretty chaotic with all the kids, cousins, extended family. Most of them have annual passes to the aquarium, so they come by often."

"That sounds like fun. I grew up with my cousins, so I know how chaotic that can be. Do you have any nieces or nephews? Or any kids of your own?" I look up from my plate as I ask the question. I hope that I'm being subtle in my nosiness.

His brows shoot up like he's surprised I would even ask that. "Me? No."

"You've never been married?"

He shakes his head. A smile teases the corner of his lips. "Have you?"

"No. No kids, either."

"You're good with kids though."

"What makes you say that?" I ask.

180

"I've seen you outside with Caitlin a few times."

I frown. "Who?"

"Caitlin," he repeats. "She's a funny kid. Loves bugs."

"Oh! Caterpillar Kid? That's her name?"

He raises an eyebrow. "You nicknamed her Caterpillar Kid?"

"She's always picking up caterpillars and coloring in a caterpillar coloring book," I say with a shrug. "I guess I should have asked her what her name is."

He drives us back to our building after dinner. My hand bumps his as we come out of the parking garage. He takes it in his and holds it the rest of the way. Just as we reach the front door, he tugs on my hand and pulls me closer to him, stealing a quick kiss and making my heart beat a little bit faster. I'm smiling up at him as we step through the doorway together. My eyes land on Joel at the security desk. I can't help but notice his judgmental stare as his gaze lowers from our faces to our hands. I wonder if Jake has noticed that our security guard seems to have a problem with us dating.

"Is Joel ever not on duty?" I ask when we make it to the stairwell.

"He doesn't have much of a life outside of work."

"Still. It seems like a lot of hours for a guy his age to work. It's a lot of hours for anyone, really."

"He must like the overtime."

When we reach my floor, he follows me to my apartment door.

"Normally this would be the part of the date where we have our first kiss," he says.

"We kind of already did that."

The corner of his mouth tilts up. His eyes wander from mine down to my lips. My body heats as I remember the way he came into my apartment and pushed me up against the wall. The way he took over my mouth with his, the way his body felt pressed against mine, the way my heart raced when I saw through his jeans how turned on he was. I can still feel the ache of wanting more. No one has turned me on like that in a very long time. I would probably try to move way too fast all over again if he kissed me like that now.

His fingers graze my arm, sending goosebumps over my skin. I'm about to ask him if he wants to come inside, but before I can, he tilts his head down and kisses me. He doesn't do it with the same intensity as before, but his lips, warm against mine, leave me wanting more of him all the same.

"Goodnight, Naomi," he says when he pulls away. My shoulders drop, the two words feeling like the most disappointing thing I've ever heard.

"Goodnight." My voice comes out as a whisper that even I can barely hear.

I let myself inside. I don't realize how worked up I am until I'm leaning against the other side of the door, catching my breath. It's been a very long time since anyone has made my heart race the way he does. I'm not sure if anyone else ever has. Even so, I can't help but think about the way my thoughts have been straying to Luca lately – even more now that I know he never got married. I don't know why I'm allowing a guy I've never met to have such a hold on my thoughts. It feels like it's out of my control. With this thought in mind, it's probably for the best that Jake isn't coming inside. As much as I want him, I know that I need to find a way to get Luca out of my head before I take things further with Jake.

Chapter Nineteen

DRESSED TO IMPRESS

I wake up sometime in the night feeling thirsty. I get up and tiptoe into the kitchen even though I live alone. I guess I don't want to make too much noise on my downstairs neighbor's ceiling. I turn on the kitchen light and pour myself a glass of water. As I'm taking a sip, my eyes wander to the stack of mail that I left on my countertop on Friday. I had been distracted with Luca's letters, and then by the hallway picnic date with Jake, and never got around to looking at it.

I sort through it now, tossing the junk mail into the trash and putting bills in a separate pile. When I get to the last envelope, I pause. From the light pouring in from the living room, I can see that there's no return address. My name and address are handwritten. I recognize the handwriting. I've been watching the evolution of this handwriting for almost twenty years. It's startling to see a letter from Luca with my home address on it rather than the news station. This means that he knows where I live. It makes me wonder what else he knows about me.

I rip the envelope open and pull out the letter. It's longer than the ones he usually sends.

Dear Naomi,

I waited until now to write again because I was hoping that you got my letter late and that's why you didn't say the magic word in your weather report. But you didn't say it at all this week, and I have to admit that I'm pretty disappointed. Is it because you can't deviate from your script, or have you lost interest in writing back to me? I guess it's been two years since you've heard from me, so maybe the letters just aren't as fun for you as they used to be. Maybe you're even annoyed that I'm writing to you now.

Do you remember when I asked if we could be friends on Facebook? I think we were both juniors in high school. I never told you that I had already looked you up before I asked. I was planning on sending you a friend request, but I didn't know how you would react, which is why I asked you first. I thought you were the most beautiful girl in the world. I wanted to know you outside of these letters, but you were so damn mean about not wanting to be my friend. Of all the mean letters you sent, that one was the first one that actually hurt me.

The second time you hurt me was when I invited you to my boot camp graduation and you didn't show up. You probably thought it was a joke, but it wasn't. I wanted you to be there. I guess you didn't know that I was the only person there who didn't have a family. I didn't tell you that because I didn't want you to feel sorry for me. I wanted you to come because you wanted to be there. Even after you rejected me in high school, I hoped that you would change your mind, and you would want to meet me in person.

I always wondered if you had looked me up on Facebook. I still wonder if you ever think about me when you're not reading my

letters or thinking of what to write back to me. I wonder if I've made
as big an impact on your life as you have on mine.

You probably think I'm crazy, or maybe you think I'm creepy for
saying all of this. Shit. Now that I'm rereading this letter, it's
definitely creepy, right? Although, it can't be as creepy as some of the
other letters I've sent. I haven't even written anything mean.

I guess I can't end a letter like that, so here goes: I hope that you
accidentally wear an outfit the same color as the green screen behind
you during your next weather report, and it looks like you're just a
decapitated head floating around the screen. Something like that
would make your boring show a lot better.

Love,

Luca

I try to process everything I just read, and find myself
reading the letter again. I remember when he invited me to his
boot camp graduation. I still have that letter. I also remember
thinking that it was a cruel joke since he had led me to believe
that I wouldn't be able to get on a plane. I had wished for just a
moment that Luca really wanted me to come to his graduation.
I might have gone if I thought that he was serious.

And now this. I stare at the letter, wondering what I'm
supposed to do with it. I've put in a lot of effort to track him
down, but after reading this letter, I know that it won't be the
same when I do find his address. Outsmarting him is supposed
to be a moment of triumph for me. It's not supposed to feel like
… whatever this feels like.

I go back to bed and stare up at my ceiling. I have a couple
more hours before I need to be up, but I know that I won't be
able to fall back asleep.

"Someone got laid," Anne says as she sets a cup of coffee in front of me.

I spin in my chair, shocked. "What? No, I didn't!"

She drops the smile on her face. Her eyes go wide, and then she smiles again. "Wait, really? I was talking about Patrick. He's in an extra good mood this morning. But this is way more interesting." She pulls up a chair. "Tell me everything. It was Husky Eyes, right?"

I roll my eyes. "Nothing happened. We just went out."

She narrows her eyes. "The look on your face told me everything I need to know."

The thing about Anne is that she can see right through me, but she doesn't know that it's not Jake who has me feeling defensive this morning.

I shrug. "We made out. That's it."

"Come on. Tell me the truth," she prods. "Was it as good as I'm imagining it was?"

I laugh, snorting out my coffee. "Quit imagining me sleeping with him. That's a little weird." I grab a napkin to pat away the coffee that spilled on my wool coat.

Anne frowns, watching me. "What's with the long coat? Don't tell me we're getting a blizzard today."

"This station is over-airconditioned. I'm always freezing in the morning."

She watches me skeptically, then shrugs it off. "Back to Husky Eyes. I want details, Gnome. I'm living vicariously through you right now. How many times?"

My face turns red. "Stop it, Anne. Someone is going to hear you."

"Once? Twice? Were you up all night? Did you have shower sex?"

She rubs her hands together, waiting for me to spill the

juicy details. Unfortunately, there aren't any to share. At least not the ones she's looking for.

I grab a pen off the desk and throw it at her. "I'm going to cancel our next San Diego trip if you don't cut it out."

She laughs, dodging the pen. "Okay. Fine. I won't ask for details. But…"

I sigh, bracing myself. "But what?"

"Do you still think it's just a onetime thing, or are you going to get serious with him?"

I think about that for a moment. I had wanted to just have fun, but I can't see it being a onetime thing now.

"You're thinking about this question a lot harder than I thought you would," Anne says.

"Yes. I do want to be serious with him."

"Are you sure moving that fast was a good idea, then? What if he thinks sex is all you want?"

I slap my hand over my face. I haven't had enough coffee for this. "For the millionth time, Anne, I did not have sex with him."

Of course Patrick chooses that moment to walk into the room. His face turns red, but he gracefully chooses to pretend he didn't hear any of what we were talking about. Anne and I exchange a look before she gets out of her chair and leaves. He reminds me that it's almost time to go on air.

"I'll be up in time," I tell him. "I just need to finish one last thing."

He leaves me alone to get ready. I'm nervous about today's report. The conversation with Anne was a good distraction, but now that I'm alone, I'm starting to sweat. I can't believe I'm about to do what I have planned. When there's only one more minute before I have to be on, I stand up and drop my wool coat onto my chair. Underneath, I'm wearing a green, long-sleeved turtleneck dress. I'm about to break the biggest fashion rule for on-air meteorologists.

I step up in front of my screen and do my report as if nothing is wrong, but I can hear the rumble of voices on the other side of the cameras. I can only imagine how this looks. And I can only hope that Luca is watching.

When I'm finished with my report and the camera turns off, Patrick storms onto the stage and grabs onto the fabric of my turtleneck. "What the hell, Naomi? What were you thinking wearing this color?"

"Huh?" I look down at my dress, pretending to not know what the problem is. "Oh God. Did I really just wear this?"

"Come to my office," he says. "We need to talk."

As I follow him to his office, we pass Anne in the hallway. She shoots me a wide-eyed, questioning look. I shrug without a word. Patrick closes the door behind me when we reach his office.

"What was the first rule you agreed to when you signed on to take Emmanuel's place?"

I bite my lip. The rule he's referring to is one that's always been laughed about, and uttered more as a joke than anything else, because none of us could believe that someone would be stupid enough to dress like a piece of broccoli in front of a green screen. And yet here I am, looking like a giant green vegetable.

"Don't wear green." I say the words so quietly that Patrick can't hear me. He cups a hand around his ear and leans in – a gesture that makes me want to roll my eyes. "Don't wear green," I repeat louder.

"And yet you are..." He gestures to my outfit.

"Wearing green."

"Oh, no. You're not just wearing something green, Naomi.

Your whole body is draped in green. Do you know what you looked like out there? You looked like a floating head bouncing around a weather map with a couple of hands flapping around below. If there's an opposite of the headless horseman, that's what you were. What the hell is the matter with you?"

"I'm sorry," I say. "I had a long weekend. I was up late and I got dressed in the dark this morning. I didn't realize what I was wearing. Please don't fire me."

He sighs heavily as if he has to think hard about whether to keep me on. So much for him being in a good mood like Anne said. "You're on thin ice, Naomi. You're lucky that ratings have been up since you came on fulltime. Now go change your clothes before you go on again. Find something in the lost and found or something."

"Thank you, Mr. Facey."

He makes a noise that sounds similar to a growl. I get out of his office as fast as I can. Anne is waiting for me in the hallway. She walks back to my desk with me.

"Are you going to tell me what you were thinking?" she asks.

"Only if you switch outfits with me."

"Funny. I was going to suggest that next."

We head to the ladies' room and lock the door. As soon as we're alone, we both burst out laughing. Once we've calmed down, we undress and put on each other's clothes. I'm lucky that Anne is about the same size as me. I had counted on her being willing to switch outfits with me this morning. If I had brought a change of clothes, this stunt might have looked premeditated.

"He told you to do this, didn't he?" Anne says when we're finished dressing.

"Huh?"

"Don't play dumb. You were going to say bologna until I talked you out of it. When did you get another letter from him?"

I sigh, realizing it's not worth it to lie to her. "I got a letter from him over the weekend."

"And he told you to wear green? I can't believe you did this, Naomi. It's one thing to wear a green skirt or a green pair of pants, but this was your whole body." She gestures to the shape of the tacky old bridesmaid dress that she's wearing now. "The only part of you that was showing was your head and your hands."

"He didn't tell me to do it."

"You can't possibly expect me to believe that you didn't do it for him. Did he promise to give you his return address again?"

"He didn't promise me anything. And he didn't tell me to do it. Not exactly."

"What do you mean?"

I take a deep breath, trying to decide how much of the letter I can tell her about. "He knows where I live, Anne."

"I would assume so since the letter didn't come here."

"We've been running around the whole country looking for him, spending all kinds of money on flights and hotels and airport food, meanwhile he knows where I work and where I live, and I can't even write back to him. I know it's all an adventure to you, but do you know how frustrating it is for me? I had to communicate with him somehow."

"By making a fool of yourself on air? If you were going to do something stupid, you should have just said it was hot as bologna outside."

"That's not what I was going to—" I shake my head, getting back on track. "He told me that if I accidentally wore something green on air, it would make my boring show a lot better."

"Seriously? That's all it takes to get you to send your career into a tailspin? You'll be lucky if you're not the laughing stock of all meteorologists after this."

"You know what? I don't regret it. Patrick didn't fire me. My career is fine. I'm sure not that many people were watching anyway."

Anne follows me out of the bathroom.

"Why didn't you tell me about the letter sooner? Were you planning to do this all weekend?"

I shush her because I don't want anyone else to overhear and know this was planned. "It was a last-minute idea."

"I can't believe you. When did you read the letter? We just spent the whole weekend together, and the whole point of the trip was to find Luca. How could you just forget to mention that you received another letter from him?"

"I didn't read it until last night. It came in Friday's mail but I didn't even notice it until yesterday."

"What did it say?"

I hesitate. "Nothing. It was just like all the other letters."

"What about the letters you were supposed to bring to Georgia? Does it have anything to do with you conveniently forgetting them?"

It's annoying how good she is at reading me. I'm starting to think she'd make a good detective. Or maybe a good palm-reader. I wonder if a palm-reading detective is a thing.

"Can we just drop it for now?" I ask. "I'm sure you have some work to do."

"Fine. Tell me about it at the café later?"

"I can't. I have ... plans."

I don't really have plans, but I hope that if I avoid the subject long enough, she'll forget about it.

I manage to keep away from Anne for the rest of the morning. She doesn't bring me any mail. I'm not surprised. I have a feeling Luca will be sending his letters to my apartment from now on. I go straight home after work and check my mail. Sure enough, there's a new letter at the bottom of my mailbox. I wait until I'm upstairs to open it. He must have sent it over the weekend for it to arrive today.

Once I'm inside, I set my things down and rip the envelope open.

Dear Naomi,

Great job on the weather report this morning. Is it weird that it turned me on to see your head floating around the screen without a body? I can't believe you did that. I guess this means that my last letter didn't scare you away.

I got a call from an old friend the other day. If you go to Georgia again, tell Maxwell I said hi. Who knew you would go that far to find me? You must like me too, or something.

Love,

Luca

I can't decide if my body is hot or cold. Of course that marine we met in Georgia would call Luca to tell him we were looking for him. It kind of annoys me that the man didn't give me Luca's number if he had it the whole time. But the whole point of trying to find him like this was so that it would be a surprise when I found his address and wrote back. Now he knows what I'm doing, and even worse: he's flattered that I'm going to such great lengths to find him.

Like his last letter, I read it again, dissecting each line

carefully. It takes a minute for it to occur to me that he must have written this letter today. I wonder how it's possible that his letter made it all the way from San Diego to Miami in less than a day.

Then it hits me: he's definitely not in San Diego anymore.

Chapter Twenty

THE BODILESS WEATHERGIRL

The realization that Luca could be a lot closer than I thought sends goosebumps over my skin. Now more than ever, I wish I could write back. I'm not sure what I would say to him if I could. I might ask him if he wants to meet up for coffee, just to see what he's like in real life. There's a lot that I want to ask him, like why didn't he follow through with getting married, and how did he end up here in Miami – if this is really where he is – and did he mean any of what he said in the letter I read last night?

Most of all, I want to know why he disappeared off the face of the planet for two years. Where did he go, and why did our letters stop mattering to him?

My phone buzzes, pulling my focus away from the letter. I check the screen and see that I'm getting a call from Anne.

"What's up?"

"I have your dress."

"We can exchange clothes tomorrow morning," I say. I fiddle with the letter in my hand, skimming over it like there might be something I missed the first time.

"Okay. Have you looked online yet?"

I pull my focus back to my conversation with Anne. "What do you mean?"

"Your segment this morning is going viral. The bodiless weathergirl is a big hit."

I groan. "Are you serious?"

"It's actually not that bad. People are loving it. I wouldn't be surprised if you start getting fan mail after this. *Real* fan mail. Not just hate mail from your penemy."

"Great. Just what I need."

"You did this to yourself, so I don't want to hear you complain. I'll send you a link to the video."

I hang up the phone, and a moment later, Anne sends me the link. I click on it and watch, cringing at first, but then I snort with laughter the longer I stay on screen. I don't know how Patrick managed to keep a straight face while scolding me earlier. I really do look like a head floating around the screen with two little hands flapping like pale birds pointing at all of my graphics. I scroll down to read the comments, and am surprised by how many there are already.

I spend a few minutes reading until there's a knock at my door. Thinking it's probably Anne showing up with my dress just to see if I was lying about having plans, I leave my phone and the letter on the kitchen counter and head to the door. When I open it, I'm surprised to find Jake on the other side.

He has a smile on his face that spreads wider when he sees me. My heart skips a beat. I never knew how good it could feel to have a man look at me like that.

"You know, I was half expecting to only see a floating head when you opened the door."

"Oh God. You saw the video?"

"Saw the video?" he repeats. "I was watching it live."

"You watched me live?"

"Every morning," he says. "It's my favorite show on TV."

I roll my eyes. "I doubt that."

"Mind if I come in?" he asks.

"Of course not." I open the door wider and step back so that he has room to move past me.

We make it to the living room and stop next to the island that separates this room from the kitchen. I glance at Luca's letter on the other side of the kitchen.

"I was thinking about you all morning," he says, pulling my attention back to him.

I smile, but inside I feel torn. He has no idea that the green screen stunt was premeditated to get the attention of another man.

"I was thinking about the weather all morning."

"Sexy," he says.

"Hot would be more accurate."

"Touché."

He looks at my countertop. A small piece of paper catches his attention. He reaches over and picks it up. "What's this?" he asks.

I step closer to him to see what he has. "Oh. Just a business card."

"Penelope Hayes," he reads. "Personal trainer." He raises an eyebrow and looks at me.

I shrug. "I met her on Saturday."

He flips the card over, reading the back. "You went all the way to Dallas, Texas?"

"It was a last-minute idea. Anne loves a good adventure."

He drops the business card back onto the countertop where he found it. "Any other spontaneous trips coming up, or can I make plans with you this weekend?"

I bite my lip. "Anne wants to go back to San Diego."

"Did you not collect as many seashells as you wanted the first time?"

I smile. "Something like that."

"Are the tickets booked?"

"Not yet."

"Then push it off. Hang out with me."

"This will be the last trip for a while. And we should only be gone for a day."

The corner of his mouth quirks up. "What if your return flight gets canceled?"

"I'll fight my way into the cockpit and fly the plane myself."

"Wow. You would hijack a plane for me?"

"Of course. Don't you have an adoption event this weekend anyway?"

He leans against the countertop. "Yeah, but only Saturday morning. I'm free all afternoon."

"Maybe you can use all that free time to go to the beach."

"I was thinking we could go to the beach right now."

I raise an eyebrow. "Now? I thought you had to go back to work."

"I decided to take the rest of the afternoon off," he says.

"Really? But who will save the walruses if you're not there?"

"The walruses will be fine. I'll keep my phone nearby. So what do you think? Want to go to the beach?"

I smile. "Yeah. Let me get my swimsuit on."

I start toward my bedroom, then pause, remembering the letter on the other side of the kitchen. I turn around and grab it, then stuff the folded letter into the back pocket of the pants Anne let me borrow. I'll have to remind myself to ask Anne where she got these pants. I can never find any that have pockets.

He waits in the living room while I change. I put on a loose white tank top and a pair of shorts over my bathing suit, then grab a bottle of sunscreen.

"Do you need to change?" I ask when I return to the living room.

He shakes his head. "I'm wearing my swim trunks already."

I look down at his legs. It hadn't occurred to me before that he wasn't dressed like someone who was heading back to work. My gaze lingers on his muscular calves for a minute. I've seen him run half naked, but I can still appreciate how good he looks in a pair of swim trunks.

We take his car to the beach. Not many people go to the beach on a Monday, so it's not hard to find parking.

When we reach the sand, I pull the bottle of sunscreen out of my tote bag and offer it to him.

"No thanks," he says as he pulls his shirt off. "I don't burn."

His skin is a nice golden tan, but I've seen darker men get sunburned. I raise an eyebrow.

"I'll be fine," he assures me.

I squeeze a large amount of sunscreen into my hand, then slap it onto his chest. He looks down at his chest, then up at me, his eyes narrowed.

"Now you'll be fine." I begin rubbing the lotion into his chest and over his shoulders. His skin is warm beneath my hands. He sucks in a breath, his eyes fixed on me. I smile at him, then return my attention to my hands as I work the sunscreen down his arms.

"Wow," I say, feeling his muscles. "Do you work out or do you get these from operating on animals?"

"It's all the water aerobics I do," he says with a smirk.

I make him turn around so that I can get his back. When I'm done, he grabs the bottle of sunscreen. I watch him, wondering what he's going to do with it.

"Shirt on or off?" he asks me.

"Huh?"

He motions to my shirt. "It's your turn. I wouldn't want you looking like a strawberry on national television."

I smile and pull my shirt over my head. I toss it onto the sand next to his. When I look back up at him, his cheeks are pink. He clears his throat and glances away from me.

"Well?" I prompt him.

He angles his head back to me, a smile teasing the corner of his lips. I can't help but laugh at how cute he is when he's flustered.

He squeezes a small amount of sunscreen into his hand and begins to rub it into my shoulders, spreading it down to my arms. When he finishes with my arms, he squeezes out another handful of sunscreen, then looks down at my waist. His eyes raise up to meet mine.

"Are you okay with this?" he asks.

It might scare him off if he knew how badly I want his hands on me. I nod, somehow managing to keep my cool. "Go ahead."

His hands close over my ribcage first, and then he works the lotion down my abdomen and over my hips. A wave of goosebumps washes over me. My belly tightens and I hold my breath. With him standing this close to me and touching me like this, I begin to wish we hadn't left my apartment. I know that I won't be able to resist doing something inappropriate at the beach if he keeps it up, so I help myself to the sunscreen and begin applying it to my chest while he moves on to my back.

"I can't believe you're finally at the beach after six whole months of living here," I tell him. His hands stroke my back, and I close my eyes for a moment, breathing in the salty ocean air.

"Me neither."

When he finishes with my back, I turn around to face him. "Are you one of those people who likes to swim all the way out past the waves, or are you afraid of sharks?"

He raises an eyebrow, and I realize how stupid my question is.

"Wow," I say. "I'm an idiot. I just asked an aquarium vet if he's afraid of sharks."

He laughs. "Hey, it's not that bad. I think everyone should have a healthy fear of any wild animal. I mean, just because you report the weather doesn't mean you're going to run outside waving a sheet of tin foil during a thunderstorm."

"Oh no. You know that aluminum doesn't attract lightning, right?"

He frowns. "It doesn't?"

It's my turn to laugh. "No. It doesn't."

"Damn. Everything I've been taught about lightning as a kid is a lie."

I kick my sandals off so that I can feel the sand between my toes. I immediately regret it. The sand is hot as hell, and it feels like my feet are frying in a hot, sandy skillet. I shriek, bouncing from one foot to another, but it does nothing to ease the burning.

His eyebrows shoot up. "What's wrong?"

"The sand! My feet!"

Without any more prompting than that, he scoops me up in his arms and carries me like a damsel in distress over a mountain of crunchy seaweed that was swept up onto the beach by the waves. On the other side of the seaweed, the sand is smooth and wet and cool. He sets me down, and I breathe a sigh of relief. My relief is short-lived when I realize he's laughing at me. I try to shove his arm, but he dodges me.

"I don't know why I thought I could walk barefoot on that sand. I should know better by now."

"You were right about the seaweed," he says, looking back at the mound that we crossed. "There's a lot of it."

"It didn't used to be like this, from what I hear. I always thought the beaches here were supposed to be pretty, but there's so much seaweed that it's hard to enjoy the white-sand beaches the way they're supposed to be enjoyed."

"Maybe you should move to San Diego."

"Oh really? Is that your way of trying to get rid of me?"

"Damn. You saw right through my plan."

I elbow him in the ribs.

"If I was trying to get rid of you, I wouldn't have knocked on your door and invited you to come to the beach with me."

"Hmm. You got me there."

"Come on. Let's go for a swim," he says.

I follow him into the water. I'm not a good swimmer, so I don't go any deeper than my knees, but he takes my hand and pulls me into the deeper water until I can hardly feel the sand with my toes.

"How do you know there aren't any sharks?" I ask.

"There could be, but we'll be safe. Sharks prefer redheads. The color reminds them of blood."

"What? I'm a redhead!"

He grabs onto a lock of my hair and examines it. "Damn.

You are. Don't worry, though. While the sharks are distracted with you, I'll swim ashore and get help."

"Oh, thanks a lot." I grab onto him, wrapping my legs around his waist and my arms around his shoulders. "If they get me, then they're getting you too."

A wave splashes over both of our heads just then, knocking him off balance and sending us both underwater for a moment. When we come back up, my mouth and nose are full of salt water and my eyes are burning. I spit out the water and gasp for air. I feel his arms lock around me, his skin warm against the cold ocean water. A moment later, I can feel the sand underneath my feet again. He swam us back to the beach. I head for my shirt and use it to wipe my eyes. When my eyes are no longer burning, and I can look at him again, I see that he's laughing at me.

"That's why I don't go any deeper than my knees," I say.

"What? Can't handle a little salt water in your eyes?"

"No. It burned. How are you okay?"

He shrugs. "I used to swim in the ocean all the time. I got used to the salt water."

"Seriously? I thought you said you've never been to the beach."

"I practically grew up on the beach," he says. "Just not this beach."

"Oh. And here I thought I was taking your beach virginity."

He laughs. "Not even close."

I sit down in the sand, just close enough to the water that the waves splash over my feet. He sits down next to me.

"I'm surprised I haven't scared you off yet," I tell him.

He smirks. "Why would you scare me off?"

"I can list a bunch of reasons." I start counting on my

fingers. "My elevator phobia, showing up on live TV without a body, my tasteless jokes about seafood..."

"Sounds like a bunch of adorable quirks to me. If you were trying to scare me off, you did a terrible job. I need more of you."

I spread my arms out at my sides, gesturing to my body. "You got me."

"I don't want just your body." He scoots a little closer to me, making my pulse speed up and my body feel a little warmer. He leans in and touches his lips softly to mine. "I want all of you."

"My head too?"

He smiles, flashing his white teeth. "Yes. Your head too. But preferably with your body attached."

For some reason that statement makes me think of Luca's letter, momentarily taking me out of this moment. I take a second to recover and remember who I'm with and where I am. This is the first time that Luca has crossed my mind since Jake showed up at my door. He has this way of keeping my mind in the present, where it should be – except for now, when Luca slips back into my thoughts, uninvited.

"Don't worry. I'm hoping to avoid being decapitated," I say.

"Good to know." He kisses me again, another light, sweet peck on the lips.

"Are you saying the same thing to any other women?"

He pulls back and looks at me, leaving me to wonder for a moment if I said the wrong thing. Then he laughs. "I'm going to assume you're talking about the 'I want you' part of what I said because the subject of decapitations doesn't normally come up in conversation. But no. I'm not seeing anyone else, if that's what you're asking. Are you?"

I shake my head, but again I find myself thinking of the two most recent letters from Luca. I'm surprised to find that I feel a little guilty. I shouldn't feel this way. I haven't promised anything to Luca. I can't even write back to him.

"So, we're on the same page?" he says tentatively.

I wonder if this is his way of asking me to be exclusive. I can't exactly say no since I'm the one who brought it up. I don't want to say no anyway. I open my mouth to say, "Yes," but then I pause, an idea coming to my mind. "I know how we can make this official."

He raises an eyebrow. "How?"

"You need to write our names in the sand. Inside of a heart."

He thinks about it for a moment. He looks down at the wet sand we're sitting on, then says, "I'll do one even better. Turn around."

"What?"

"Turn around. I want it to be a surprise."

I stand up and turn around, my back to him and the ocean. "What kind of a surprise?" I ask.

"You'll see."

"Oh God. You're not going to propose to me, are you? I mean, I like you and all, but I haven't even met your parents yet."

I can hear the laughter in his voice when he responds. "Now if we're talking about scaring someone off, that would be the way to do it."

"That or show up decapitated on live television," I offer.

"I don't think there's anything you could do to scare me off, Naomi."

"What if I just started peeing? Right here. Standing up. Through my shorts."

"I would assume you got stung by a jellyfish and I just didn't notice."

"What if I told you that I was a robot?"

"Then I would say whoever built you did an excellent job."

I can hear his hand scraping the sand as he writes our names in it.

"What if I told you that I hate kids?"

"Then I hate them too."

"And if I told you that I want a baby right now?"

"I would say 'let's start trying' but if you're a robot, then we might have to adopt."

I snort, biting back a laugh. I've never met anyone like him before. I'm starting to wonder where this guy has been all my life. I think of the last guy I went on a date with, who didn't seem to think anything I said was funny. Then I think of Luca and all of the ridiculous letters we sent to each other over the years. I wonder what he's like in real life. I wonder if we would get along like this. I put those thoughts away. I shouldn't be thinking of Luca when I'm having such a good time with Jake.

"Can I turn around yet?"

"Almost. Just a second." I can hear him scraping the finishing touches and then smoothing the sand with his hand. "Okay. Turn around."

I do as he says. I'm surprised to see that he didn't write our names, but instead drew what looks like a terrible portrait of us in the sand. He drew two big smiley faces: one with hair made of crunchy red seaweed, and the other I assume is supposed to be him. He drew a stick figure body under his own face. A big heart is drawn around both, with several smaller hearts filling in the extra space.

"You didn't finish," I say, pointing at the one that's supposed to be me. "You didn't give me a body."

"It's finished," he says. "I'm sure anyone who comes across this will know exactly who this is supposed to be."

"Who knew you were such a great artist?" I say. "You should have gone to art school."

"Yeah, but then who would save the walruses?"

"I'm sure you could draw them a nice picture."

A wave rolls in, splashing over our feet, and when it recedes into the ocean, it takes my seaweed hair with it and leaves only a faint trace of his drawing.

I reach out and touch his shoulder, which has a slight pink hue. "Oh no. Looks like I missed a spot. I thought you said you didn't burn."

He looks at his shoulder, seeming surprised. "That's a first."

"Maybe we should head home," I suggest. "Unless you wanted to stick around and build a sandcastle."

"As fun as that sounds, I should probably go home. I promised the kittens I would take them bowling."

I put on my sandals to walk back across the hot sand toward the parking lot. "Can't disappoint the kittens. I haven't heard any noise upstairs in a while. I thought maybe you gave up on bowling."

"I've been trying to keep it quiet for you."

"So considerate."

He takes my hand and holds it the rest of the way to the car. When we get back to the building, Joel is at the front desk.

"Good afternoon, Joel."

He responds with a half-grunted "Hi" and a frown. My smile falters a little. I'm not sure if I'm imagining it, but he doesn't seem happy to see me lately. I turn to Jake and see that he's frowning back at Joel. At least he finally notices the old man's attitude toward us. I wonder if he's going to say anything, but he doesn't.

"Do you need to check your mail?" I ask.

His frown dissolves and he smiles at me. "Nope. Got it earlier."

When we reach my floor, he pauses, and I get the sense that he's waiting for something.

"I had a good time today," I tell him.

He leans down and touches his lips to mine. He pulls away slowly, his eyes on my mouth. "Me too." He glances at my apartment door, then returns his eyes to me. "Can I come in?"

As much as I've been dying to hear him ask that question, I find myself feeling torn. I want my mind to be fully on him when we're together, and I can't do that when my thoughts keep straying back to Luca and his letters.

"Maybe we should take it slow." It kills me to hear these words come out of my own mouth. "Is that okay?"

He smiles. "Of course it is."

He kisses me one more time, then heads back down the hallway toward the stairs. I go inside my apartment alone. I pick up Penelope Hayes's business card on the kitchen counter, look at it for a moment, and then flick it into the trash.

Something rolls across the floor above me, making my ceiling rumble. I picture Jake up there, playing with the kittens, and I smile.

Chapter Twenty-One

FAN MAIL

"**Y**ou're a genius."

These are the first words that Patrick Facey says to me when he sees me Tuesday morning. His face is flushed and his eyes are brighter than I've ever seen them. It's a little bit scary. I didn't know the man could look this elated.

"Can you put that in writing?" I ask. "Because yesterday you were pretty close to firing me."

"Our station has never been more popular," he says. "We got over a thousand new followers on our Facebook page yesterday, and we're still getting more coming in. Everyone loved your floating head."

"Fine. I'll take a raise, if you insist."

"Very funny. I actually wanted to talk to you about extending the amount of time you're on air. You wouldn't be required to stay any later, but viewers would get to see more of you and your shining personality."

I know that this isn't his idea. I read through the comments on the news station's social media page last night, where commenters were begging the station to let them see more of me.

I lean back in my chair and cross my legs, putting on a show of thinking about it. "How much more airtime are we talking?"

He shrugs. "Maybe a minute or two per segment. You could engage in some banter with the anchors. I've heard you and Anette talking. I know that you can be funny when you want to be, and I think our viewers want to see that too."

"An extra minute or two would require more planning on my part. It would also give me less time to plan. Sounds like more work. What's in it for me?"

"You would get more exposure. All of Miami would be watching you."

"You're right. More exposure could be a good thing. Maybe I'll even get another job offer with higher pay, and take all your new viewers with me to another station."

He tightens his lips, and his semi-bald head turns redder. "I'm sure we can work out a deal that will make us both happy. What are you thinking, like, a five percent bump?"

I glance up at the ceiling, pretending that this is the first I've thought about it. Then I look him in the eye and say, "More like twenty percent."

"Tw-twenty percent? Really?"

"Twenty percent," I repeat, keeping my tone even. I raise an eyebrow.

"Okay. Well. I'll see what I can do."

He leaves the room, and I swivel my chair to face my desk again. Seconds later, Anne marches into the room with my green dress draped over one arm and a coffee for me in her other hand.

"What's with Patty-boy? He seemed really flustered."

"He wants me to spend more time on air to help keep our new fans watching. I told him I'd do it for a raise. I don't think he liked how much I asked for."

She sets the coffee cup next to me, then places the dress next to it. "They didn't give you much of a raise when you came on air full-time. I'm sure that with Emmanuel gone, they can afford however much you asked for."

"That's assuming Patty-boy didn't already give himself and the anchors a raise when Emmanuel left."

"True." She peeks into the tote bag I brought her clothes in. "Are these mine?"

"Sorry I didn't wash them."

"No big deal. I didn't wash your dress either. The tag said dry-clean only. That, and I wouldn't expect you to spend all your quarters to wash such a small load."

"That's what I'm looking forward to about the house I'm buying. A washer and dryer. Well, at least the hookups."

"Yes. That's a must-have. Get a washer and dryer, and I'll be at your place once a week to do my laundry."

"Maybe I'll conveniently forget to give you my address."

"No big deal. I'll just follow you home."

"Stalker."

Anne takes the tote bag with her clothes, leaving me to focus. I go on air wearing regular clothes and wonder if any of our viewers will be disappointed that I'm not just a floating head anymore. Maybe Patrick will turn the green dress into my new uniform.

I wrap up my last report for the day, then head back to my desk. I'm surprised to see Anne standing next to a bouquet of flowers with a stack of paper in her hand.

"Are those for me?" I make a show of clasping my hands together. "Oh, Anette. You shouldn't have."

"You got a ton of fan mail, too. And not from your penemy. You got real fan mail."

"Already? It's only been a day."

"That's the magical thing about the internet," she says. "It allows us to use email. I think you're the only person I know who still uses snail mail for anything other than paying doctor bills."

She hands me the stack of paper. "You printed the emails?" I ask. "Why not just forward them to me?"

"I thought it would be more fun to read them this way."

I read over the first email, the gist of which is the same as the comments on my bodiless weather reporting video. I hand it back to Anne and turn my attention to the flowers.

"Who sent these?" I lean in and take a deep breath, enjoying their fragrance. It's been a long time since anyone has sent me flowers. I wonder if they're from Jake.

I pull out the small white envelope, open it, and take out the card. I recognize the handwriting.

"Luca," I say out loud before I start reading.

Dear Naomi,

   A million microscopic bugs live inside these flowers, and when you smell them, all the bugs will get sucked up into your nostrils and eat away at your cartilage until you don't have a nose anymore.

   Xoxo,

   Luca

"He sent you flowers? Interesting."

"He also told me that I'm going to lose my nose."

I hand her the note. She reads it and laughs. Then she turns the card over and frowns.

"What?" I ask.

She hands the card back to me. "This is a local florist."

"So?"

"So, that's his handwriting, isn't it?"

I examine it carefully. His handwriting was the first thing I noticed when I pulled the card out of the envelope. "I guess it's possible that he called it in and the florist happened to have the same handwriting as him."

Even as I say it, I know it's not likely. I remember the letter he sent yesterday, which I received the same day. I don't want to tell Anne about it, because then she'll want to know what the letter said. It probably doesn't matter. I can tell by the look on her face that she can see right through me.

"What do you know that I don't?" she asks. "Did he send you another letter?"

It's annoying how hard it is to keep a secret from her. "I don't think he's in San Diego."

"You think he's in Miami?"

"I don't know. He sent a letter yesterday. There's no way it came all the way from San Diego in a day. He mentioned my floating head. He couldn't have known ahead of time that I was going to do that."

"I can't believe you didn't say anything earlier. When were you going to tell me about that?"

"I'm telling you now."

She narrows her eyes, her lips curling up in a suspicious smile. "What are you hiding?"

"Nothing!" My face heats. I take a drink of water, hoping it will dissolve my blush.

"He sent you flowers. That's something."

"He only sent them as part of a joke. Didn't you read the note?"

She touches one of the petals. "This is a beautiful

arrangement. It couldn't have been cheap. That's kind of an expensive joke, don't you think?"

"It would be just like him to go all in on a joke like that."

Even as the words come out of my mouth, I'm not sure I believe them. I picture Luca walking into a florist and picking out a bouquet for me. I wonder if he chose the first one he saw, or if he put some thought into it. As much as I want to deny it, I wonder if Anne is right. I worry that Luca might be after more than just writing letters.

"Did you keep the envelope he sent the letter in?" Anne asks. "Maybe the postmark will show where it was mailed from."

"I don't keep the envelopes. I threw it away, and then I took out the trash. I'm not about to go dumpster diving to find it."

Anne sighs heavily like I'm inconveniencing her. "Hang onto the next one. Maybe if we find out where they're coming from, we won't have to go back to San Diego this weekend."

"Good, because all these trips are starting to take a toll on my bank account. That, and Jake wants me to himself this weekend."

"I bet he does." She wiggles her eyebrows. "Want to get lunch?"

Joel is at the security desk when I come in after lunch. He smiles as I walk through the door. "Good afternoon, Naomi."

I'm surprised by the friendly greeting. I feel like the last few times I've seen him he's been cold to me.

"Hey Joel. How are you?"

"Just wonderful." He nods toward the mailboxes, where

214

the mail carrier is filling them up. "You got here just in time. Lots of mail coming in today."

"Perfect."

I open my mailbox and pull out a short stack of mail. I flip through it: bills, junk mail and more bills. I feel a leap of excitement when I get to the bottom of the stack and see my name and address written in that familiar handwriting. Then I remember what Anne said. I turn to the mail carrier, who is just finishing up, and show him the newest envelope from Luca.

"Can you tell me where this letter would have been mailed from?"

He leans in to look at the envelope, frowns, then snatches it from my hand. He turns it over, shrugs, then hands it back to me. "Didn't come through the post office," he says. "No postmark. There isn't even a stamp."

"What?" I turn it over and realize that he's right. "It was in my mailbox, though. How is that possible? Maybe because there's no return address?"

He shakes his head. "It would have been held at the post office, and you'd be notified that you need to pay the postage in order to receive it. Someone else must have put that in your box."

I stare at the envelope for a moment. I'm aware of the mail carrier watching me for a few seconds before he turns around and heads out of the building. I can only think of one explanation for this: Luca has been in my building. Or maybe he had someone else drop it off. Either way, he has to be in Miami.

"Something wrong, Naomi?"

I look up at Joel, remembering that I'm not alone. Then I have an idea. "You're here pretty much all day, right?"

"Pretty much."

"Have you seen anyone who doesn't live here come into the building? Maybe someone hanging around the mailboxes?"

"Can't think of anyone out of the ordinary," he says. His gaze shoots down to the stack of mail in my hands. "Can you describe what they might have looked like?"

I shake my head. "No idea." I realize how ridiculous I must sound. "Could you keep an eye out for anyone who doesn't live here and might be putting things in the mailboxes? I don't want to get them in trouble. I just want to know who it is."

He smiles. "That's my job."

"Right. Thank you."

I head upstairs, and when I get inside, I set the flowers on my kitchen table and rip open the envelope.

Dear Naomi,

Did I mention that I'm sorry that I didn't write to you for two years? Because I am. By the time I found the last letter you sent, you had already moved and all the letters I sent got kicked back to me. I guess maybe the same thing happened when you wrote to me. That's just an assumption on my part. Maybe you didn't try to write to me again. I hope you did.

I still have the last letter you sent. My ex had intercepted it and hid it from me for seven months. I guess she didn't like that you told me not to marry her, and that I could come hide away with you. I wish I had received that letter a lot sooner. I wouldn't have stayed with her for so long, and I would have taken you up on your offer.

Speaking of that offer, is it still valid? Because I'd like to come hide away with you if you'll have me. Just say the word and I'm yours.

Love,

Luca

I don't know why my knees feel so weak. I don't understand why after all these years his words are making me feel this way. I remember that last letter I sent him two years ago. I had prepared myself for what I would say when he inevitably made fun of me for inviting him to come hide away with me. At the time that I wrote it, I had meant it. Maybe I hadn't expected him to take me up on my offer, but I was feeling lonely, and maybe a little adventurous when I wrote it.

I had wanted a change of scenery, so I started looking for a job in other cities. My boyfriend at the time didn't want to uproot his life to move with me, so we made the mutual decision to break up. It made sense. We hadn't been dating long. I received the letter about Luca's engagement a few days later. Breakup season was in the air, and it didn't sound like he wanted to get married. Maybe a selfish part of me was afraid he would stop writing to me once he settled down. That fear seemed to have been confirmed when I didn't hear from him for the next two years.

For a while, I wondered if he would show up at my doorstep after I sent him that last letter. But then I moved to Miami, and I knew that wouldn't happen unless he had my new address. But the next letter I sent was kicked back, and so was the next one. It took longer than I care to admit to accept that Luca had gotten married and wasn't interested in writing to me anymore.

I wish that I could write back to him now. I wish that I didn't have to use my weather reports as a ridiculous way to send messages to him. I look at the torn, unstamped envelope, and an idea comes to me.

I've been overthinking it.

I find a notebook and a pen in my bedroom, then return to the kitchen table and start writing.

Dear Luca,

   How long have you been in Miami? I know that you were in my building. I'm not sure if I should be creeped out or just happy that I can finally write back to you. Maybe you wanted me to figure that out so I wouldn't go back to Georgia and bug your old friends. Is that why you didn't bother to put a stamp on the envelope?

   I did try to send you my new address when I first moved here, but you must have already moved because the letter was sent back to me. I kind of hoped that you would show up at my door one day. In fact, I still hope you will.

   Love,

   Naomi

I fold the letter and stick it in an envelope. My hands are shaking by the time it's sealed. I stare at it for a moment, trying to decide if I really want him to read this. I'm scared that he might actually show up. I don't know why that scares me. What's the worst that will happen? He's had my address for years and he never showed up to murder me. But that's not what I'm afraid of. I don't really know what I'm afraid of.

I write his name on the envelope. Nothing else, no address. I put on my shoes and head downstairs. I walk past Joel and stick the envelope on the shelf on top of the mailboxes, where Luca will be able to see it if he comes back into the building.

Joel is frowning at me when I turn around. "What's that?"

"Bait," I say. "Let me know if you see who grabs it."

He harrumphs in response. I head back upstairs.

Chapter Twenty-Two

THINK ABOUT ME

I dream about Luca tonight. It starts off innocent enough. I walk out of my apartment building and he's there, standing on the sidewalk, facing the road. I don't know how I know that it's him, but I do. I call his name, and he turns around, but before I can see his face, I'm somewhere else. I'm in my apartment, and he's here. It's dark, so I can't see him. He's evasive. One moment, he's right next to me, and the next, I'm reaching for him, but it's like trying to grab smoke. My hands slip right through him and then he's on the other side of me, laughing. I fall to the floor, and the next thing I know, his legs are tangled with mine. I try to touch him, but he moves, and all I feel is a blanket. My floor is covered in blankets.

His hands slide over my body, and he whispers into my ear about how it turned him on to see my head floating around on the news. I reach for him again, and even though he's so close to me, all I can feel is the fabric of the blanket. He laughs at me, then asks why I never tried to find him sooner. I start to get frustrated. I just want to touch him, to know that he's real, but the harder I try, the more tangled I become in these blankets, until I can't feel him at all anymore.

I'm startled awake when I hear a knock at my door. I have my blackout curtains drawn, so it feels like it's the middle of the night, but when I look at my bedside clock, I see that it's only seven in the evening. I've been in bed for an hour. I groan. My first instinct is to shout through the door at whoever interrupted my dream. I was so close to finding Luca. My whole body feels flushed. I don't know what I would have done if I could have reached him in my dream. I feel tense, like I was on the verge of uncovering something important. There's this warm ache between my legs, and I realize I know what it is. I wanted him here in my bed with me. I was about to have a sex dream. About Luca.

Whoever disturbed my sleep did so just in time, though I'm not sure knowing this is any better. I cover my face, but when I close my eyes, all I see are the images from my dream. My whole body feels hot and a thin layer of perspiration glazes my skin. As much as I don't want to think about what just went on inside my head, I know why it happened. It's all the time I've been spending with Jake – the touching, the flirting, but never taking it any further than that – combined with the letters from Luca, hinting at him wanting more. My body is confused again, and it's trying to trick my mind into having thoughts I shouldn't have.

As my mind begins to wake, I wonder who could be at my door. I start thinking up a list of possibilities. Maybe there's a fire in the building and the alarm didn't go off. Maybe there's an emergency that only a meteorologist can help solve. I'm sure if it's an emergency, they'll knock again. Maybe it's someone who doesn't live in the building, who doesn't know I'm in bed by now.

I sit up straight, my blanket flying off of me. I think of the letter that I left for Luca on top of the mailboxes. Could it really be him? Did he come back already just to check if I left a letter for him?

I turn on all the lights in my apartment on my way to the front door. I think about stopping by the bathroom to make sure I look presentable, but decide against it and settle for patting down my hair in front of the hallway mirror. I take a deep breath before I open the door.

I don't know why I'm so surprised to find Jake on the other side. I should have known that it would be him. I immediately feel guilty for what I was dreaming about a minute ago.

"Sorry I'm here so late," he says. "I had a bad day, and I just... I needed to see you."

I open my door a little wider, letting him in. He stops at the end of my hallway, looking around the room. Knowing that he had a bad day makes me feel even guiltier about my dream, like I somehow contributed to his day being shitty, even though he couldn't have known what was going on inside my head. I wonder if Joel mentioned I left a note for another man in the lobby.

"Why was your day bad?" I ask. I lean against the hallway wall opposite him.

He reaches his hand up and rubs the back of his neck. "Family stuff," he says with a sigh.

He had mentioned before that he has a big family. I've always been envious of people with siblings, but I guess it's not without its own challenges.

"I'm sorry to hear that. Do you want to talk about it?"

He shakes his head. When he speaks again, his voice comes out in a whisper so quiet I can barely hear him. "I just want to live like nothing is wrong for a little while longer."

I may not know what's wrong, but I think I know how I could help him feel better. Just as I'm thinking it, his eyes wander over my body, and I remember the last time we both stood in this hallway. The spark that was awakened in my dream about Luca is reignited. Maybe this is what I need to put a stop to that dream and those unwelcome thoughts about Luca.

I step closer to him, letting my hands rest on his waist. He sucks in a breath, like even a touch as light as this does something to him. I raise up on my toes to reach him better. He angles his neck downward, and our lips meet somewhere in the middle. It's soft and sweet, but it doesn't stay that way for long. His arms wrap around me, his hands moving from my ribcage to my waist, down to my hips, and lower. I'm not sure when he moves me to the wall, but the next thing I know, my back is against it, and his body is pressed against mine. He doesn't hold back this time. I can feel the weight of him pushing into me, fitting perfectly between my thighs. When he rocks his hips against mine, I can feel the shape of him.

I reach down and feel him through his sweatpants.

"What happened to taking things slow?" he asks.

"I changed my mind. Is this okay?"

He nods, breathing out a barely audible, "Yes."

"I'm on the pill," I tell him. "Are you clean?"

He nods. "I've been tested."

"Me too." I tug his waistband down and... "Oh, wow. That's..."

I want to say that it's big, but I can tell by his smug smile that he already knows it. I take him in my hand and stroke him. His skin is smooth and hot, and he's so hard that just the thought of what he could do to me sends a pulse through my body and down between my legs.

"I like that," he mumbles. He presses his face into my hair. I can feel his hot breath against my neck.

His hand trails down my hip until his fingers are poking under my waistband, but he pauses there. I take his hand and guide it a little farther until he moves the rest of the way down on his own, reaching that sensitive spot between my legs. His fingers curl in, and my body responds with a shudder. He does it again, and this time I gasp.

"Take this off," he says, pulling at my shirt with his other hand.

I let go of him to pull my shirt off, but my action is delayed when he goes in deeper, making me cry out and cling to his shoulders involuntarily. I try again, but I'm forced to drop it when he does it again.

"I can't take it off if you keep—" I bite his shoulder to keep myself from being too loud.

He releases me and pulls my shirt over my head, then pulls his own shirt off and drops them both to the floor. He lifts me up so that he's holding me against the wall and my middle is pinned against his. I wrap my legs around his waist. He kisses a trail from my ear down my jaw, my neck, and down to my chest. He focuses his attention on my breasts for a minute, giving them each equal attention. My fingers are in his hair, and when he takes my nipple into his mouth, I squeeze, wrapping my legs around him tighter. He keeps going, his tongue moving over my nipple until I can barely hold on anymore. I've never been brought so close to an orgasm this way before. I didn't know it was possible.

Unable to bear it any longer, I pull myself away from his mouth. He looks up at me with a primal look in his eyes.

"I need you," I tell him. "Now." In my head, I calculate the distance to the bedroom. It's too far. "Take me to the couch."

Keeping me wrapped around his waist, he carries me to the couch. When we get there, he lays me on my back, then pulls my pajama shorts down. My panties come off with them. When he sees me completely naked, he shudders out a breath.

"Are you sure about this?" he asks.

"Yes. Get over here." I sit up and pull him down onto the couch with me.

He eases himself between my legs until I can feel his tip against my center. He doesn't push into me right away. He holds it there for a moment, his lips against my neck, on my ear, trailing down my cheek to my mouth. His teeth pull at my lower lip.

I wrap my legs around his back, pulling him closer and trying to get him inside of me. He holds back, and I think I might go crazy from how close we are.

"Please," I whisper against his ear. He inches in just enough to make me beg. "More."

He takes his time, and with each new inch he gives me, I'm pushed closer to an edge I've never been on before. No one has ever teased me quite the way he does. By the time he's snugly inside of me, I'm already halfway there. My fingers tighten on his shoulders, feeling his muscle as he rocks against me.

He buries his face in my neck, his breath hot against my skin. When he makes love to me, it doesn't feel like it's the first time. He moves like he knows exactly what I like. I'm not sure I even know what I like until we're there, and he's diving into me, taking me higher and higher until I can't hold on anymore. He doesn't stop when I reach my climax. With each rock of his hips against mine, he takes me to a whole new level I've never felt before. I lose all control, and I still can't get enough. My arms tighten around his shoulders, my legs pulling him closer as my body pulsates around his. I cry out, not caring anymore that my neighbors might be able to hear me. The only thing that matters in this moment is him, and how good this feels, and how I could live in this moment right now for the rest of my life.

Just as the sensation begins to taper off, he locks his lips with mine and presses deeper into me, sending one last surge of pleasure through my body.

We lie there for a moment, his weight on top of me, my legs still wrapped around his back. Both of us breathe heavily, unwinding slowly. He separates himself from me, then angles his body so that he's between me and the edge of the couch.

Once I've recovered a bit, I sigh, but it comes out as more of a laugh. He smiles, amused by my reaction.

"That was good," I tell him, not caring that I'm fueling his ego. "So fucking good."

We watch each other for a moment. Even in the dim light of the living room, the blue of his eyes is piercing. I don't think I could get tired of looking into those eyes.

My eyes wander past him to the coffee table where I left the bouquet of flowers. Just as I'm wondering if he noticed them, he follows my gaze over his shoulder and looks at them. I wait for him to ask me who they're from, but he doesn't.

"Sorry if I woke you up," he says, turning his attention back to me.

"I'm not complaining. Though I have to say that you didn't seem like you were sorry a minute ago."

He shakes his head. "You caught me. Guess I'm not that sorry."

"I do need to go back to bed, though. Feel free to hang around if you don't mind watching me sleep."

"Do you have a chair that I can sit in at the foot of your bed?"

I snort out a laugh. "I do, but I'd prefer if you watched me from the other pillow. It's a little less creepy that way."

"Good," he says. "Because I'm not done with you just yet."

He follows me into the bedroom, but stops me from turning off the light.

"I like seeing you," he says. "All of you."

We were so close before that I didn't get to fully appreciate the view. I've seen him shirtless twice before, at the beach and when Anne and I saw him running the morning we got back from San Diego. Even so, seeing him like this in my bedroom makes my breath catch in my throat. I slide my fingers across his firm chest and down his sculpted abdomen. His eyes darken with my touch.

"Are you even real?" I ask, making him smirk.

"I could say the same about you," he says. He cups my breast, then moves his hand down to my hip, tracing my curves with his fingertips. "Look at you."

When we finally make it to the bed, he takes his time with me, but he doesn't tease me the same way he did the first time. This time he explores my body with his hands and with his mouth, kissing every inch of me until I'm squirming and begging for more of him. He parts my legs and enters me, giving me what I want.

It's slower and sweeter than it was the first time, but it's no less passionate. When it's over, he wraps his arms around me. I lean my head against his chest and close my eyes. I can feel the rhythmic thumping of his heart, a steady beat that makes the rest of the world seem a little quieter. I've never fallen asleep easily with someone else's arms wrapped around me, but I do now.

This time I dream about blue eyes, and airplanes, and unanswered letters.

I wake up sometime later when he gets up to turn off the light. It's not quite midnight, so I don't have to be up for another few hours. For a moment, I think that he's leaving, but then I feel the mattress shift and the blankets move as he climbs back into my bed. His arms close around my waist, and his head rests against my chest.

In the dark, I breathe him in. I run my hand over the smooth skin of his back and over his firm arm. He trails his fingertips up and down the back of my thigh, sending a delicious tingle between my legs. I should be getting some sleep before work in the morning, but the way he's touching me has me feeling restless. I want him. I never knew until now how badly I needed him.

He inches a little closer and nudges me with his thigh. I part my legs for him. His hand snakes its way between my legs, and he touches me, gentle strokes at first, and then he massages deeper, like he knows just what to do to get me to climax. I reach for him again, but in the dark, I only get a fistful of the blanket. I try to move the blanket out of the way, but it's wrapped around him now and all I succeed in doing is tangling us up more. It feels like I'm back in the dream I was having before he came over, only it's so much more real now. He's touching me but I can't reach him because this blanket is in the way. He lets out a couple of quick breaths, amused and laughing at the way I can't get the blanket off. He keeps on touching me, not bothering to help free me. I gasp, climbing higher and higher, and I'm right on the verge of tipping over when Luca's name slips out of my mouth. It comes out in a whispered moan, so distorted that even I don't entirely understand myself. But I hear it. It's the only sound in the otherwise quiet room, and I know that he hears it too, because his fingers stop moving. *Shit.*

For a moment I just lay there in the dark. I can still feel his body pressed against mine, and his hand is still resting between my legs, but not moving. He begins to move, and I'm about to apologize and try to explain myself until I realize that he's rolling on top of me. He must have not understood me. He probably thought it was just a weird moan. He pushes the blanket off of me, and the next thing I know, he's parting my legs wider and he's inside of me. He moves slowly, not like someone who is angry about being called the wrong name. He steadily brings me back to where I was when he was touching me. When I climax, I bite his shoulder, afraid of what else might come out of my mouth.

He finishes shortly after, and he stays on top of me, his body pinning mine to the bed. In the dark, I can't see his face, but I can feel his breath, and I know that he's watching me. Our chests rise and fall together with each heavy breath. I wait for him to ask me who Luca is, or at least ask what it was I said, but he doesn't. He finally rolls over and falls asleep next to me.

Chapter Twenty-Three

IT'S A PROBLEM

Dear Naomi,

I've been in Miami for a while. Imagine my surprise when I learned that you live here too. Such a small world. I'm glad you finally figured out how to write back to me. I was getting pretty close to giving in and putting my return address on the next letter. I guess now I don't have to.

Is that a dare or an invite? Because if it's an invite, I want you to make it clear. I want you to tell me that you want me.

Love,

Luca

Dear Luca,

Sorry if I led you on. I should probably mention that I'm seeing someone. I didn't mean to flirt with you, and I think you should stop trying to flirt with me.

Love,

Naomi

Dear Naomi,

I bet he's not as hot as me. I can send a picture if you want to compare?

Xoxo,

Luca

Dear Luca,

I see you're still just as full of yourself as you've always been. Are you this perverted in real life, or only when you're hiding behind a pen and paper?

Love,

Naomi

Dear Naomi,

I just meant an innocent picture of my face. Did you think I meant a dick pic? Come on! We're not in high school anymore. All kidding aside, does your boyfriend know about our letters? Because I've learned the hard way that they can really destroy a relationship. I think anyone who reads them would know that I'm in love with you.

Love,

Luca

Dear Luca,

How can you say that you're in love with me when we've never even met? If that's how you think you feel, you should have told me a lot sooner. It's too late now.

Love,

Naomi

Dear Naomi,

It's not too late.

Love,

Luca

The letters come more often now that I know how to write back to him. On Friday morning, I'm still thinking about the last letter he put in my mailbox. I don't know what to write back. It doesn't seem to matter how mean or dismissive I am. He keeps writing back, and I can't stop thinking about him.

"I found something interesting when I was doing the laundry."

I thought I was done letting Anne scare the crap out of me, but when I hear her voice, I scream and almost fall out of my chair. I swivel around and glare at her.

"That's it. I'm buying you a pair of stilettos with a metal heel," I tell her. "Your shoes are too damn quiet."

"I'm a sneaky snake," she says. "But you're even sneakier."

"What are you talking about?"

"This."

She tosses a wrinkled sheet of notebook paper at me. It floats toward my lap, but misses me entirely and lands on the floor. I pick it up and straighten it out. "Shit."

I forgot to take this letter out of Anne's pocket before giving her clothes back. I remember sneaking it in when Jake showed up at my apartment the day we went to the beach.

"This ranks right up there with all the creepy messages I get on my dating apps. It turned him on to watch your news report? You didn't think this little development was worth mentioning? What about all the other letters he's been sending to your place? What else is he saying to you?"

I fold the letter and tuck it under my keyboard. "None of your business."

"I traveled to three different states with you looking for this guy. You let me read all the letters he sent to you in high school. Since when is this not my business?"

I groan. "Since it became a problem."

"What do you mean? What's going on?"

I sigh, trying to decide how much I want to tell her. "I've been writing back to him."

Her eyes widen. "He gave you his address? Where does he live?"

"No idea. I figured out that his letters to my apartment weren't postmarked. He's somewhere in Miami."

"Okay. How are you writing back to him then?"

"I leave the letters in my building. He takes them and writes back."

Her eyes are so wide I'm afraid they might pop out of her head. "Are you kidding me? He's been in your building? Holy shit, Gnome. How long have you been holding onto this little tidbit?"

"That's not even the worst part." I close my eyes. I can't believe I'm telling her this, but it also feels good to get it off my chest. I don't have anyone else to confide in.

"Go on," she prods.

"I can't stop thinking about him."

She purses her lips. "Thinking about him in what way?"

I cringe, bracing myself for her reaction to what I'm about to say. "I had a sex dream. Or, not really a sex dream, but it was close."

"About *Luca*?" Her voice is so high and loud that I'm sure everyone in the building can hear her.

"That's not all. Jake came over right after and we, you know—"

"Had sex," she says, filling in the blanks.

"I said his name."

She frowns. "Whose name?"

"I said Luca's name in the middle of a moan. I don't know what came over me. It's not like I was thinking about him. I feel awful about it."

"Ouch. That had to hurt his ego."

"I don't think he understood me. Thank God." I breathe out a sigh.

She looks at me seriously. "So, you don't think it's just a fun fling anymore? With Jake?"

I shake my head. "I don't know. It's more than that. I have feelings for him, but why can't I stop thinking about Luca?"

"Because you have feelings for Luca, too," Anne suggests.

I let out a desperate laugh. "I can't have feelings for two guys at the same time."

"What are you going to do then? If you continue dating Jake and writing to Luca, you're just going to keep saying his name at inappropriate times."

I sigh. I know that she's right. I've thought about it myself. But after not hearing from him for two years, and now finally being able to write back, I can't bring myself to let him go just yet.

"I just can't shake the feeling that I'm missing out on something. I've been writing to Luca since fifth grade. Somehow, we both ended up in Miami. I've never believed in fate, but what if this is it? What if this is the universe telling me that I need to give him a chance?"

I hope that she'll tell me I'm being ridiculous and that I

should just leave things the way they are. I've never met Luca and I don't know what he's really like. Besides, I already admitted that I'm falling for Jake. Unlike Luca, who has only ever been words on paper, Jake is real, and he's here, and I know him.

"I think fate and soulmates and all that are bullshit," she says. "But come on, Naomi. You've been writing to Luca for longer than most people are married. Don't get me wrong. I'm not telling you to dump Jake. But maybe give Luca a chance. Meet him."

"You were just comparing his letter to the creepy dudes in your inbox, and now you're saying I should meet him?"

She shrugs. "You're always going to wonder if you don't. And who knows? Maybe you'll like him better than Jake."

"I don't know. It feels wrong. I already told him I wasn't seeing anyone else. We basically agreed to be exclusive. And I'm not going to break up with him just to find out that Luca's a total creep in real life. Plus, I really, really like him. I haven't felt a connection like this with anyone in … well, ever."

"Then tell Luca that you want to meet him platonically. I'll even tag along if you need a third wheel. But you need to choose between them, Gnome. You can't be having sex with one guy while you're thinking about the other. That's not right."

We hear a throat clearing behind us. I swivel my chair around to see Patrick standing there, his face redder than ever.

"I certainly walked in on the wrong part of that conversation," he says. "Anette. Get back to work."

"Yes, boss," she says with a mock salute. She leans toward me and whispers, *"Choose between them,"* before she follows Patrick out of the room.

Chapter Twenty-Four

COME TO MIAMI

Luca

When I left Dallas, I wasn't sure where else to go. I ended up back in San Diego. All I had were my clothes, my basic necessities, and a box full of letters from Naomi. Most of my furniture had been sold before the move, and the rest I left behind because I didn't feel like fighting Penny over it. I was able to get my old job back. I had only been gone for a month and they hadn't replaced me yet. Someone else had moved into my apartment, so I ended up living in Ben and Yvette's spare room.

It wasn't the ideal situation. Ben and Yvette had married right after college and they had their first kid nine months later. By the time I moved in, they had just had their third. There was a lot of screaming and crying, toys all over the house, and it seemed like everyone was always rushing to get somewhere. It was chaos.

I wasn't sad about the breakup with Penny, but everyone

else seemed to think I should be. It was more of a relief than anything else. I should have ended things a lot sooner.

I wrote back to Naomi as soon as I was settled into my new temporary home. I sat at the kitchen table during one of the rare moments that all three kids and their mom were napping at the same time. Ben walked into the room and did a double-take when he saw me sitting there with a pen and paper.

"Don't tell me you're still writing to that girl from fifth grade."

I didn't have to look up at him to know that he was joking. I could tell by the tone of his voice.

"Naomi Light," I said.

"Wait. Are you serious? You still write to her?"

"I never stopped."

"Does she still write disturbing shit about getting hangnails and losing fingers?"

I shrugged. "Sometimes."

"You are so weird. I can't believe you still write to her." He sat down across from me. "What did Penny think about that?"

"She wasn't a fan. She hid Naomi's last letter from me. It's kind of the reason everything blew up when it did."

"Have you ever met Naomi in person?"

I shook my head. "Maybe one day."

"I think it's crazy that you've been writing to her for this long and you've never even met her. Do you still stalk her Facebook page?"

"I tried. She set everything to private. I can't even see her photos anymore."

"She probably knew you were looking at them and wanted you to stop."

The newborn started to cry in the other room just then. Ben left to go check on the baby, and I finished writing my letter. I put it in the mail and waited. And waited. A few weeks went by, and the letter was returned. Undeliverable. She had moved.

I hung onto the letter for about a month before I tried again. I mailed the next one to the last address she had lived at as a teenager before she headed off to college. I hoped that maybe her parents still lived there and they would be able to get the letter to her. That one came back about a month later.

I tried to look her up on Facebook again, but her page was still set to private. There were no clues offered as to where she lived or where she worked. I didn't even have the option to send her a message or a friend request. I didn't want to give up on finding her, but I was beginning to lose hope. Maybe it was too late. I took too long to write back to her, and our long history of writing mean letters had finally come to an end.

I thought that maybe it was for the best. I had held that girl up on such a high pedestal that no one else I dated ever measured up. If I hadn't been comparing everyone to what I fantasized Naomi might be like, I would have been happily married by now.

Then one day, I got a new letter in the mail. My name and Ben's address were written with such sloppy handwriting that I would have known it wasn't from Naomi even if the return address hadn't been included. I stared at the envelope for a while before I tucked it away, unopened, into my nightstand.

I wasn't sure at first how my dad got my address. It had been more than ten years since he left me and my mom. I hadn't heard a word from him since then. He had told me when he left that he was moving to Montana, but he had never given me an address to write to him, and he never bothered writing to me or even calling me. I had grown numb to his abandonment. There were more important things to worry about.

I didn't want to read his letter and feel compelled to forgive him for all the years he was absent. I didn't want to read it and find out that he was poor now and was hoping that I was well-off enough to loan him some money. I didn't want to open that envelope and find a tacky invitation to a wedding I wouldn't attend in a million years. I didn't want to find out that he had terminal cancer and that he was trying to make amends with me before he died. It made me angry that he thought he could come back into my life just by writing me a letter.

I left it unopened in my nightstand drawer for a few months. I thought about burning it or ripping it up and throwing it away without reading it, but I decided to hold onto it. Maybe one day I would be ready to read it.

I was living with Ben and Yvette for ten months when I learned how my dad must have found my address. Penny had found it the same way. She started calling Ben's home phone and leaving harassing messages on his answering machine. She must have finally figured out that I blocked her number and that's why I wasn't returning any of her calls or texts. Desperate to reach me, she had looked me up in an online database that listed Ben's address as my residence, along with Ben's home phone number.

I paid every database I could find to remove my information, and then I deactivated my Facebook account too. I didn't want to take the chance that she might find me on there even after I blocked her. Ben was able to block her number, but soon after, she began sending vulgar letters and postcards to his address. Yvette told me to write 'refused' on all the letters that came in, and eventually they stopped. I could only hope that she would look me up again and, seeing that my name was no longer listed at that address, she would assume that I had moved.

I had already felt like I was wearing out my welcome before Penny started harassing us. Ben and Yvette never complained about me being there, and they never asked me to leave. I paid rent for my room, and I babysat the kids a couple times a month so that they could have a date night. Even so, I knew that they probably wanted their place back to normal. I decided to look for an apartment, and I started to pack up my room so that I would be ready to go when the time came.

When I opened my nightstand drawer, I remembered the letter I hid in there several months ago. I didn't feel as heated as I had when I first received it. I picked it up and stared at it for a moment. For the first time since I received the letter, I was curious about what was so important that after all these years, he finally wrote to me. I slid my finger under the flap and opened the envelope.

Dear Luca,

I know that no words will ever be enough for you to forgive me for walking out on you when you were a kid. In many ways, I was still just a kid myself, but I know that that's no excuse. There were things that happened between me and your mother that you couldn't have understood at that time. I don't know if she ever told you what happened, but if she did, she probably didn't tell you the whole story. I wouldn't blame her if she didn't.

If I could change things, I would have fought harder to take you with me when I left. The only reason I didn't was because I knew that she was a good mom, even if she wasn't a good wife. You probably don't want to hear this about her. I know that it's wrong to say bad things about people who have passed away, so I will leave it at that. She was lucky to have you there to take care of her when she got sick.

I can't go back in time and fix things. I wasn't there for you, and

I regret it every day. I hope that one day we can work it out and be a part of each other's lives again, but I'll understand if it's too late.

I've sent a lot of letters to you over the years. I don't know if that makes any difference, but selfishly I hope that it does. It's been difficult to track you down with all the moves you've made. I can only hope that this letter will make it to you. I have a lot more that I want to tell you, but there is only so much I can say in a letter when I'm afraid it will be kicked back like all the others.

If this letter should make it to you, I hope you will give me another chance at being your dad.

Much love,

Joel Pichler

Chapter Twenty-Five

THE INTRODUCTION OF MR. PICKLES

Naomi

I reach the bottom of the stairs at the same time the elevator doors open and Caterpillar Kid and her mom step out. I guess I should start calling her Caitlin now that I know her real name. Caitlin is holding a jar of pickles, and her mom has a caterpillar coloring book clutched against her chest. I slow down to let them cross my path on their way to the security desk where Joel is sitting. The man has to make killer overtime with all the hours he sits at that desk.

"Pickles for Mr. Pickles!" Caitlin announces as she slides the jar onto his desk.

I look at them as I walk past them toward the mailboxes. When I hear her nickname for Joel, my mind wanders back to my trip to Georgia. I remember Maxwell's nickname for Luca, and how he had said that his ex-fiancée wanted to be Penny Pickles.

The letter I left for Luca is gone, but there isn't a new one in my mailbox. I look out the window to see if Anne is outside yet, but she's not. I can see Caitlin and her mom and Joel out of the corner of my eye. I try not to make it obvious that I'm listening to them.

"You're the best," Joel says to Caitlin as he accepts the jar of pickles.

"No, you're the best," Caitlin's mom says. She sounds a little out of breath. The kid must wear her out. "I'll be down in an hour. Thank you so much for watching her."

"It's my pleasure," Joel says. He pops the lid open and pulls out a pickle. Caitlin watches him with wide eyes, and when he takes a big crunchy bite, she giggles.

The mom hands the coloring book to Caitlin, then heads back into the elevator. Caitlin runs to the front door, while Joel calls after her: "Stay next to the window where I can see you!"

Once we're the only two people in the lobby, I approach Joel. He finishes the pickle he's eating, then closes the jar and smiles up at me.

"Is that your payment for babysitting her?" I gesture toward the jar.

His smile widens. "It would seem so."

I force a laugh that I hope sounds natural. "Why pickles?"

He shrugs. "Who knows? I think Ms. Bayer shops at the surplus store. She must've bought too many jars."

"Oh," I say, realizing that I must be overthinking the nickname. "I thought that maybe it had something to do with what she called you."

"What's that?"

"She called you Mr. Pickles," I remind him.

"Did she?"

There's something about the way he asks the question that gives me pause. He says it with an air of nonchalance that makes me think he's hoping I'll drop the subject. Maybe I'm reading too much into it.

I tug the corners of my lips up into a smile. "Yes."

"Oh. Well, huh. Kids say the funniest things sometimes."

I look over my shoulder at the mailboxes. "I left another letter on top of the mailboxes last night. You didn't happen to see who took it, did you?"

He shrugs. "Sorry. I didn't see anything there this morning."

"And you haven't seen anyone strange coming into the building?"

"No one who's been hanging around the mailboxes."

The front door swings open before I can ask anything else, and Caitlin pokes her head in. "Gnome! Your friend is here."

I look out the window and spot Anne's car parked at the curb. I head outside and get in. She's blasting music so loudly that I can't hear my own thoughts. I turn off the radio.

"I didn't get a new letter from Luca."

"Did you write what we talked about?"

"Yes."

After work yesterday, Anne and I had stopped at the café for lunch and went over how I should approach meeting Luca in person. I kept the letter straight and to the point. I told him that I wanted to meet him in a public place, and that I didn't want him to expect anything more from me.

"The letter was gone this morning," I continue. "So he's been in the building sometime between then and now."

"But nothing new from him."

"No." I chew on my lip, considering whether I should bring up whatever else is on my mind. "Hey, do you remember when we went to Georgia and met that guy who knew Luca?"

"Maxwell. He was cute."

"Of course you would think so. Do you remember what he called Luca?"

She twists her lip as she thinks about it. "Pickles, right? Because his last name is Pichler."

"That's what Caitlin calls Joel. Pickles. Well, Mr. Pickles, but still."

"Who? And who?"

"Caitlin is Caterpillar Kid's name. And Joel is the security guard. I've told you about him."

"You think that Joel could be Luca?"

"No. He's the wrong age. But he's at that desk pretty much all day, and he doesn't seem to notice whoever is coming in and taking my letters and sticking things in my mailbox."

"Maybe Luca is the mailman."

I laugh. "Doubt it. My building has been on his route since long before I moved here."

"I wouldn't read too much into the nickname. She calls you Gnome."

"Yeah, but that sounds close enough to Naomi."

She drives us to the pet store where the adoption event is being held. The humane society has several pens set up at the front of the store. The most adoptable dogs are in these pens, excitedly greeting the people who are grouped around them. We pass a pen of about eight brown and white puppies that look like they can't be any older than two months. The young puppies seem to be getting the most attention.

We go inside and make our way to the back of the store where there are several more cages lined up with cats and kittens of all ages. I spot Jake standing by one cage. Inside the cage is an orange tabby kitten and another that's mostly white with patches of gray and orange on its back. He's talking to one of the other volunteers. When he notices me, he smiles and gives me his full attention.

"You came," he says.

"Are these the kittens?" I poke my finger through the bars of the cage. Both of the kittens approach to sniff me.

"These are the famous bowling kittens," he confirms. He points at the orange one. "That's Roland. The calico is Phoebe."

Anne steps up and extends her hand to him. "I don't think we've been properly introduced. I'm Anne."

He reaches over the cage to shake her hand. "Nice to finally meet you, Anne."

"And you are?"

He laughs and lets go of her hand. "Very funny."

I frown at her and mouth, "Why are you being weird?"

Jake turns his attention back to the kittens.

"Has anyone looked at the kittens today?" I ask him.

"A couple people have passed by and played with them through the cage, but no one has filled out an application for them."

"They're so cute. How could anyone pass them up?"

He shrugs. "Do you want to play with them?"

"Can I?"

He shows me and Anne to a small room that's designed to be a quiet space for families to meet animals that are available for adoption. He brings the kittens in a moment later. Anne and I sit on the floor as the two kittens bounce around the room wrestling each other.

He hands us a box full of toys, then sits down next to me. Anne picks out a plastic stick with a feathery toy at the tip, which she dangles over the kittens. They both launch themselves at the toy at the same time, crashing into each other and missing the toy entirely.

I laugh. "How old are they?"

"Four months," he says.

The orange kitten jumps into my lap just then and stretches his paws up, swatting at my hair.

"He must think my braid is a toy," I say. I wiggle my braid and the kitten swats at it again, but this time he doesn't let go. The kitten pulls back, yanking my head down with him.

"Oh. Ouch."

"His claw is stuck," Jake says. He leans over me as he lifts the kitten, carefully untangling the tiny claw from my braid.

From this angle, all I can see are his chin and his throat. His jaw is speckled with short stubble. I watch as his Adam's apple bobs up and down once. I know what the skin of his neck feels like against my lips, between my teeth. If I didn't have a kitten stuck in my hair right now – or an audience of Anne, watching us – I might push him down to the floor and have a little fun with him.

When he pulls away, his eyes meet mine for a second, and in that brief moment, they narrow just enough to make me think he knows exactly what I'm thinking. I can't help but wonder if I'm really that easy to read, or if he has the same thoughts going on in his head.

He sets Roland back down on the floor, but the kitten returns to my lap, this time settling down instead of playing with my hair.

"He likes you," he says, nudging my arm with his elbow.

"Are you jealous?" I wiggle my eyebrows.

He smirks. "A little."

The calico kitten pounces from a few feet away and tackles Roland off my lap. I watch, amused, as the kittens wrestle for a minute. Then, as quickly as they started, the play session ends and the two kittens begin to lick each other's faces, purring.

"Do they do this all the time?" I ask, gesturing to the kittens, whose faces are now wet with each other's saliva.

"Oh, yeah. When they're not wrestling, they're making out with each other. It's a little weird considering they're brother and sister."

I laugh, startling the kittens, who stare up at me, and then return to wrestling each other.

"I can't believe you've kept these kittens from me this whole time," I tell him.

"Judging by the look on your face right now, it was the right decision. You probably would have kidnapped them and we never would have made it to this adoption event."

He's right. I can't picture myself going home without these two kittens now. "Would it be crazy if I adopted them?" I ask.

Anne frowns, snapping her head in my direction. "Have you ever had a cat before?" she interrupts.

"No. I've always wanted one."

"You don't have to feel guilted into doing this just because no one else has adopted them," Jake says. "That's not why I wanted you to come."

I reach over and pet Phoebe while she swats at my shoelaces. She grabs one in her mouth and pulls, untying my shoes. "I don't feel guilted into it. I've been thinking about getting a pet for a while. And I've always wanted a cat ever since I was a little kid. Did you really think you could throw me in a room with these two and not have me fall in love with them?"

I look up and meet his eyes as I say it. It's not until I notice his slight frown that I wonder if my choice of phrasing is a little weird to use with someone I've just started dating. I probably shouldn't have said that I love a couple of kittens I just met before I even say those three words to him. The room is so quiet for a moment that it has me questioning everything, and I wonder if I should backtrack or if that would just make things weirder.

Before I have the chance to embarrass myself or make this situation weirder, his frown dissolves and the corner of his mouth tilts up in that crooked way that I like so much. "If you're serious about adopting them, I'll have someone get the paperwork."

By the time I make it home, I'm the proud new owner of two kittens, one cat carrier, a litterbox, a bag of kitten food, and way more toys than these kittens will know what to do with. Anne helps me carry everything inside. She stops me when she sees me heading to the stairwell.

"Uh, excuse me? Gnome? Don't you think the elevator would be easier?"

I turn around and look at her. She's holding most of the items I just bought. Her arms are full. All I have is the carrier with the two kittens inside. I remember the last time I took the elevator and got trapped. I really don't want to take it again, but I also don't want Anne to trip and fall down the stairs while her arms are full of all my things.

"You take the elevator. I like the exercise."

We reach my floor at the same time.

"You are so weird," she says when we get to my door. "Did Luca write a traumatizing letter about elevators when you were a kid?"

"No. I got trapped in there once. Well, twice. I haven't ridden it since."

I unlock my door and she follows me inside.

"Where do you want this stuff?" she asks.

"Just set it down wherever. I'll find a place for everything."

I set the cat carrier on the floor but I don't open it yet. There are still a few more things to grab from Anne's car, but I have something I want to do first. I grab my notebook and pen and head to the kitchen counter.

"What are you doing?" Anne asks when she sees me start to write.

"I'm writing a letter to Luca."

"Right now?"

She hurries over to watch over my shoulder.

"In the first letter I ever wrote to him, I told him that I wanted a cat. He told me that cats were boring. I figure he'll get a kick out of knowing that I just adopted two."

I finish writing the letter, then tuck it into an envelope.

"The litterbox and litter are still in my car," Anne says. "I can go down and grab them."

"I'll go with you," I offer. "I need to drop this letter off anyway. Then I can help you carry everything."

I leave the kittens in the carrier so that they can't get into any trouble, then step back into the hallway. I head toward the stairwell again.

"Are you serious?" she says. "The elevator isn't going to break."

I ignore her and head down the stairwell. I don't realize that Anne is behind me until she starts talking. She somehow doesn't make a sound even when she's jogging down the steps right behind me.

"Is this why you have such killer calves?" she asks. "Climbing two flights of stairs at least twice a day seems like such a workout."

"I'm used to it. I'm pretty sure it's faster than the elevator anyway."

We reach the lobby. I walk past Joel and leave the envelope on top of the mailboxes like I usually do. Anne is already outside trying to juggle the big litterbox I bought with a case of heavy litter. I run outside to help her.

I let the kittens out of their carrier when we get inside the apartment. We play with them for a few minutes before Anne heads out. The kittens watch curiously as I set their new litterbox up. It's one of those self-scooping litterboxes. Anne talked me into buying it because she couldn't fathom why anyone would want to kneel over an open box and do the dirty work themselves. The thought reminds me of the first few letters that Luca and I exchanged all the way back in fifth grade. I smile at the memory. I had been so upset by those first couple letters from him.

I think about the letter I left on top of the mailboxes a few minutes ago. I wonder what he'll think of this turn of events. He'll probably tell me that I was always destined to be a crazy cat lady. I slip my shoes back on and head downstairs. I know there's no way he already came into the building in the short amount of time since I left that letter, but I haven't checked the mail yet today, and it won't hurt to see if he's been here.

I come out of the stairwell and get halfway across the lobby when I stop in my tracks. Joel is standing next to the mailboxes, holding the envelope that I just left for Luca.

"What are you doing? Put that back."

He doesn't move. He looks from the envelope in his hand to the mailboxes.

"Joel?"

"I, uh…" His shoulders slump and he sighs.

"Have you been taking all of the letters I put up there?"

I try to make sense of it, but I can't. Joel is too old to be Luca. But if he's the one taking my letters, then who is writing back to me? And then it hits me. I feel like the rug has been swept out from under me. The room starts to spin as I realize that Luca hasn't been in my building like I thought.

"You know him." I mean to phrase it like a question, but it comes out as a statement instead. I can tell by the look on his face that I'm right. "Where is he? How do you know him?"

He shakes his head, snapping out of the initial shock of getting caught. I have so many questions, primarily about why the security guard in my building is acting as a middleman delivering letters between me and Luca.

"Did he pay you to do this?" I ask.

Joel clears his throat. "No. He didn't pay me."

"How do you know him?" I repeat.

Again, he hesitates. He averts his gaze, choosing to look at the envelope rather than meet my eyes.

"He's my son," he says.

Chapter Twenty-Six

THE FAMOUS BOWLING KITTENS

"**Y**ou're Luca's *dad*?"

Rather than confirming, Joel shoves the envelope into his back pocket and steps around me on his way back to the security desk.

"So ... what? Have you been delivering all of my letters to him?"

He glances up at me for a split second before returning his attention to his desk. He organizes a stack of paper that was already perfectly straight.

"Did you read any of them?" I ask. "Where is he?"

He ignores my questions altogether, not even bothering to look up at me this time. He opens a drawer, shifting the contents around like he's looking for something. I watch him, waiting for him to answer me, even though it's clear he doesn't plan on it. I guess this is why he watches disapprovingly every time he sees me going out with Jake. He's rooting for his son, and Jake is getting in the way.

"I don't know what Luca might have told you about me,

but it's none of your business who I date. I'm seeing Jake and it's pretty serious. You can tell Luca that. I don't care."

He stops digging through his drawer and looks up at me. I've always thought I was pretty good at reading people, but I can't decipher the look he gives me now. He mumbles something about making his rounds, then steps away from his desk and disappears into the elevator. I'm still processing this when I get back upstairs.

Caitlin's nickname for him makes a lot more sense now. I knew there was more to it. I have so many more questions I want to ask. I want to know how Joel figured out that I'm the person his son has been writing to all these years. Did Luca come to visit him here and see me? I still don't know if Luca lives here or if he's just visiting. Maybe that's why he hasn't given me a return address.

The kittens are inspecting their new home when I hear a tap at the door. I open it and let Jake inside. It's been a couple of hours since I learned that Joel is Luca's dad. I feel a little calmer now, but I'm grateful for the distraction of Jake coming over.

As soon as the door closes behind him, he pins me against the wall using only his body, no hands. The sudden movement steals my breath. His closeness sends a rush of warmth over me. His lips hover just above mine, teasing me. I tilt my chin up just a little. My lip grazes his softly, but I don't go in for the kiss just yet. The soft touch makes his eyes darken, pushing him over the edge. He makes the move, pressing his lips into mine. Somehow he makes it feel like this is our first kiss all over again. It's been a couple of hours since I've seen him, but it feels like days, even weeks.

When he finally pulls away, I notice that the reason he's not touching me is because he's holding something behind his back. I angle my head to try to see what it is, but he turns, blocking my view.

"How are the kittens settling in?" he asks.

"They're already acting like they own the place. Now all I need is a miniature bowling alley to make them feel right at home."

"I have to tell you something, Naomi."

"What is it?"

He takes a deep breath like he's bracing himself for what he's about to say. He exhales slowly before he speaks. "The kittens don't know how to bowl."

"What?" I stomp my foot. "This is a rip-off. I want my money back."

He smiles, then pulls a small skateboard from behind his back. It's about half the size of a regular one, like it was made for a child.

"You skate?" I ask.

"No. It belonged to my brother. He outgrew it, and when I started fostering the kittens, he gave it to me. We were teaching them to skate."

I look back at the skateboard. "The kittens skate?"

"Sort of. They like to sit on the skateboard while I push it across the floor."

To demonstrate, he sets the skateboard on the floor. Both the kittens come running. He picks up each kitten and places them side by side on the skateboard, then gives it a gentle shove. The kittens stay on the board as it rolls across the floor, their small heads bobbing around as they look at all the things that are interesting and new to them in my apartment.

"Are you serious? So when I asked if you were bowling upstairs, this is what I was hearing? And you didn't think to tell me that you had two tiny kitten versions of Tony Hawk skating around up there all day?"

"I thought you would think I was crazy. Or making it up. Anyway, I don't need the skateboard anymore. I thought it should stay with the kittens."

I look at the kittens, who are taking turns pouncing on each other from the skateboard and sending it rolling around the room as they do so. I look back at him. "I can tell you right now that my downstairs neighbor is going to hate me for this."

"It's okay. Maybe they can drown out the noise with some loud music."

"It's a pretty effective method," I agree.

He takes my hand and pulls me toward my bedroom. "Now let's finish what we started a few minutes ago."

———

Dear Luca,

I know that Joel is your father. I don't really know how to feel about this. I really hate being lied to, and to find out that Joel has been keeping this from me for weeks is pretty hurtful. I'm not sure if he gave you the letter I left for you Friday night. I feel like I can't trust him now, but hopefully he will get this one to you. I want to meet you. Are you going to show your face, or are you afraid that I'll find out you've been ugly all this time?

Love,

Naomi

———

I'm at work, focusing on my computer when I get the unsettling feeling that someone is watching me. The skin on the back of my neck prickles. I turn around. Anne is standing behind me. Somehow, I manage not to gasp or show any sign that I've been startled.

"Creep," I say. "Why are you just standing there?"

She purses her lips. "How was the rest of your weekend?"

I shrug and face my computer again. "It was good. I took a long nap on the couch with both of the kittens yesterday."

"Did you talk to Luca?"

"Talk to him? No. I didn't hear from him all weekend, so I wrote another letter."

"Oh. He didn't, like, show up at your door or anything?"

I frown. "Don't you think that would be the first thing I'd tell you?"

She sits down with a thud in the chair next to mine, and sets the coffee she brought next to me. "I never know with you, Gnome. You can be so secretive when you want to be."

"I'm not keeping any secrets from you."

As I say it, I think about what I found out about Joel. I take a moment to think about whether to tell her. "Actually."

She raises an eyebrow.

"I did learn something new this weekend," I continue.

"Go on," she prods, leaning forward.

"Luca hasn't been in my building."

She frowns. "But what about the letters you left on top of the mailboxes?"

"His dad took them."

"His dad? I thought his dad abandoned him when he was a kid."

"That's what his old neighbor Carol Bell said. We don't actually know that they didn't stay in touch. Besides, even if that was true, they could have reconnected at some point."

"How do you know it's his dad, though?"

"Remember when you told me that I was overthinking Caitlin's nickname for Joel?"

"Yes," she says slowly.

"It turns out there was a very good reason she was calling him Mr. Pickles."

"Wait. Luca's dad is the security guard in your building?"

I nod. "Imagine my surprise when I went downstairs and caught him grabbing the letter I left for Luca."

"That's insane. Do you think he's still giving the letters to Luca? Maybe that's why you haven't heard back."

I take a moment to think about it. "I don't know. My first thought was that maybe he was only in town for a couple of weeks, and that's the end of the letters, but that doesn't make any sense. He has my address. He could still write to me. And he implied that he lives in Miami."

"Maybe you can follow Joel next time he takes one of your letters. He's bound to lead you to Luca eventually."

"Don't you think that's a little creepy?"

She rolls her eyes. "You flew all the way to San Diego to try to track him down. You tried to drive onto a military base, and you flew out to Texas and lied to his ex-fiancée about who you are. Explain to me how spying on his dad is suddenly taking it too far?"

"Okay, you're right." I sigh. "I'm just tired of playing all these games to find him. And I'm afraid that's all this is to him. A game."

"What makes you think that?"

I think about the last letter I sent to him before he disappeared and I didn't hear from him for two years. I had invited him to come hide away with me after he complained about his fiancée. For months after I sent that letter without hearing back, I had stewed over my choice to invite him, even if I had done it in a roundabout way that could be taken as a joke. I guess I knew that deep down, it wasn't really a joke. I wouldn't have admitted it to myself then, but I hoped that he would take me up on my invitation. His lack of a response felt like a rejection.

And now it's happening again. I told him that I want to meet him, and now he's not writing back. I'm not sure how to explain all of that to Anne. I decide to keep it simple.

"I don't think he really wants to meet me."

She frowns, looking doubtful. "I think he does."

I roll my eyes. "You're not the one who's been writing to him all these years. But you read the letters. This has never been anything more than a joke between us. We've been one-upping each other since fifth grade. He never wanted to meet me. He just wanted me to admit that I want to meet him."

I won't admit to Anne that I feel so torn about him and Jake. It might be a good thing if I don't hear from him again. How can I build anything real with Jake when my mind keeps straying to Luca? I've spent a lot of time trying to track him down – time that I could be spending with Jake, who doesn't play these childish games.

Maybe it's for the best that I leave this all behind when I buy my house and move in a couple of weeks. Putting in the effort to follow Joel around might not have been taking it too far a few weeks ago. But now that things are getting serious with Jake, it feels wrong, especially when the result of spending all this time and energy on tracking down Luca is that he pops into my head at the most inappropriate moments.

"I don't believe that's true," Anne says about Luca not wanting to meet me. "And I don't think you really believe it's true, either."

"Why not?"

She hesitates as she tries to think of a reason. "He sent you flowers," she says.

"You remember the note he included."

"I think you're being a little ridiculous. Maybe he was just surprised that you want to meet him. He's probably just trying to figure out how to make it happen."

"I'm not going to keep my hopes up while he takes his sweet time."

"Are you going to write to him again?"

"I left another letter with Joel this morning. If there isn't a new one by the time I get home, then I'll leave it at that. Besides, I probably shouldn't be focusing so much energy on Luca when I have a boyfriend who I like very much."

A boyfriend who doesn't deserve to be called the wrong name, even if he didn't hear me. I had thought that being able to write back to Luca would take away the excitement of the chase and I would be able to get him out of my head. Instead, he's taking up more room than ever. Writing to him is one thing, but he has no place in the bedroom with me and Jake.

"Are you sure he likes you? He seems pretty secretive to me. I'm not sure I trust him."

"Secretive?" I repeat, frowning. "How did you come up with that conclusion?"

"I think that you should tell him about Luca," Anne says, ignoring my question.

I almost spit out my drink. "What? Why?"

"You don't want to start this relationship off on a lie, do you?"

"It's not a lie. It's just..."

"An omission of the truth?" she supplies.

"Exactly."

"That's still a lie. You've been writing to Luca for years. Do you really want that hanging over your head if things get serious? And what if Luca is who you're meant to be with? You don't want to cheat on Husky Eyes with him. You need to be honest."

"His name is Jake," I say with a roll of my eyes. "I don't think he'd take it very well. We both already said that we're not seeing anyone else. We basically agreed that we're exclusive."

"You haven't been dating that long."

"You just want him to break up with me so that you can have a shot at him."

"Gross. That ship has sailed. As soon as you two started dating, he became off-limits. Girl code, you know?"

"Either way, I don't think it's going to go as well as you think it is."

"Maybe he's a romantic." She clasps her hands together and presses them against her cheek. "Maybe he'll tell you to pursue your long-lost penemy."

"I'm not sure that's what I want."

"Maybe he'll be into it. Maybe you can have a threesome with them."

I catch movement out of the corner of my eye, and look over to see Patrick watching from the doorway. His face is red right up to his receding hairline.

"Wrong part of the conversation again, huh, Patrick?"

Anne's eyes become so large they look like golf balls. She whips her head around to look at him and make sure I'm not messing with her.

"Jesus, Mr. Facey, did you steal my shoes or something?" she asks. "Normally I'm the one sneaking up on people."

"I'm sure you have work to do, Anette," he says.

She slides out of her chair, but I place my hand on her arm, stopping her. I'm fed up with him always pronouncing our names wrong.

"Anne," I say, looking at Patrick.

Anne looks at him, and then they both stare at me expectantly.

"Excuse me?" Patrick says.

"Her name is Anne."

He frowns. "That's what I said, isn't it?"

"I must have misheard you. Can you say it again?" I don't think I've ever heard him say her name correctly. I don't know if it's a weird power move or if he's just really bad with names, but I want to force it out of him.

"Annie ... Anna. Anette," he stammers.

"None of those were correct. In fact, all of those are more syllables than her actual name."

"It's okay," Anne says with a forced smile in my direction. "Mr. Facey can call me whatever he wants."

"Anita," he says.

"Anne," I repeat loudly at the same time as Anne says, "Yeah, sure, that's fine."

He frowns. "Arnie?"

"Okay, now you're throwing in an entirely different letter. What is the matter with you?"

"What do you mean? What's the matter with *you*?"

"You've been pronouncing both of our names incorrectly for the last two years. Do you not hear the difference in what you call us versus what everyone else calls us?"

He has the audacity to look taken aback. "Wait, you're serious? I thought this was a running inside joke we had going."

When neither of us responds, he shrugs, then says, "Isn't that why you call me Mr. Facey all the time?"

Anne and I exchange a glance. When we look back at Patrick, I can see a look of realization dawning on him. "It's Pacey," he says, enunciating the first letter with a pop of his lips. "Patrick Pacey."

He stares at us for a moment. Neither of us says a word. It's the most awkward silence I've ever been a part of. It's Patrick who finally breaks it. "Did you really think my name was Facey? *Facey?* What kind of name is that?"

"I'm sure it's a real name," I say.

Anne isn't looking at either of us. Her wide eyes are locked onto the far wall between me and Patrick.

"Jesus Christ," Patrick mumbles. "Anne, get to work. Naomi, I'm sure you need to finish your report before you go on air."

I think that's the first time I've heard him pronounce my name correctly. He turns around and leaves the room. Only then does Anne look at me again. Her face is almost as red as Patrick's was when he heard her suggesting I have a threesome.

"You really thought his name was Facey?"

I'm confused. "What do you mean? You thought the same thing."

She shakes her head, and her mouth widens into a smile. "You really are terrible with names, aren't you?"

"You thought his name was Facey, too!"

"No, I didn't. He's Patrick Pacey. He's always been Patrick Pacey. That's what his nameplate says on his office door."

"Then why do you always call him Mr. Facey?"

"Because that's what you called him on your first day here, and I thought it was hilarious. I've called him that ever since. I think he thought it was funny, too. That's when he started calling me Anette."

"You mean this really was a running inside joke, and I just didn't realize I was a part of it? Are you kidding me?"

She shrugs, then turns toward the door. "I better get to work before he comes in here and yells at me again."

"Wait. Why didn't you speak up just now? Why let him think you really thought that was his name?"

"Because you had already embarrassed yourself enough. I couldn't let you go down alone."

I feel oddly touched by the sentiment. Anne is almost out of the room when I realize I haven't responded.

"You're a good friend, Anne," I say.

She looks over her shoulder and smiles at me. "Quit messing around and finish your report," she says, mocking Patrick's tone.

Chapter Twenty-Seven

DOUBLE LIFE

It's been a few days, and I still haven't heard from Luca. I ask Joel every day if there are any new letters, but he shakes his head and pretends to be busy with something else. I wonder if he even gave my last letter to Luca. I haven't seen much of Jake, either. I spotted him through the window the other day when I was coming home, but by the time I got inside, he was already in the elevator, heading up to the fourth floor.

On Friday I head home after eating lunch with Anne. I'm not really sure what to do. I don't have any letters to look forward to reading. Anne and I canceled our plan to go back to San Diego. Now that I know who Luca's dad is, there's no point in tracking down Ben Toole. I sit on the floor with a laser pointer and send the kittens chasing the little red light around the room.

It's starting to feel like I've lost Jake. I think that maybe he was only after one thing, but that doesn't seem likely. The time that we spent together isn't something that can be found in a one-night stand. Maybe he only kept me around so he could trick me into adopting the kittens. It's a ridiculous thought, and I dismiss it almost as soon as I come up with it. The only other thing I can think of is that Joel told him about Luca and the letters. I can imagine that he would be upset about me keeping that from him, but I wish he would at least talk to me.

I start to type out a text message to him, even though the last two I sent went unanswered. I'm interrupted by a wailing, screaming cry coming from upstairs. I look up at the ceiling. Roland and Phoebe do the same. The godawful sound has to be coming from Jake's apartment. I try to ignore it. I return to playing with the laser light, but the kittens aren't interested anymore. Their focus is on the noise upstairs.

I'm able to ignore the cry for another minute, but it becomes unbearable. I slip on my shoes and I head out into the hallway. No one else seems concerned. I must be the only one who can hear it. I go upstairs and follow the screeching sound to Jake's apartment. I haven't been up here before, but I can tell by the placement of the door that it's the apartment right above mine. I tap on the door. The screeching doesn't stop. I tap again. No one answers. The terrible noise continues. I try the doorknob, but it's locked.

I dial Jake's number, but it goes straight to an automated voicemail. I know that I won't be able to focus on anything until this noise is gone. I go downstairs to the lobby. Joel is eating out of a jar of pickles. I look out the front window and see Caitlin doing a cartwheel.

"Joel," I say. He looks up, seeming startled that I'm addressing him. His cheeks are bloated with the pickle he just stuffed in his mouth. "There's an animal making a lot of noise in the apartment above mine."

He finishes chewing the pickle, then wipes his mouth with

a napkin. "It's a puppy. Are you here to file a noise complaint?"

I shake my head. "Can I get a spare key?"

"I'm not so sure that's a good idea. I heard you two were taking some time off on account of you seeing someone else."

I thought that Jake might be avoiding me, but to hear someone else say it makes it feel real. It's like a punch to the stomach. On some level, I hoped that I was overthinking things. I guess I thought that he would be mature enough to tell me it was over in person.

"Did he say that?"

Joel gives a noncommittal grunt.

"You told him about Luca, didn't you? You know, it makes sense now why you were always frowning at us when we were together. I know you feel like you're doing your son a favor, but you can't go messing with my personal life like that."

He rolls his eyes, which annoys me even more. "This is exactly why I shouldn't give you the key."

"Come on, Joel. I'm not going to trash his apartment. I'm just going to take the puppy for a walk before it drives me and all my neighbors insane."

He watches me with narrowed eyes like he's skeptical of my intentions, and then he glances at a lockbox he has sitting on his desk. "Don't make me regret this," he says. He unlocks the box, sifts through a pile of keys, and then pulls out one that has a tag with Jake's apartment number.

I take the key and head back upstairs. As I reach the fourth floor, I can hear the puppy's high-pitched whine all the way from the stairwell. I'm surprised that no one else has complained yet or even poked their heads out of their apartments, but I guess most people are at work at this time of day.

I unlock the apartment and step inside. The layout of his apartment is the same as mine, but his is decorated more sparsely. I spot the source of the noise sitting inside a dog crate in the corner of the living room. The puppy stops crying when he sees me. He begins to jump against the side of the crate, whimpering and wagging his tail like he knows I'm there to rescue him.

I think I recognize him from the adoption event last weekend. His body is mostly white. He has a brown spot over one eye, and another brown spot that covers half of his back. He looks like one of the puppies from the pen that was getting the most attention on Saturday. I wonder why this one didn't get adopted.

"You poor thing," I say as I kneel down to unlatch the crate. The puppy stumbles out and launches himself against my legs, squirming and begging for attention. "Aren't you cute? And soft." I run my hand over his body. "So soft."

I pick him up before he has a chance to pee on the floor, then turn around, looking for a leash. I find a harness and leash on the kitchen counter. I struggle a little to put the harness on the puppy. I've never had a dog, so none of the straps make any sense to me, but I figure it out. I hook his leash to the harness, and then I head downstairs, still carrying him because I don't want to clean up a mess in the hallway. I may have never had a dog, but I know that puppies as young as this one are prone to accidents.

I set him down on the sidewalk when we get outside. Caitlin squeals with excitement and comes running just as the puppy lowers his hips and pees on the sidewalk. Caitlin doesn't seem to notice, or maybe she just doesn't care. The puppy doesn't seem bothered by her squealing either.

"You got a puppy!" she exclaims. "What's his name?"

"He's not mine," I tell her. "I'm just taking him for a walk."

"Can I come?"

"You should probably stay by the window where Joel can see you."

"I'll go ask him if I can come with you," she says.

"I don't—"

Before I can finish protesting, she's already through the door and talking to Joel. When she comes back out, she skips over to me. "Mr. Pickles says that I can come with you as long as we don't go too far. How far are we going?"

I sigh. "Not far. Just to the end of the block and back."

"Can I hold the leash?"

"I should probably hold it just to be safe. There's a lot of traffic on this road and I don't want to put the puppy in danger."

"Okay. I heard Mr. Pickles and Fishman talking about you."

I frown. "Fishman?"

She shrugs. "Your boyfriend."

It takes me a second to realize she calls him Fishman because he works at the aquarium. I'm surprised that she knows I'm dating Jake – or rather, *was* dating Jake. I'm not sure where we stand now. Her out-of-the-blue statement seems to confirm that Joel told him about the letters. I'm so frustrated that I could cry, but I'm not about to let myself break down in front of a kid.

"How old are you, Caitlin?"

"I just turned eight."

"Happy belated birthday. Why do you call them Fishman and Mr. Pickles?"

She shrugs. "I'm bad at remembering names. It's easier when I make them up."

I feel like I'm talking to a young version of myself. "No one is going to know who you're talking about if you call everyone by nicknames that you made up. Do you do that at school, too?"

"Oh. Sometimes. I just don't know how I'm supposed to remember everyone's names."

"You don't have to remember everyone's name right away. There's no shame in saying, 'Sorry, I didn't catch your name, can you remind me what it is?' It's better than just making one up and then not knowing." I know that this is hypocritical considering I called her Caterpillar Kid for the longest time, and I had no idea that my boss's last name was Pacey and not Facey. I figure I can help her learn from my experience now so that she doesn't have to make the same mistakes I did. "You know what my real name is, right?"

"Uh. Naomi?" She stumbles over the syllables.

"That's right. And Mr. Pickles is...?"

"Joel," she says. "But his last name sounds close enough to Pickles. Can't I keep calling him that?"

I think about it for a moment. Joel doesn't seem bothered by her calling him Mr. Pickles. "Yeah, I guess that's fine. What about the guy you call Fishman?"

She gives me a rueful smile. "I can't remember."

"It's Jake," I tell her.

"Oh. What's the puppy's name?" she asks.

"I don't know. What do you think his name should be?"

"I can make it up?"

"Sure."

"Bruno," she says.

I look at the puppy. He's waddling ahead of us, stopping every few paces to chase a leaf or sniff an old black piece of gum hardened into the sidewalk. "He does look like a Bruno," I agree.

"Don't you want to know what they were saying?" Caitlin asks.

"Who?"

"Mr. Pickles and, uh..." She hesitates, looking up at me for help.

"Jake," I supply.

"Oh, right. Mr. Pickles and Jake. Don't you want to know?"

As much as I don't want to talk about this with an eight-year-old, my curiosity gets the best of me. "What were they saying?"

"They were talking about you and your letter. I think Fish — sorry, Jake – was mad, because he didn't say hi to me or my mom. They were arguing about it. They said a lot of other things, but that's all I can remember. What did you say in your letter that made him so mad?"

I'm not sure which letter Joel showed him, but it can't be good. No wonder he's avoiding me. I think I might throw up. I'm sweating, yet I feel cold at the same time, despite the Miami sun beating down on me. Anne was right. I should have just told him about Luca. Now it's too late, and I've probably lost both of them.

We reach the end of the block. I stand on the corner for a moment, watching the traffic pass us, and thinking about what Caitlin said. I can be angry at Joel all I want, but it's my fault that this is happening.

"Does this mean you're breaking up with him?" she asks.

"It's complicated," I tell her. "You're too young to understand."

"That's what my mom said when she got divorced from my dad, and also when she broke up with her last boyfriend. I just don't get what's so complicated about it, and why I'm always too young to understand. I'm starting to think that people say that because they don't understand it either."

"You might be right," I say. "Or maybe sometimes we don't want you to think badly about the other person."

In this case, the person she would think badly of is me. This realization hurts. She frowns up at me as we turn around. "Do you think that my dad did bad things to my mom?"

"Maybe not. I don't know them, so I couldn't tell you. But I'm sure when you're a little older, you can ask your mom and she'll tell you why it didn't work out."

When we reach the building, I leave Caitlin outside to continue her sidewalk acrobatics. I bring the puppy inside and stop by Joel's desk on my way to the stairwell. I think about confronting him about the letter he showed to Jake, but I'm afraid that I'll make a scene. He watches me wearily.

Without a word, I turn and take the puppy into the stairwell. He struggles to make it up each step, so it takes us a while to make it to the fourth floor. I could have easily carried him, but I want to wear him out so that he'll go to sleep once I put him back in his crate.

We make it back to Jake's apartment. This time I have more time to look around because I'm not in a hurry to get the crying puppy out of here. His apartment isn't messy like I imagined it would be. His furniture isn't the best, but it's not trashy or tacky either. There's no evidence of a woman's touch, no sign that he's living a double life. It's funny how Anne had suggested that he was the secretive one, and yet it turns out I'm the only one living a double life.

I return the puppy to his crate, and then, without disturbing anything else in the apartment, I step out into the hallway. As soon as the door is closed behind me, the screeching, wailing, crying starts. I wait a minute, hoping that he'll stop, but he doesn't. I consider going back inside and bringing the puppy downstairs to my apartment. If I do, Jake will have to come see me, and then I can try to explain myself to him.

I hesitate, my hand on his door. On the other hand, I want him to come for *me*, not because I forced him by taking his dog. I'm not above this idea if that's all I have, though. I know that I'm in the wrong here, but he's the one who has been avoiding me without a word. I shouldn't have to hear the reason I'm being ghosted secondhand from a kid.

The puppy quiets down a bit, and I take my hand off the doorknob. I decide to walk away for now. I need to figure out what I want.

Chapter Twenty-Eight

THE RANSOM NOTE

"I told you."

Anne isn't very good at sparing my feelings. She had warned me that I should tell Jake about the letter, and now she needs to make sure that I know she was right.

"You also told me he was hiding something from me. You were wrong about that. I've been in his apartment."

I think about the puppy and wonder if he's crying again. I heard him a few times over the weekend, but the crying never lasted long because Jake was home to take care of him. There were a few times that I wished the crying had lasted a little longer. It would have given me an excuse to go up there and see him again. I can't bring myself to go up there and pretend that nothing is wrong, though. I'm not sure I can stand in front of him and lie and tell him that Luca and the letters mean nothing to me. I'm torn, because I still have feelings for both of them. As much as I hate the way he's cut off contact with me, I still feel like he deserves an explanation. I just don't have a good one. Not one that he will like, anyway.

"Speaking of which, I should probably go home and check on the puppy."

She rolls her eyes. "Do you really think you can win him back by walking his dog? I mean, you called him by another man's name while you were having sex with him. Maybe this is for the best, to be honest. With him out of the picture, you can see where things go with Luca."

"Things are going nowhere with Luca, because he won't even write back to me."

"Have you tried writing to him again?"

I sigh. "How many times do I need to write to him before I give up? This feels like it did two years ago all over again. I invite him to meet me and he ghosts me. I wouldn't be surprised if it's another few years before I hear from him at this point."

"I doubt that. Maybe he just needs to know that you're serious about meeting him."

"I'm not even sure what I want anymore. I thought that I wanted to meet him, but now I'm afraid of losing what I had with Jake."

"News flash. You already lost what you had with him. Just write to Luca again."

I finish off my coffee. "I'll think about it. I need to go home."

I can already hear Bruno crying when I reach the stairwell. I never gave Joel the key back, so I head up to the fourth floor. I tap on the door to make sure Jake isn't inside. I wait a moment, then unlock the door and let myself in.

I rip a sheet of paper out of a notebook, and scribble a note: *I have your dog.*

I stick the note to the refrigerator with a magnet, then reread it. On second inspection, I realize that it sounds a little cryptic. All it's missing is a request for ransom. I grab the pen I used to write the note, and add: *Come get him.*

I read it again, but it still doesn't feel right. The short, clipped sentences might make him think that taking care of Bruno is a burden. I'm probably overthinking it, but I add to the note again anyway: *What's his name by the way? I've been calling him Bruno.*

I put the pen down and head to Bruno's crate to let him out. I take him downstairs and outside to use the bathroom, but he doesn't seem to have to go. He must have gone for a walk already. I take him back inside. Joel looks at me once, but doesn't remark on me having the puppy again.

Bruno is excited to meet the kittens when we reach my apartment. Roland and Phoebe don't seem to mind his never-ending energy. They play for a little while, and then Bruno stops without warning, lowers his hips, and pees on my floor.

"Bruno!" I exclaim. "No!"

He doesn't seem to think he's done anything wrong. As soon as he's done peeing, he trots away from the mess and rejoins the kittens. I clean the mess, then sit down on the couch and watch the three of them play. Not five minutes later, Bruno squats and poops right on my rug. I'm lucky I bought a special spray for removing pet stains when I adopted the kittens. I haven't needed to use it until now. With the second mess cleaned up, I return to the couch, relieved that I can relax now because surely this puppy has it all out of his system and won't be having any more accidents.

I couldn't have been more wrong. Bruno pees on my hardwood floor again, and while I'm cleaning that up, he pees a third time. I groan, then throw his harness and leash back on him and take him outside. We walk up and down the block several times before it's finally clear that he got it out of his system in my apartment.

"You are going to drive me crazy," I say to him as we go back inside.

I make him climb the stairs with me again. Last time, the extra exercise didn't do much to wear him out, but this time, he's knocked out almost as soon as we get inside. He's on my lap on the couch, so at least I'm comfortable.

I don't realize that I've drifted off to sleep until I'm startled awake by someone pounding on the door. Roland and Phoebe are curled up and cuddling with each other on the other end of the couch. I take a moment to appreciate how cute they are, and then slide the sleeping puppy off my lap to go answer the door. I already know that it's Jake. I wonder if he'll talk to me or if he'll only say the bare minimum to get his dog back.

He's leaning on the door frame when I open the door. I'm reminded of the day he came to my door before taking me out to dinner. I remember the way he came through my doorway, pushed me up against the wall, and kissed me. The memory makes my body feel warm. I wish that we could go back to that moment.

"Bruno?" He sounds skeptical of the name. At least I know that he read my note. That, and he's talking to me again.

I shrug. "Caitlin named him."

"Of course she did. Where is he?"

"On the couch. What's his real name?"

I step away from the doorway, hoping that he'll come in. He hesitates, looking down at the threshold like there's a physical barrier stopping him from entering my apartment.

"He doesn't have one," he says. Then, as if he has to force himself to do it, he steps through my doorway, but pauses in front of me in my hallway. For a moment, he stands so close to me that I think that maybe nothing is wrong and I imagined the last several days. My heart begins to beat a little bit faster. I can see his chest rising as he takes in a deep breath. He doesn't release it before turning away from me and stepping into the living room.

"How does he not have a name?" I ask.

"I'm only fostering him, and he's deaf, so it's not like it matters if he knows his name or not."

"He's deaf?" I'm surprised. "Are you sure?"

"That's why the family that adopted him gave him back to the shelter. They couldn't handle his nonstop crying, and nothing they did worked. He wouldn't respond to any of their commands."

"They didn't have him long. Maybe he's just stubborn. Did he have a hearing test?"

"No, but watch this." He claps his hands. Roland and Phoebe both pop their heads up, but Bruno doesn't respond. He's lying on the couch, sleeping soundly.

"That doesn't mean he's deaf," I argue. "Maybe he's just really tired. He should have a hearing test done."

"The shelter can't afford to pay for it, so we're treating him like he's deaf. I'm going to foster him until he's housebroken and knows enough hand signals to be adopted by someone experienced with deaf dogs."

The way he explains it is so casual that it feels like he's not mad at me anymore, like he's letting me into the wall he built when he found out that I lied. I begin to feel my own guard dropping.

"Speaking of housebroken," I say, "he had four accidents in my apartment today."

I start to laugh it off, but his face turns serious. Just like that, the wall is back up.

"That's what happens when you don't watch him. I'm crate training him for a reason. If you would have just left him up there—"

"I was watching him," I interrupt. "And if I had left him up there, someone would have called in a noise complaint."

"Pay more attention next time. When you see him start walking in circles or sniffing around, it's time to take him outside."

He walks to the couch and nudges Bruno. The puppy jolts awake, then perks up when he recognizes his foster dad. I watch as he picks the puppy up, then scans the room for the leash and harness. I point to the armchair where I left them. He sets the puppy down just long enough to put the harness on, then picks him back up and heads out the door.

I let out a breath once I'm alone. Maybe he's not ready to give me another chance, but at least he doesn't expect me to stop taking care of Bruno while he's at work. Or maybe I'm reading too much into the way he said "next time". I watch the door for a minute, wishing that it could give me answers.

As I hear the elevator doors opening and closing behind him down the hall, my mind wanders to Luca. I think of all the times I've turned down his invitations to meet him, all the times that I might have given him a chance if I hadn't been dating someone else at the time. Maybe Anne is right. Maybe this is a sign that I'm supposed to meet Luca.

If there was ever a time to make this work and not feel guilty about it, it's now. I look at my notebook, which is sitting open on my coffee table. I sit down and grab my pen.

Chapter Twenty-Nine

GOOD IMPRESSIONS

Dear Luca,
Come hide away with me.
Love,
Naomi

I wasn't going to write another letter, but the fact that I haven't heard from him is driving me crazy. I decide to use the same words I used when I invited him to leave his fiancée for me two years ago. I know it's a longshot, but I hope that he's just been waiting for me to use these words again.

I don't bother leaving the letter on top of the mailboxes. I drop it on Joel's desk. He looks at the envelope, then up at me.

"Please make sure it gets to him today."

Joel nods. I head back to my apartment. I feed the kittens, and then they play by my feet while I make dinner. I've hidden the skateboard that Jake gave me inside a closet. I'm reluctant to take it out and subject my downstairs neighbor to the level of noise those kittens can make with a skateboard.

I just finished eating dinner when I hear a tap at the door. I know that it's unlikely that Joel already gave my letter to Luca. Even so, my heart rate picks up. I comb my fingers through my hair, suddenly conscious of the fact that I haven't looked in a mirror in the last hour. I slide my tongue over my front teeth to make sure I don't have food stuck in them. I don't know why I'm doing these things. Since when have I wanted to make a good impression on Luca?

When I open the door, it's Jake on the other side. I'm surprised that he came back.

"Hey," I say.

Without responding, he pushes my door open wider and steps in and kisses me.

"I'm sorry that I've been so distant," he says when he breaks away from me.

"You're not the one who should be sorry," I argue. "I should have told you about the letters. I feel like I need to…"

I trail off as he walks past me and into the living room.

"I want to explain myself," I say, following him.

He drops down onto the couch. I hesitate. I get the impression that he doesn't want my explanation, but I feel like I owe it to him anyway. I sit down next to him.

"I know that you said you wanted to be exclusive, but I feel like I should tell you that I've been—"

"Who is Jake?" he interrupts.

I frown, feeling stumped by the odd question. "What do you mean?"

"Joel told me that you mentioned you were seeing someone named Jake."

I shake my head. I'm even more confused now. "I was talking about you. Did you think there's another Jake?" My eyes widen as realization hits. I feel like laughing, but I'm not sure it's appropriate, so I hold it in. "That's why you've been avoiding me?"

He stares at me, his expression remaining serious. My smile dissolves as I try to figure out what's going on.

He clears his throat. "That's not my name."

For a moment I think that he's messing with me, but there's no hint of amusement on his face.

"I don't understand." I think about the name badge he was wearing when we first met. I know I didn't read it wrong. "What's your name, then?"

He looks from me to the coffee table, where I left the notebook that I use to write my letters to Luca. He reaches for it and pulls out the pen that's tucked into the spiral binding. Half of the pages in the notebook have been ripped out, and the few that are left are blank. Seeing him hold my notebook that I've used to write countless letters to Luca makes me feel uneasy. I watch, waiting, as he writes something on the first blank page. I'm curious about what he has to say that he can't say out loud.

He has the notebook angled away so that I can't see what he's writing. When he finishes, he rips the page out, folds it up, and then hands it to me. I hold the folded page for a moment. I don't know why I'm nervous to open it and read what he wrote. I look up at him and see that he's watching me, waiting. I unfold it.

Dear Naomi,

I hope that you forget to change the litterbox tonight, and Roland poops in your laundry basket.

Love,

Luca

I stare at the letter, trying to process what this is. For a second, I think that it's a trick, but it's the same familiar handwriting that I've been reading for years. I raise my gaze slowly from the letter to him. Now I understand why he interrupted me.

I feel like the rug has been swept out from under me.

"You're Luca."

"Yes. I know that I should have told you—"

"Get out," I say before he can continue. My body is trembling with anger. I scramble to get off the couch. I can't believe I've been so stupid. I stand up and point to the door. He stays on the couch, watching me like he's not sure if I'm serious.

"Get out," I repeat. "Leave. Now."

"Don't you want to talk about this?"

"No. I don't even know who you are. Get out of my apartment."

"It's me, Naomi. I haven't changed. Everything that we've talked about, that we've done together – that was the real me."

I look him over, from his dark hair to his ice-blue eyes, to his body, sitting on my couch, and even though I've spent so much time with him, seen him and touched him so many times, it feels like I'm looking at a stranger. I can't make sense of the fact that he's the same person I've been writing to for years. He's not Luca, he's—

A new wave of anger crashes over me. He must have known that I had his name wrong this whole time. He took advantage of the fact I didn't know who he was. He lied to me.

He stands up, which feels unfair because now he towers over me.

"Please, Naomi. Let's talk about this."

His tone is reasonable, which makes me even angrier.

"How am I supposed to believe anything you're saying when you've been lying to me since the beginning?"

He steps toward me, reaching out his hand. His fingertips graze my arm, and I feel my resolve drop just a little. I take a step back, not wanting to be drawn into him. I need to be able to think clearly so that I don't fall for any more lies.

"Don't touch me," I warn him. "Where did you even get that fake name badge?"

He frowns. "What fake name badge?"

His act of pretending not to know what I'm talking about makes me even angrier. "That badge you wore when we first met to trick me into thinking your name was Jake Dubois."

His brow remains furrowed. It's almost believable that he doesn't know what I'm talking about. Then his eyes widen. "Jake Dubois is the other vet at the aquarium. I borrowed his scrubs once when mine got soiled taking care of an injured—" He shakes his head, cutting himself off. "It doesn't matter. I didn't mean to trick you. I didn't realize his badge was on me."

I don't believe anything he's saying. "You should leave."

"Naomi—"

"Leave. *Now!*"

I shout the last word. I can feel tears burning my eyes. I don't want him to see me cry or try to stay and comfort me when he's the reason that I feel betrayed.

"Can't we just—"

He's still standing too close to me. I press both hands against his abdomen, pushing him away. He could easily overpower me, but he lets me push him all the way to the door. When we reach the front door, I open it, shove him into the hallway, and then slam the door behind him.

Chapter Thirty

OF ALL THE BUILDINGS

Luca

When I flew out to Miami, I hadn't planned on forgiving Joel. I refused to even think of him as my dad. He had abandoned me and didn't deserve the title. I didn't plan to stay long. I only went because I wanted to talk to him face to face, to hear him try to explain why he thought he could waltz back into my life after all these years. I couldn't believe he would imply that my mother was to blame for him abandoning our family.

I got a rental car at the airport because I wanted to be able to leave whenever I felt like it. I didn't want to be at anyone else's mercy. Joel had texted me the address of a coffee shop where I could meet him. I was glad that this reunion wasn't taking place at his home, and especially glad that he wasn't trying to impress me or win me back by taking me to some five-star restaurant.

He was already sitting in a booth when I got there. I almost didn't recognize him. He had put on a few pounds and his hair had turned gray, but his eyes were still the same. He was wearing a security uniform. I could tell that he didn't recognize me until I was standing in front of his table.

He stood up. "Luca?"

I nodded. He spread his arms slightly like he was going to hug me, then thought better of it, and extended his hand for me to shake. We sat down.

"I got you a coffee," he said, pushing the cup toward me. "I don't know how you take it, so…" He gestured toward the cream and sugar packets he had grabbed.

I took a sip of my coffee without adding anything. He watched me, eyes wide and expectant. I realized that he had no idea what he was supposed to say to me. After a tense moment of silence, I asked the only question I could think of: "Is this where you've been the whole time?"

He shook his head. "I started out in Montana. I only moved out here a few years ago."

"Let me guess. You started a new family and abandoned them, too."

"I understand why you're angry," he said.

I didn't respond. I was done asking questions. It was his turn to provide an explanation.

He continued: "I met a woman shortly after I moved to Montana. Cheryl. We got married and we had three kids together. Twin girls and a boy."

There were a few times over the years when I wondered if my dad had ever remarried or had another kid. When I was younger, when my family was still intact, I would have loved to have a brother or a sister. This wasn't how I imagined it would happen.

"I have siblings," I said. I thought that if I said it out loud, it would feel more real, but it didn't.

He averted his gaze. "Things didn't work out between me and Cheryl. It was a mutual breakup. Cheryl got a job offer out here shortly before our divorce was finalized. I helped with the move, then never went back to Montana."

I smirked, but I found it far from funny. "So, let me get this straight. You break up with my mom and take off running to another state, never to be seen or heard from again. You break up with Cheryl and not only do you help her move, you uproot your life so that you don't have to be far from your new kids."

"I know that I was a terrible father to you—"

"No," I interrupted. "You weren't. That's what always confused me. You used to take me to the beach every day. We built a home gym and worked out together. Every goddamn memory that I have of you is a good one. But then you up and left for no fucking reason, and I hated you for it. You don't know how many times I wished that you were an asshole so that I wouldn't have to miss you so damn much. What is so damn different about your new family that you could make it work with them and not me?"

"It had nothing to do with you."

"It sure felt like it did when I didn't hear from you for fifteen years."

"Your mother and I—"

"Right. Blame her. She can't defend herself now that she's dead."

"I was sorry to hear about her passing, despite what she did to me."

I stared at him, waiting for him to elaborate, but he didn't. He was waiting for me to ask. I didn't want to hear him pass the blame onto my mother, but I traveled all this way, and I needed to know what his excuse was.

"What did she do to you?" The question tasted bitter in my mouth.

"You don't want to hear this about your mother," he said.

"You brought it up."

He sighed, glanced out the window at the building across the street for a moment, then looked back at me. "Your mother was having an affair. We fought about it. A lot. We tried marriage counseling. Things were getting better for a while, but one day I…" He paused, pursing his lips. "She gave me an STD. I couldn't even look at her after that. I filed for divorce and I left. Every day I'm sorry that I didn't take you with me. I was so angry when I left that I just wanted to keep going and never turn around. There are so many things I wish I could have done differently. I would have left your mother a lot sooner. I probably would have stayed in San Diego if I had, but then I never would have met Cheryl and had the twins and Caden."

"When did you finally remember me? It took you fifteen years to write to me."

"I thought at the time that it was best to wait until you were grown up to reach out to you. I didn't want to cause any tension between you and your mother. And then I heard about what happened to her, and by the time I tried to get in contact, you were long gone. I had no idea where you had gone. A few years ago, Cheryl showed me how I could find your address online, but it seemed like every time I wrote to you, you had already moved. When you took seven months to call me, I thought my letter had been lost in the mail."

I didn't want to believe a word he said. I was ready to get up and go back to San Diego when something caught my eye in another booth. It was a flash of blond hair and blue eyes. I craned my neck to see better. Two identical faces were watching me from a few booths down. Next to the twin girls was a boy, a little younger, watching me with equal interest.

I had decided when Joel told me about my siblings that I was never going to meet them. It wasn't fair to expect me to. It would have felt like a betrayal to my mother, to accept this life that my dad had created away from us. But everything changed when I saw them in the coffee shop that day. I looked at Joel, and then back at the kids. They were waiting to see if their older brother would accept them.

I didn't even know them, but I already knew that I couldn't abandon them.

I moved into the building where Joel worked a week later. I flew back to San Diego to get my things, then drove through eight states to get back to Miami. I made sure to stay far away from Dallas on my way.

I didn't have much. Just my clothes, my car, and a few boxes of personal belongings. I opened the trunk of my car and pulled out my box of Naomi's letters. I headed for the front door of the building. I wondered if I would ever be able to write to her again. I would have to ask Joel how he found my address. Maybe I could find hers the same way.

As the thought crossed my mind, a woman stepped through the door and stopped to hold it open for me. Her red hair caught my eye. I almost tripped and dropped my box. It felt like time slowed as I approached. All I could do was stare at this woman and try to remind myself of what Naomi looked like. I knew that this wasn't her. Naomi had never moved out of Oklahoma. Miami was a big city and there were probably thousands of redheads here. It was just a coincidence that I happened to be thinking of Naomi at the exact moment this beautiful woman opened the door.

"Thank you," I said as I walked through. She let go of the

door and went on her way. I stood there in the middle of the lobby, watching her through the window until she disappeared.

"She's a looker, huh?" Joel said from the security desk.

I turned to face him. "Does she live in this building?"

"Yep. She's kind of a local celebrity. She covers for the weatherman sometimes, so we get to see her on TV once in a while."

I knew that it couldn't be her, but I had to ask anyway. "What's her name?"

"Naomi Light," he said.

I must have heard him wrong. He couldn't have said her name. I was convinced that it was my own mind that planted her name in his mouth when he spoke. "What?"

"Naomi Light," he repeated.

I looked at the box of letters that I held, then back out the window. She was long gone, but it was her. Of all the apartment buildings in all of the world, I had just moved into hers.

"No fucking way."

The sound of the door slamming behind me solidifies every doubt I had about whether this was a good idea. I can hear the click of the lock, like she's scared I might try to come back inside. I'm not really sure what I expected, but I guess I hoped it would go better than that. In her letters, she's been asking to meet me for a while. Every time I show up, she doesn't seem to remember that she invited me. I guess it's not fair to say that she doesn't remember. The truth is, she didn't know that I was the one she was inviting over. There were many times I was about to tell her, but I chickened out every time until now.

It kills me that she thought that she was the one deceiving me. I had never meant to drag this out as long as I did. I tried to put some distance between us the last few days, but the damage was already done. I had lied to her.

It had hurt her enough that Joel had lied to her. What I did was so much worse. I knew that no amount of distance would make the lie any less hurtful. I could only hope that it wasn't too late to tell the truth. I thought that writing a letter might make it easier. I thought she liked the real me enough that she might be glad we were the same person. I realize now that I was being naïve. Writing that letter was a stupid idea.

I turn around and step toward the door so that she can hear me through it.

"Naomi? Can we please talk?"

"About what?" she snaps. I can tell by the closeness of her voice that she's right on the other side of the door. "About how you've been lying to me? Or about how you've been stalking me for the last six months?"

"I didn't stalk you," I say. "And if that's the reason you're mad, then I feel like I should remind you that you went to at least three different states to try to find me."

"Bullshit. Do you expect me to believe that you didn't know who I was either and you just happened to move into the same building as me? Is Joel even your real dad? Do you even have siblings? I thought you were an only child. Is everything you told me a lie?"

"He is my dad."

"Carol Bell said that your dad left you when you were a kid."

"He did. We reconnected six months ago, which is why I

ended up in Miami. I didn't lie about that. And I do have three half-siblings. Who the hell is Carol Bell?"

"She was the old lady who lived on the corner of your street in San Diego."

I want to point out how hypocritical that statement is, but I decide against it. I don't want to fuel the fight. I just want her to talk to me.

"None of it was a lie," I say. "Well, except for me not telling you my name."

"You knew damn well that I didn't know your name that whole time. If your goal was to make me feel like an idiot, you succeeded."

I think about when she said my name while I was touching her in her bedroom in the middle of the night. I had thought in that moment that she knew who I was, but by the morning it was clear that she didn't. I still think about it often. I wonder if I misheard her. It doesn't feel like the right moment to bring it up now.

"I know," I tell her. "I'm sorry. That wasn't my intention."

She doesn't respond. I can't tell if she's still standing on the other side of the door. If she is, she's breathing quietly. I decide to continue, hoping that she can still hear me.

"I'm sorry that I didn't tell you my name sooner. To be honest, I was scared that you wouldn't want anything to do with me. You never wanted to meet me, and then I came to Miami and found out you lived in the same building as me. I wasn't supposed to know what you looked like, but I did. When I was a teenager, I spent hours clicking through all of your photos on Facebook. What were the odds that I would end up in the same apartment building as you?"

"Pretty slim. I don't believe you."

I'm surprised to hear her voice, but glad to know that she's still listening to me.

"I should have introduced myself right then," I continue. "I chickened out."

"You had plenty of time to introduce yourself, and you chose not to. Why did it take you six months?"

"I was scared."

"Of what? I didn't know who you were."

"I was afraid of exactly this. That I would tell you who I am, and you wouldn't want anything to do with me. I was scared that you still felt the same way you did when you told me that you didn't want to be my friend on Facebook, or when you told me that you would never come to my bootcamp graduation. I guess I thought it was easier if you didn't know who I was at first."

"Because lying to me is so much better."

"It wasn't my plan to deceive you for so long. I was going to send that first letter to you at the news station, and then I was going to tell you who I was. I saw you almost every day on my lunch break. But the day I planned to do it, you were sitting at that table with Anne, and you were looking up my name on Facebook. So, change of plans. I asked you out to dinner instead, and I was going to tell you then, but then you postponed dinner—"

"Oh, so it's my fault that you didn't tell me."

Her tone is dripping with sarcasm. I continue anyway. "No. Not your fault. You told me that you were going to San Diego, and it occurred to me that you might be trying to find me."

"So, instead of telling me, 'Hey, I'm Luca, and I'm right here in Miami,' you decided to keep dragging it out and let me travel all over the country looking for you?"

"That's not why I didn't tell you. I was scared that I had already waited too long and that you would be mad at me."

"I wouldn't have been nearly as mad as I am now."

"I'm sorry, Naomi." I press my forehead to the door. I wish that she would let me back in and we could talk this through without the whole third floor hearing us.

"So you've said."

"Can you please forgive me?"

"No. Go home."

"I can't lose you, Naomi."

"You just did."

"Please. I promise there won't be any more secrets."

"Secrets? Is that what you think this is about? Secrets? You let me feel like an idiot, and you took advantage of me. How am I supposed to know that you weren't laughing behind my back every time I had sex with you, not knowing who the hell you really were? I wish I had never written back to you. I wish I had chosen a different name out of that damn hat back in fifth grade."

It hurts to hear her say that.

"Do you really mean that?"

"Yes." Her voice sounds lower now, like she's sitting on the floor. I lower myself to the floor so that we're at the same level.

"Your letters were the only consistent thing in my life for a long time," I say. "My parents were always fighting when they were together. After my dad left, my dog got out of the house and we never saw him again. Then my mom got sick, and she passed away the same day I graduated high school. All I had after that was the military and your letters. I moved around a lot for four years, but your letters always found me. They were the only good thing in my life, and then ... and then they just stopped one day. I don't know what I would have done if you

296

hadn't written back after I wrote that first mean letter to you, or if it had been someone else who wrote to me in the first place. I don't think any of the other kids in our classes continued to write to each other past those first couple of months. I guess in the grand scheme of things, it might not have changed much. My mom would have still cheated on my dad. My dad would have still left, and my mom would have still died. I don't know if I would have joined the military or dated Penny. I would have had much lower standards if I didn't know you existed, and maybe I would have married someone else. But maybe not. My dad would have still reached out to me, and I would have come to Miami and met the three siblings I didn't know I had. I would have moved into this building anyway, and had no idea who you were the day you held that door open for me." I wait a moment to see if she has anything to say, but she's quiet. "I probably would have asked you out a lot sooner."

I lean against the door and wait for her to respond, but she doesn't. I probably wasted my breath. She must have walked away a while ago. She didn't hear a word I just said. I stay by her door for a while longer. I regret the way I handled this whole thing. I wish for a moment that I could go back in time and introduce myself that day she held the door open for me. If I had, I might not have had the time that I did with her these last few weeks. In the end, lying to her wasn't worth it, but I wouldn't trade the time that I got to spend with her for anything. I wish that I could tell her that without it sounding like I'm minimizing what I've done to her. After a while, I decide that it's best if I leave her alone. I stand up and head for the stairwell.

Chapter Thirty-One

SAY MY NAME

Naomi

It takes me a while to respond because I don't trust my voice. I'm so angry with him, but even more so at myself for falling for any of what he just said. I wipe my eyes, and then take in a shaky breath.

"You wouldn't have seen me in Miami," I say. "I never thought about becoming a meteorologist until you suggested it. I would have been somewhere else with some other job."

Some other job that I probably wouldn't love as much, but I don't say that out loud. I realize that it's been a moment and he hasn't responded. I wait a while longer. Still nothing. I stand up and open the door. He's not there anymore.

I don't get much sleep. I'm sure it shows on my face. I pack on my makeup in the morning, but I'm afraid that the dark circles under my eyes will still scare away the new viewers I brought in when I wore that green dress. It's days like this I wish our station had a makeup artist.

I'm more grateful than ever for the cup of coffee Anne brings me. I know I said that she would be the first person I'd tell if Luca showed up at my door, but I feel too ashamed to tell her now. I still can't believe I was stupid enough to not realize it was him the whole time.

"You look tired," she remarks as she hands me my coffee. "Someone keep you up all night?"

She says this with a wink, her tone suggestive. I'm not sure how to respond without giving myself away, so I choose to ignore her. Nothing gets past her, though. She sits down, rolling her chair forward so that she's right next to me.

"You're upset," she says. "Talk."

"I really don't want to." I lock my gaze onto my computer screen, but I can't focus on it. My vision blurs as my focus lands somewhere in the air between my head and the monitor.

"Hey." Her hand touches my arm. "You know I'm here for you."

"I have work to do."

"It's Luca, isn't it? Did he ... show up?" She slows her speech mid-sentence.

I turn to look at her. I shouldn't be surprised that she would guess this is about Luca, considering he's all we've been talking about the last few weeks. I wish that she would let me process this on my own, but I guess it might be helpful to talk to her about it.

"Jake wasn't his real name," I say. I pause a moment. She doesn't prod, just watches me patiently. "He's Luca."

It takes a moment for her eyes to widen, and then, in a hushed voice, she says, "Oh my God, really?"

It's the fakest look of surprise I've ever seen. I feel even dumber now. I roll my eyes. "You already figured that out, didn't you?"

She shrugs. "Maybe."

"How long have you known?"

"I've had my suspicions since the day you adopted the kittens. There was just something about him. I'm good at reading people."

I hate that she's always right. "Why didn't you tell me that you thought it might be him?"

"I didn't want to make you paranoid if I turned out to be wrong," she says.

"I feel like an idiot."

"You're not. You just – well, I am surprised that you didn't suspect it, but—"

"Jake had three siblings and a dad he saw every day. Luca was an only child and his dad abandoned him. How could I have known they were the same person?"

"How did it go when he told you? Were you mad?"

"Of course I was fucking mad," I snap. "He's been lying to me the whole time. He slept with me, allowing me to believe he was someone else. I don't even know who he is now. How am I supposed to trust him after that?"

I see Patrick poking his head through the doorway behind Anne. He looks like he's about to speak up, but I cut him off. "Not now, Facey. I'm talking to Anne."

He mumbles something about his name, then turns around and leaves. Anne watches him go over her shoulder, then looks at me, her eyebrow raised. "Facey," she repeats with a giggle. Then she gets serious again. "Maybe you should give Luca another chance. After all the years of mean letters you wrote to each other, he was probably just scared that you wouldn't want to meet him."

"Seriously? You're taking his side?"

"Not completely. He's an asshole for keeping the lie going for so long, and I definitely think he shouldn't have slept with you until he came clean about who he was."

"I don't date liars," I say. "And this is so much bigger than any stupid white lie any of my exes has ever told me."

Anne twists her lips in a way that indicates she's about to disagree with what I just said. I brace myself for it.

"In a way, I think little white lies are worse," she says.

"Now you're reaching. He lied about his entire identity. I hardly think that's more forgivable than a white lie."

"Let me explain," she says. "I'm not talking about when a guy tells you that your ugly dress looks okay – although, screw anyone who lets me walk out of the house looking terrible. I'm talking about little white lies like telling your boss that you're sick because you don't feel like coming to work, or telling someone that your car broke down because you don't want to hang out. One little lie here and there isn't a big deal, but someone who tells a lot of little lies like that usually makes it a habit. I dated a pathological liar before. It started off with him making excuses to cancel our dates instead of just telling me he didn't have enough money. It was always little things, where if I confronted him, I would sound paranoid, but it got to the point that he was lying so much that I felt like he was never telling the truth. And there was no reason for it either. He would tell me that he was helping his mother with something when in reality he was drinking with a friend. I wouldn't have been mad if he had just told me what he was doing."

"I dated a guy like that," I say. "I couldn't trust anything he said."

"I don't think that Luca is like our exes. He's not a

pathological liar. Have you felt like he was lying to you about anything other than his name?"

"How can I be sure? I feel like I don't even know him."

"You worked so hard to find him. And you had such a good connection with him. You told me so yourself. I really doubt that he was faking all of that. He was showing you the real him. So what if he didn't tell you his real name? He was afraid that you would freak out. And guess what? He wasn't wrong."

"I wouldn't have freaked out if he had come right out and told me who he was."

"Are you sure? Imagine how you would have felt if he came up to you out of the blue before you ever met him and said that he was Luca and that he was the person you had been writing to all those years."

"We'll never know how I would have reacted because it didn't happen that way. Instead, he lied to me and now I can't trust him."

"You lied to him too."

"No, I didn't."

"How did you explain our trips to San Diego and Georgia and Texas?"

"Okay, that's different."

"How? I'm sure you didn't tell him that you were trying to track down your old pen pal."

"I didn't really lie, though. I kept the details to a minimum. I told him that I wanted to see what the beaches were like in San Diego, which was true."

"So, you lied by omission. Much like…"

"Don't say it."

"Much like he did," she continues, louder, "when he avoided telling you his name."

"It's so not the same thing."

"You also didn't tell him about the letters. You were flirting with someone you thought was another guy while you were getting serious with him."

"That doesn't count. I was writing to him, and it's his fault that I didn't know it. Plus, I was trying to tell him about the letters last night when he interrupted me and told me who he was."

"Maybe if you had told him about the letters sooner, he would have confessed sooner."

I open my mouth to argue, but I realize she has a point. I had written that last letter to Luca hoping that he would show up at my door. I'm not really sure how I expected it to go from there. If he had turned out to be someone entirely different, then I would be the one in the wrong right now.

"Maybe you're right," I say with a sigh. "You should probably get back to work. I need to finish up here before I go on air."

The last thing I want is to run into Luca while I'm still processing everything that happened last night and over the last few weeks. But of course nothing can go my way. He's standing by Joel's desk when I walk into the building after work. Both men are in the middle of a conversation that halts when I walk through the door. I keep my glance in their direction brief, and then I head the other way toward the mailboxes. I'm considering taking the elevator so that I won't have to walk past them again. I'll be buying my house and moving in just a couple of weeks and then I won't have to deal with facing him anymore.

Before I can finish unlocking my mailbox, Luca appears next to me.

"Can we talk?" he asks.

Without looking at him, I open my mailbox and pull out the stack of mail that was delivered this morning. I sift through the envelopes. When I find a letter from him at the bottom of the stack, I pull it out and shove it against his chest. He's startled by my action. He takes the envelope and looks at it before turning back to me.

"You're not even going to open it?"

Ignoring him, I turn away from the mailboxes, but he steps in front of me, blocking my path. I hate that my heart rate picks up even now, like it hasn't gotten the memo that I'm mad at him.

"Talk to me," he says. "I know I fucked up, but this can't be the end of what we had. We have something special, Naomi. I know that you feel it too."

Ignoring my pounding heart, I glare at him, waiting for him to move out of my way.

"I think that somewhere deep down, you knew that it was me," he continues. I raise an eyebrow, curious about where he's going with this. He lowers his voice. "You said my name."

"Excuse me?"

"You said my name while we were having sex. I think you knew that it was me."

I had tried to bury that memory, but now he's bringing it up and I can feel my face flush.

"I said your name because I was fantasizing about a person who I thought was someone else," I say, trying to keep my voice quiet because Joel looks like he's trying to eavesdrop from across the lobby. "Maybe if you were better in bed, I wouldn't have had to do that."

305

Chapter Thirty-Two

BAD IN BED

"Ouch."

This is Anne's reaction to me telling her what I said to Luca yesterday. I feel pretty damn proud of myself for coming up with that, but Anne seems to think I took it too far.

He wasn't really bad in bed. I just wanted to shut him up. I don't really care if it's a blow to his ego. He's always been cocky and I know that he'll get over it. Still, I know that words can be pretty hurtful. I hope I haven't done any permanent damage.

"He's not the victim here," I say, more as a reminder to myself than to Anne. "And he hurt me first. What I said pales in comparison to what he did to me."

We both turn our heads when Patrick walks into the room. I can tell that he's a little hesitant to order Anne around after I snapped at him yesterday.

"Maybe we can ask a guy's opinion," Anne says. "Hey Patty—"

"Don't call me that," he interrupts.

She continues anyway. "Has anyone ever told you that you were bad in bed?"

I don't think she really thought that question through. Patrick begins to stammer, and his face turns bright red. "What … why would you ask that?"

"Naomi told her boyfriend that he's bad in bed," she explains. "I told her that it was a pretty mean thing to say. What do you think? Has anyone ever said that to you?"

"This isn't an appropriate thing to be talking about at work," he says.

"And with your boss," I add.

Anne's eyes widen. "Oh my God. I'm sorry. I didn't mean to embarrass you. You don't have to tell me if someone said that to you."

"No one said that to me," he says. "I just … it's just … not appropriate."

He mumbles something about getting back to work as he walks away. Anne watches him leave the room. Once he's gone, she looks at me and smiles.

"He's so cute when he's all flustered," she says.

I almost choke on my coffee. "Did you just call Patrick cute?"

She shrugs. "In a bossy, balding teddy bear sort of way."

"None of that sounds cute except for the teddy bear part, and I don't think I've ever equated Patrick to a teddy bear."

"You're reading too much into what I said. The point is, he got all upset at the mere thought that someone might think he's bad in bed. You straight-out told Luca that he sucks."

"I don't think that's what Patrick was upset about. He was upset because his employee was asking him about his sex life."

"You're changing the subject because you know that I'm right."

"I'm not changing the subject at all. Do you realize how weird that was?"

"It wasn't that weird. He's walked in on plenty of awkward conversations before."

"True, but we've never dragged him into any of them."

Anne slaps her hand over her face and groans. "Ugh. That was weird, wasn't it? You don't think he's going to fire me, do you?"

"Probably not for that, but maybe if you keep spending your whole morning talking to me, he'll have a valid reason."

Anne takes the hint and gets up. "Now I'm going to have to avoid him the rest of the day. Or the rest of the week."

———————

I stop on the third floor of the stairwell and look at the steps leading up to the fourth. Normally I would be heading up there to check on the puppy. Now that I know who Luca is, I hesitate. I'm mad at him, but that doesn't mean that I've stopped caring about Bruno. After a short deliberation, I head upstairs.

His apartment is messier now than it was the other times I've been in here. There's a stack of papers on his small kitchen table. I step closer to see what it is. I recognize my own handwriting. These are the last few letters I wrote to him. I lift the pages and realize that these are *all* the letters I wrote to him. He kept all of them. At the bottom of the stack is the very first letter I wrote in fifth grade. I read it, and feel a little sad. I was so nice. So innocent. I had no idea that I was going to get such a mean letter in return, and that it would turn into years of the weirdest pen pal friendship I imagine has ever existed. I couldn't have predicted that it would all end the way it did.

I set the letters back down the way I found them, and then spot an unopened envelope addressed to me. It looks like the one he had left in my mailbox yesterday. I decide to take it with me. After all, it is addressed to me.

I take Bruno for a walk, and then I sit down on my couch with the envelope. Giving it back to Luca yesterday was a knee-jerk reaction that I regret. The thought that I would never know what's inside this envelope has bothered me all day. I rip it open. I'm surprised to find two more sealed envelopes inside. The first one is addressed to my last address in Oklahoma City. I recognize the second address as the house my parents owned before I left for college and they downsized. There's a yellow label affixed to each envelope, indicating they were undeliverable.

Dear Naomi,

I know it's been a while since you heard from me. Life has felt like a rollercoaster lately. It started when you didn't write back. Or, at least I thought that you didn't. My ex-fiancée intercepted your letter and hid it from me for several months. She was also batshit crazy, and for a while I thought that she was the best I could do in life. And then she threw your letter at me, and I realized that you did write back. Come hide away with you? Is that invitation still open? Because if it is, I'll be on the next flight.

I know that we say mean things and joke around all the time (at least I hope you're joking) but I want you to know that I mean it.

Love,

Luca

Dear Naomi,

I guess in the time it took me to move to Dallas and back to San Diego, you also moved. It's a little weird to realize that I have no idea where you live now. I'm sending this letter to your parents' address on the off-chance they still live there. I hope that they can get it to you.

Long story short: I didn't get married and I never saw your last letter until months after you sent it.

Update on my life: I currently live with the guy who told me that I shouldn't just ignore the very first letter you sent back in fifth grade. I also live with three screaming children and their mom who takes a lot of naps. I need to escape. Any suggestions on where I should go?

Love,

Luca

I thought that I was sad before. I thought that I was angry. What I feel now is something new, and I can't explain it. I wish that I had seen these letters sooner. I wish that I hadn't shoved them into Luca's chest when he tried to give them to me yesterday, and I wish that I hadn't insulted him.

If I had known to set up a forwarding address, these letters would have made it to me. The postmarks on the envelopes indicate they were written around the time that I first started to give up on hearing from him again. That was back when I hoped that he would show up one day out of the blue. I guess I never stopped hoping that he would.

When Luca knocks on my door, I turn the letters over as if I'll get in trouble for reading them. I head over to the door to let him in. The blue of his eyes looks ice cold, and there's no hint of a smile on his face. I don't think I've ever seen him look this angry.

"I could have you arrested for dognapping," he says. He steps past me and grabs Bruno's harness and leash. I turn to watch him, frowning.

"I still can't believe that he's deaf," I say.

He doesn't respond. He slips the harness onto the puppy.

"He seems like a normal dog to me."

He clips the leash to the harness.

"Are you ignoring me now? Is that it?"

"My bad," he says. "I didn't want to subject you to any more mediocrity."

I roll my eyes. "Oh. You're mad at *me* now? Is that how this works? You lied to me, Luca. You tricked me. You don't get to be mad at me."

He turns away from the door and steps toward me. My heart rate picks up. I hold my ground, refusing to be backed into a corner. I have to crane my neck up to look at him. He's still holding the puppy, who is excitedly licking his chin. He's glaring at me, but it's a little hard to take him seriously when he's holding such a cute puppy. I press my lips together to stop myself from smiling.

"I have every right to be upset," he says. "Do you really think you're the only one who's hurting over this? I fell in love with you, and I lost you."

There are those words again, catching me off guard. My heart pounds so hard that I think it might rip out of my chest. My hand raises up against my will, reaching for him. I force it back down to my side before I can touch him. His gaze drops down to my hand before he meets my eyes again. There's something about the look in his eyes that makes me wonder if he would have backed away from my touch.

I want to believe that he's only saying this to try to win me back, but he doesn't seem like he's trying to win me back anymore. "How can you say that you fell in love with me? You barely even know me."

He sighs, angling Bruno away from his face. "You're wrong

about that. I've known you for most of my life. Maybe it was just the idea of you at first. I thought that you had to be just as funny in real life as you were in your letters."

"That's not love, that's—"

He cuts me off, continuing. "I fell so hard for you that I couldn't even enjoy anyone else's company, because I had already decided that you were the one. I tried to tell myself that I was holding you up on a pedestal, that you couldn't be as funny, or beautiful, or amazing as I imagined you were. Before I came to Miami, I had convinced myself that I was wrong for thinking I could be in love with someone I had never met. And then I met you in person, and it turns out I was right. Everything that I thought I felt was real. I fell in love with you all over again."

I don't have a chance to respond before he turns back to the front door.

"Luca…"

He opens the door, then looks back at me. "It's too bad you're also just as mean in real life," he says. "I guess I dodged a bullet."

Chapter Thirty-Three

WORLD'S WEIRDEST FRIENDSHIP

Luca

I stand next to the only patch of grass on the block, waiting for the puppy to do his business so that I can go back inside and be miserable without any witnesses. I told Naomi that I dodged a bullet, but maybe I was wrong.

Maybe I'm the bullet.

I shoot right through every relationship I have, leaving nothing but pain and bitterness behind. I've been that way since I can remember. I always thought that if I met Naomi, things would be different. I never cared about making any of my past relationships work. It wasn't that I was the type of guy who didn't want to settle down. It was because I was waiting for the one girl who measured up to what I imagined Naomi would be like.

There would be no lying, no pretending, no faking the way I felt just so that I wouldn't look like a heartless asshole. I thought that when I met Naomi, everything would be real. And it was, right up until the moment I told her my name.

I guess it's just as well that it ended so soon. I'd rather know now than later. I can pretend that it doesn't hurt as badly as it does.

I take the puppy back inside. Joel is off duty, but he's sitting at the security desk anyway. I don't think he has anything better to do. It's a little pathetic. I assume I'll end up like him one day.

"She didn't trash your place, did she?" He asks the question without taking his eyes off the book he's reading.

"No. Just stole my dog again."

It's been six months since I've talked to Ben, so I'm surprised when I get a call from him out of the blue. For a moment, I wonder if Naomi found him during her search for me, but that probably would have come up sooner. I answer the call.

"This might sound totally random, but how far is Boca Raton from Miami?"

"Not far. Are you in Boca Raton?" I ask.

"They're flying me out there to fix a project my team keeps messing up. What are you doing on Monday? I thought maybe I could sneak away long enough to grab lunch."

"I can do lunch," I tell him. "As long as it's close by. I have a foster puppy, and I usually come home to walk him during my lunch break."

He agrees to meet me at the café. He says it's because he looked up their menu while we were on the phone, and the food looks good, but I have a feeling he wants to see my place and make sure I'm not living in a dump like I was when I was in college.

On Monday, I get home in time to walk the puppy before

Ben shows up at my door. I show him that my place is in at least somewhat decent shape. It's a nice building, but my furniture came from thrift stores. After a quick tour, we head downstairs to the café.

When we get inside, I spot Naomi at the booth where she normally eats lunch with Anne. I thought she might avoid this place after everything that happened between us. I'm glad that she isn't. I don't want her to miss out on the things that she enjoys just because of me. And maybe I'm a little masochistic, because as much as it hurts, I like seeing her even if it's from a distance.

"I have something I need to tell you," I say to Ben.

"Is it about that redhead you've been staring at since we walked in?"

I can tell that he's joking.

"Do you remember my pen pal?"

"How could I not? You were the last person I expected to still be writing to your pen pal long after the rest of us stopped." We take a step forward in line. "Why? Did you finally hear from her again?"

I gesture toward Naomi. "That's her. Naomi Light."

He whips his head around to look. "The redhead? Seriously?" Then he looks at me, eyes wide. He lowers his voice. "Wait. Did you track her down here?"

"Not exactly."

"What do you mean, 'not exactly'? You either tracked her down or you didn't."

"I didn't. I was moving into the building and she was just … here."

"Does she know you?" Ben asks. "Please tell me she knows who you are."

"Yeah, well, I kind of screwed things up."

"You? Screwing things up? I can't imagine."

I ignore his sarcasm. "I didn't tell her who I was at first. Now she doesn't trust me."

It's clear he doesn't understand the extent of how badly I screwed up, because he says, "I have to meet her," and then steps out of line and heads for her table. I curse under my breath, and then follow him.

"Naomi Light," he says, sliding into the seat next to Anne so that he's across from Naomi. "You are an absolute legend."

She looks confused and a little bit scared. Anne leans away from him, clearly put off by the stranger intruding on their lunch date.

"You must have seen her weather report," Anne says.

"Weather report?" He looks back at Naomi. "What, are you on TV?"

Naomi looks from Ben to me. I can tell by her expression that she's putting together that we must know each other.

"She reports the weather here," I say to Ben.

Anne looks over her shoulder at me. Ben continues, addressing Anne this time. "This girl here has been writing to my friend Luca since fifth grade. Can you believe that?" He turns back to Naomi, clutching his own hand dramatically. "I'm still traumatized by that one about the hangnail."

"You read the letters?" Naomi asks.

"Only a couple of them." He extends his hand across the table. "I'm Ben."

She shakes his hand. "Ben Toole?" she asks.

I'm surprised she knows his name. He seems surprised too. "I didn't know Luca told you about me."

"Penny told me."

Ben's eyebrows shoot up. He looks at me, then back at her. "You met Penny?"

I realize this isn't going to be a quick meet and greet, so I slide into the seat next to Naomi. She slides over, making room for me, but she doesn't move fast enough and my leg bumps hers as I settle into the seat. She inches away from me, but I can still feel the spot on my leg that touched hers briefly. It's almost enough to distract me from the heat of her glare on the side of my head.

"She tracked Penny down while she was stalking me," I say to Ben.

"I was not stalking you."

"You basically were," Anne counters.

"He was writing letters to me at the news station with no return address," Naomi explains to Ben. "I was just trying to find a way to write back to him."

"What was Penny like?" Ben asks. "Still crazy?"

"So crazy," Anne says.

"We didn't talk to her for very long," Naomi says. "Only long enough to figure out Luca didn't live there anymore."

I'm not looking at her, but I'm aware of every little move she makes. She brushes her fingers through her hair, and I can smell the familiar scent of her shampoo just as strongly as if my face were buried in her neck. It takes everything in my power not to bump her leg with mine just to see if she would move away again.

"And that Naomi is the reason the wedding never happened," Anne chimes in.

"You went pretty far to find an address," Ben says.

"She went to San Diego and to a base I was stationed at in Georgia, too," I add.

"At least I didn't lie about who I was," she says. Then, turning to Ben, she says, "He sent me a death threat at the news station."

Ben snaps his head in my direction. He looks horrified.

I direct my response to Ben, because I can't bring myself to turn my head and look at her when she's this close to me. I'm afraid that I might do something stupid. "It wasn't really a death threat," I argue. "I just said that I hoped she got struck by lightning."

"To be fair, Naomi read it and laughed," Anne says. "I was ready to turn the letter in to the station manager."

"You guys are so weird," Ben says, shaking his head. Addressing Naomi again, he says, "Did you know that if it wasn't for me, Luca wouldn't have written back to you that first time? I guess you have me to thank for the world's weirdest friendship."

"They're hardly friends anymore," Anne says. "Can't you sense the tension between them?"

Ben looks from Naomi to me, his brow furrowed, like he didn't notice how awkward this was for both of us. I turn to look at her in time to catch her staring at me, but she quickly turns her head in the other direction.

"Wow, you really did screw up, didn't you?" Ben says. "Just apologize to her." He looks at each of us again, and curiosity gets the best of him. "What did you do? Rip a hangnail off her hand? Threaten to kill her yourself?"

"He lived here for six months, wrote letters to her, and took her out on dates while letting her think he was someone else," Anne says.

"Six months? Damn." Ben looks at Naomi. She's glaring out the window next to her.

Before I can stop myself, I reach under the table and rest my hand on her leg. She doesn't slap my hand away, but she doesn't look at me either.

"I guess I should have known that he would be as big of an asshole in real life as he was in his letters," she says.

Her words are more painful than a slap would have been, but they have the same effect. I take my hand off her thigh. She looks at me for just a moment before facing Ben and Anne across the table again.

"I wasn't lying to her for a whole six months," I tell Ben. "I only got the courage to talk to her for the first time a few weeks ago."

"I'm not surprised. You're a big wuss when it comes to talking to women," he says. Then, addressing Anne and Naomi, he adds, "Which is weird considering he was a player all the way up until junior year in high school. I never saw him with anyone else until Penny came along."

From the corner of my eye, I can see Naomi turning her head in my direction. I dare to turn my head and meet her eye. Her brow is wrinkled in a slight frown, her lips parted just a little, like she's thinking about saying something, but then she thinks better of it and her mouth closes. I wonder if she remembers that junior year was when I asked her if we could be friends on Facebook. I wonder if she'll put it together that I lost interest in my classmates because of her.

She holds my stare for a moment before she turns her attention back to Ben. "You've really known Luca since fifth grade?"

He nods. "Since fourth, actually."

"But you were in the same fifth grade class? Did you have a pen pal, too?"

"Of course. His name was…" He scratches his chin like he's thinking hard. "Andy, I think. Something like that."

It's clear that she recognizes the name by the way her eyes brighten. "Andy Nicoletti?"

Ben smirks. "Do you remember the first and last name of everyone in your fifth-grade class?"

Her mouth widens into a smile. "No, but I grew up with Andy. We dated for a while in high school."

I know that high school was a long time ago, but I can't help but wonder why she looks so happy when she thinks about Andy Nicoletti. Then her eyes flash over to me for the briefest second, and I think I know why. She must be trying to make me jealous.

"No way," Ben says. "I can't believe I was writing to the future ex-boyfriend of the legendary Naomi Light."

She rolls her eyes, still smiling. "I'm not that legendary."

"You wrote to this guy for damn near twenty years and didn't go insane. That's pretty legendary if you ask me."

She leans forward on the table, resting her chin in her hands. "How long did you write to Andy?" she asks. "Most of the kids I knew only kept up with it for a couple of months."

"I'm pretty sure the last letters we wrote to each other were about what we hoped to get for Christmas that year." He looks at me and adds, "You were the last one in the class to get a letter, which was funny because you didn't want to write them at all in the beginning." Addressing Naomi again, he says, "This guy kept the letters a secret until eighth grade when he showed me that one about the hangnail."

"No wonder you're so fixated on that one. It's not even the worst one," Anne says.

"I can't get a hangnail without thinking about that letter," Ben says. "Does that mean I'm traumatized? I feel like I might be traumatized."

"I'm curious about Andy Nicoletti," Anne says. She steals a glance at me before turning to Naomi. "How long did you two date?"

"A couple of years. We broke up right before college."

"Was he cute?"

Naomi leans back in her seat again and releases a sigh like this is bringing back good memories. I know that they're only talking about Andy to make me jealous, but I can't help but feel annoyed at the thought of Naomi swooning over some other guy.

"He was *very* cute," she says.

"Ugh. He's probably the one that got away," Anne says. "We should track him down next."

"Let me know if you do," Ben says. "Maybe I can send him a death threat."

The girls both giggle.

"I'd like to send him one," I say before I can stop myself.

"Whoa, guys," Anne says. "That took a turn."

"There won't be any death threats," Naomi says. "We're not tracking him down."

"You're no fun," Anne complains. "Is it because he was bad in bed?"

As soon as Anne says it, my face flushes. I thought that Naomi had only said that out of anger, but if she told Anne... I need to get out of here. I stand up before anyone can respond.

"There's a Spanish diner down the street," I say to Ben. "The food is better there. Let's go."

Chapter Thirty-Four

THE EXHUMATION OF NAOMI LIGHT

Naomi

"Did you really have to say that?" I ask Anne.

"Say what? The bad in bed comment?"

"Yeah. That."

"I don't get you. I thought you were mad at him."

"I am, but now he probably thinks I told you about our sex life."

She frowns. "So, it's okay for you to be mad at him, but you don't want him mad at you?"

"He's already mad at me. Couldn't you tell? Every time he had something to say to me, he said it to Ben as if I wasn't sitting right next to him."

"It was a little hard to get a read on him," Anne admits. "One moment, he was looking at you with those pretty puppy dog eyes, and the next he was glaring at you like he wanted to make good on his death threat."

"I think it's because I told him that he's bad in bed. And

you just reminded him of that. Am I the asshole in this situation?"

"You're both the assholes."

"Why do you say that?"

"He kept his identity a secret from you. That was an asshole move. You didn't tell him about the letters. Also an asshole move."

"I feel like faking his identity was a little bit worse than some innocent letters."

"Innocent? Then explain all those sexy letters and the secret meetup you were trying to plan."

"It wasn't a secret sexy meetup. I just wanted to meet the person I had been writing to all this time. And I feel like he should get another asshole point for totally ignoring those letters. He led me to believe he wanted to meet me, then stopped writing back."

"Maybe he wasn't ignoring them," she says. "Maybe he was responding to your invitation by showing up at your door."

"Which leads us back to him being an asshole for not telling me who he was. Can we give him a third point for that?"

"Only if you get another point for lying to him about all those trips you went on. And another for the 'bad in bed' comment."

I sigh. "That puts us at an even score."

"Not everything has to be a competition. Save the one-upmanship for the mean letters and just be real with him."

I stare through the window at my building. Luca and Ben walked past a while ago toward the other diner. Maybe Anne is right. This shouldn't be a competition. I don't want it to be. I just want...

I pause, thinking about what it is that I want. I miss writing letters to Luca, but even more, I miss what I had with him when I thought his name was Jake. I hate that the reason I have neither now is because they're the same person.

I guess I just want it back. All of it.

I'm still thinking about Luca when I get home. I pull my box of letters out of the closet and look through them. I had wondered for a long time if Luca held onto any of the letters I sent him. I didn't see them the first couple of times I was in his apartment, before I knew who he was. I wonder if he keeps them in a box in the closet like I do. Maybe he plans on burning them.

No matter how angry I am with him, I know that I could never bring myself to destroy the letters. I imagine that I'll keep them with me through every move. I'll probably still have them stowed away in my attic when I'm an old widow. I'll be ninety-seven years old by then, and my late husband will have never known what was in the box. When I pass away, I'll leave my mansion to my grandchildren – yes, I plan on being rich and living in a mansion by the time I'm that old. My grandkids will go through my house, choosing which things to sell and which things to keep when they come across my box.

They'll think for a moment that they've stumbled upon Grandma Naomi's secret stash of love letters until they actually read some of them and realize that no, these are not love letters, but something far juicier. This is hate mail. Grandma Naomi had an enemy who wrote awful letters to her for decades. But why did she keep all these letters? Perhaps she was afraid that one day this person would track her down and poison her. The grandkids would then take the letters to the police station and have an investigation launched on what was once believed to be a death of natural causes. My body would be exhumed and a new autopsy would be performed.

This is the type of thing that I might have written in a letter to him. I'm suddenly hit with the realization that we might never write to each other again. I don't like the thought of that. I leave the box of letters in my living room and go downstairs. I'm not sure what I'm expecting to find. It's not like he's going to leave another letter in my mailbox at this point.

When I get to the lobby, I spot Luca standing next to the elevator. Ben isn't with him anymore. He watches me for a moment after the doors open, then pulls his gaze away and steps inside. I force myself to get inside the elevator with him. We stand side by side, facing the door.

"Luca, I'm sorry," I blurt out when the doors close.

He turns to face me, and I do the same. He frowns. "For what?"

I'm annoyed that I have to explain myself. I'm not annoyed at him, but at myself for bringing it up. I sigh. "For what I said the other day."

He raises an eyebrow. "Can you be a little more specific?"

The elevator feels hot. I wonder if it's too late to take back my apology. I decide to tough it out. "I may have implied that you were bad in bed. I didn't tell Anne that you were, if that's what you were thinking when she made that comment earlier. I had only told her what I said to you."

He stares at me, his expression unchanging except for a tiny hint of a smile at the corner of his lips. I hate that he thinks this is funny while I've been stewing over it.

"You don't have to apologize for that," he says. For a moment, I think that's all he's going to say. But it isn't. "You were just mad." His gaze wanders down my body before returning to my face. "I know that you liked it."

I'm so mad and embarrassed that I let out an actual growl. This only serves to amuse him more, and the hint of a curved lip becomes a full-fledged smile. His smile makes me hate him even more, because damn it, it looks so good on him.

"I hate you," I say.

He tries to frown, but he can't seem to undo the smile. "Why would you say that?"

"You've always been so damn cocky, ever since we first started writing to each other. I kind of hoped that you would turn out to be an ugly troll, but … ugh. You must have felt so damn smug when you met me and all I wanted to do was jump your bones."

His smile fades. "If I was cocky, it was only because I wanted to impress you. You were right though, you know."

"About what?"

"Fifth grade," he says. "I wasn't hot. I was just skinny."

The elevator door opens on my floor. I begin to step out, but he reaches his hand out, his fingers grazing my forearm. I stop and turn toward him, his touch lingering on my skin. His brow is furrowed, his lips parted, like he's debating whether to say what's on his mind.

"Luca?"

"You didn't have a panic attack," he says.

It takes me a second to remember my fear of this elevator. I look at the walls, and then out at the hallway before I return my gaze to him. "You're right," I say with a nod. "I guess I felt safe."

His hand slides further down my arm, until he reaches my hand, and he intertwines his fingers with mine. I give his hand a small squeeze before I let go.

The elevator door begins to slide shut and I back out so it doesn't hit me. We make eye contact as the door closes, both of us frozen in place. I wonder if he's as torn as I am about letting the door close between us. I think about reaching my hand out to stop it, but I'm not sure what I would say if I did. I let the door close, and so does he. I stand in the hallway for a minute, still staring at the door, still feeling his fingers on mine, and hearing the echo of what he said before the door opened. I can hear the rumble of the pulley as the elevator brings Luca up to his own floor.

I turn away from the elevator, and as I walk back to my apartment, I think about that first year of letters. I wonder if he reread them recently like I did, or if the words I once forgot I had said were powerful enough to stick with him all this time, waiting for an opportunity to be spoken again.

Chapter Thirty-Five

THE PEN PAL ZONE

Maybe I'm crazy, but I want him to write to me again. I'm not really sure how to bring it up. It might be a little weird to go from sleeping with someone, to not talking at all, to telling him that I want to go back to being pen pals. It feels a little like friend-zoning, but worse. I wonder if pen-pal-zoning is a thing.

Then again, I don't think it would be called the friendzone if I already dated him. Maybe the ex-zone would be more accurate. Some people stay friends after they break up. Some never talk again. I usually fall into the latter group, but that's not how I want things to end with me and Luca.

I reach over and pet the kittens, who are sitting next to me and grooming each other. Maybe instead of asking him if we can go back to writing letters, I can just make the first move and write to him. After all, I rejected the last letter that he gave me. He's probably afraid to make the next move. He doesn't know that I've forgiven him.

This last thought gives me pause. Have I forgiven him? I haven't really given it much thought. I'm not angry anymore. I find myself missing him more with every day that passes by. I just need to find a way to tell him.

I wait until Bruno starts crying before I head upstairs to get him. I'm not avoiding Luca, but I don't want to run into him just yet. I'm afraid he'll convince me to leave Bruno alone, or worse, take his key back so that I don't have a choice.

The note I left on his refrigerator before is gone. I wonder if he tossed it or if he added it to his box. I think about snooping around his apartment to see if I can find where he keeps it, but I decide against it. I brought a new note with me. I leave it on his refrigerator with the same magnet.

Dear Luca,
    I took something from your apartment. Can you guess what it is?
    —N

I take Bruno for a walk, and then spend the afternoon researching deafness in dogs. I try to prove that he can hear, but he doesn't react to any of the noises I make. I think it's time to accept that this puppy really can't hear anything. I sit down and watch several videos on training a deaf dog using hand signals, and then I attempt some of them with Bruno. It's going to take a lot of work, but I think I can do it. I'm fully committed to this by the time Luca knocks on my door.

"What did you take from my apartment?"

He doesn't waste time on pleasantries; he gets straight to the point. Even so, I think of the last time we were this close together, how his hand grazed mine, sending goosebumps over my skin that I can feel even now.

"You're not supposed to answer a letter verbally," I scold him.

"Should I have written that question down and handed it to you without speaking?"

I shrug. "Probably." I step aside and let him into the apartment.

"Seriously, though," he says, this time smirking a little. "What did you take?" He looks into the living room where Bruno is playing with the kittens. "Bruno?"

"No. Well, yeah, but that's not what I was talking about. I trained him to sit, by the way."

He looks skeptical. "How? He's stubborn as hell."

"He'll do anything for a piece of cheese."

I go to the kitchen and grab a package of cheese. Bruno smells it and comes running. I do the hand signal from the video. The puppy lowers his bottom to the floor and stares at me expectantly. I give him the piece of cheese. He eats it, then runs to the other side of the room to join the kittens.

I can tell by the look on Luca's face that he's impressed and maybe a little bit jealous.

"I didn't know you grew up with dogs," he says.

"I never had a dog."

"Seriously? So, you're just a dog whisperer by accident?"

"I watched a lot of videos this afternoon," I say. "Plus, I had a ferret when I was a kid. I loved teaching him new tricks."

Luca smiles. He leans against the armrest of my couch. "I guess your fifth-grade dream came true, then. Didn't you mention that you wanted a ferret in the first letter you ever wrote to me?"

"I also wanted a cat. Now I have two."

He snorts out a laugh. "What did I say about cats back then?"

"You said that cats were boring, and that's why they'd be a perfect fit for me. Something like that."

We both look at Roland and Phoebe, who are in the living room ganging up on Bruno.

"I might have been wrong about that." He steps away from the couch and toward me, but then passes me, making me have to turn around as he makes his way to the kitchen island.

"You were wrong about a lot of things," I remind him. "For one, my parents aren't brother and sister."

I follow him to the island and pull out a stool to sit down. When I cross my legs, one of my feet bumps his knee. He looks down at my foot, but he doesn't move out of the way. I don't move either. My foot feels warm where it touches his leg. It's all I can focus on. The heat spreads up through my leg to the rest of my body.

I watch as his Adam's apple bobs up and down before he meets my eyes again. "I was a little shithead back then, wasn't I?"

"Back then? You mean you're not anymore?"

His smile fades just a little. For a moment I wonder if I went too far. I move my foot away from his knee, bringing his attention back down to my legs.

"You've been reading the letters again," he says without looking up, "haven't you?"

"Yeah. So have you."

"I figured you might have seen my box."

"I was surprised that you kept all those letters. I've always wondered if I was the only one saving them."

"I threw away the first one," he says. "Then I regretted it and I took it out of the trash. I couldn't bring myself to get rid of them."

"I really thought that you hated me that first year," I say. "It wasn't until I realized nobody else was still writing to their pen pals that I thought maybe you didn't hate me as much as you wanted me to think."

He looks back up at me, and it feels like it's the first time I've seen those ice-blue eyes in ages. "Why did you keep the letters if you thought that I hated you?"

I shrug. "Hard to say. I'd like to think that I was too sentimental, but I was probably just a hoarder. I used to keep all of my birthday cards for years until my mom forced me to throw them away."

"I have two more letters upstairs if you want them," he says. "They were the letters that I tried to send to you after you had already moved. I tried to give them to you the other day, but I think you were still pretty mad at me."

He says this tentatively, like he's wondering if I still am.

"Oh. Uh. This is awkward."

"What?"

"That's what I took from your apartment."

He frowns. "You took the letters?"

"They were addressed to me." I shrug.

He tilts his head, the corner of his lip curving up. "I'm surprised I didn't notice they were missing. When did you take them?"

"The day after you tried to give them to me. They were right next to all the other letters."

He raises an eyebrow. "Why didn't you say something before?"

"You weren't in a very friendly mood that day, remember?"

He sighs. "I might have been overreacting to your comment about my bedroom skills."

"Ha! I knew you were upset about that." I don't know why I feel so smug about it. While Luca kneels to put Bruno's leash and harness back on, an idea occurs to me. "Do you want to read our letters?"

He looks up at me. "What do you mean?"

"I mean we could read them all together. I've reread some of them recently, but I only have the ones from you. What if we read them in order?"

"I have to take Bruno for a walk."

"Oh. Forget it. I just thought that—"

"Let's read them after my walk," he interrupts.

I smile. "I'll grab my box and I'll meet you upstairs?"

"Sounds like a plan."

Chapter Thirty-Six

SWEET AND INNOCENT

Luca

When I come back upstairs, Naomi is already waiting at my door with a box in her arms. I don't know why she didn't just let herself in. She has a key to my apartment. I let us both inside. I feed the dog while she settles down on the couch. My furniture isn't as nice as hers. I bought it all from a thrift shop when I moved here. It's not raggedy, but nothing really matches.

I go into the bedroom and grab my box of letters. I return to the living room and sit down next to Naomi on the couch. I leave plenty of space between us so that she won't feel like I'm crowding her.

She leans forward to open her box, which she left on the floor. She pulls out a stack of old letters. I recognize my old childish handwriting. It feels weird to see it. Sitting up straight again, she scoots a little closer to me. I tell myself not to read too much into it, but I can smell her hair from here and it makes me want to lean a little closer and just breathe her in. I know what the skin on her neck looks like when it's covered in goosebumps after I've kissed her there. I want to see it again. She probably wouldn't be sitting so close to me if she knew that this is all I can think about.

She pulls her feet up underneath her, then hands me the stack of letters.

"You can read these," she says. "I'll read the ones from me."

I hand her the stack of letters from my box. They're in reverse chronological order. After Penny dumped all my letters out of the box, I spent hours putting them back in order and distracting myself by reading them. I flip through the stack that she gave me. Hers are in the same order.

She pulls the first letter from the bottom of the stack that I gave her, and begins to read.

"Dear Luca. I am really excited to be your new pen pal. My teacher says that you—"

"Stop," I interrupt.

She looks up at me, eyes wide. "Why?"

"Don't read it in that tone."

She frowns. "What tone?"

"You know what I'm talking about. You're making yourself sound all sweet and innocent. Now I'm going to sound like a major asshole when I read mine."

"Newsflash. You were a major asshole. This is the tone I imagined when I wrote it, so it's the tone I'm going to use."

She finishes reading the letter, and then it's my turn.

"Damn," I say. "My handwriting was awful."

"It was," she agrees. "Imagine how I felt having to decipher that madness only to discover how mean your words were."

"You must have been so devastated."

"I was." She pouts, exaggerating a sad face.

It takes everything in my power to not lean in and kiss her.

She smiles, and for a second, it feels like we're back to where we were before I deceived her. I'm not stupid enough to think she's forgiven me that easily, though. Her eyes drop to my mouth for a split second, so fast that I think I might have imagined it. She moves a lock of hair, tucking it behind her ear, then smiles again, and turns her attention back to the letters.

"Your turn," she says.

We take turns reading our letters to each other, laughing at things we wrote that we forgot about, and cringing over others. Time passes quickly while we're reading, and before I know it, it's dark outside. We only take a break long enough for me to walk Bruno again. While I'm outside, Naomi helps herself to my kitchen, and I come back to a fresh grilled cheese sandwich. We eat in the kitchen, and then return to the living room.

I sit down on the couch, and she drops herself down next to me, so close that her arm is against mine. She pulls her feet up underneath her, bending her leg so that it rests over my own. I tilt my chin down to look at her, but she's not paying any attention to me. She has a stack of letters in her hand, ready to keep reading.

Dear Luca,

Do you want to know something weird? Someone left a box full of bananas on my porch today. I'm really confused. I've had Christmas cookies left on my porch during the holiday season. We're nowhere near the holiday season now, so I'm not sure what's going on. I'm trying to figure out if there's a banana related holiday I should know about.

Love,

Naomi

Dear Naomi,

Someone mistook you for a monkey, which doesn't surprise me. That's why they left you the bananas. Speaking of fruit, I went to an orchard for the first time today. Did you know that people pay a ridiculous amount of money to pick their own apples when they could buy them much cheaper at the store and have someone else do all the work? Anyway, it made me think of you. I bet you eat your apples without removing the sticker that the grocery store puts on them. You probably eat the whole thing, all the way down to the core. Stem, too, if it's still attached.

Love,

Luca

Dear Luca,

That's exactly the way I like my apples. I have a really strong digestive system. That's how I can stomach writing to you all the time.

Love,

Naomi

Dear Naomi,

I have an idea. If we're still single by the time we're both twenty-five, let's get married. What do you think? By the way, what kind of name is Naomi Light? It sounds like a weird superhero made up by a guy who hasn't had a haircut in 3 years, and uses nail clippers to trim his split ends.

Love,

Luca

Dear Luca,

You're making it sound like twenty-five is a long time away. It's not. I turn twenty-five next month, and I'm not single by the way.

Also, how are you going to give me a half-ass proposal in one sentence and insult my name in the next, and expect me to say yes? You must be drinking salt water again.

    Love,

    Naomi

She sets the letter on her lap and looks up at me. Our faces are so close that if I leaned down just a little, I could reach her lips.

"This was only a few years ago," she says. "Weren't you already engaged to Penelope when you tried to make that married-by-twenty-five pact?"

"No. I was trying to get away from her when I wrote that letter."

She's quiet for a moment. I can tell that she's thinking. I hold my breath, waiting for her next words. "You were with her for a long time. You two met while you were in the military. That's what Maxwell said."

My body tenses. I don't like talking about Penny. Naomi starts to pull away, but I put my arm over her shoulder, and she stops moving. "We dated casually for a while. We were one of those on-again-off-again couples," I say. "I never wanted to commit to her."

"Then why did you propose to her?" She doesn't take her eyes off mine. I hold her stare.

"I didn't."

She frowns. I can tell that she thinks I'm lying. I wish I hadn't broken her trust by hiding who I am.

"She used my credit card to buy herself a ring, then started planning our wedding," I continue.

Naomi rolls her eyes, then leans away from me to pull one of the most recent letters out of the stack in front of me. It's the last one that I wrote to her before Penny and I moved to Texas.

"That's what you said in this letter," she says. "Do you actually expect me to believe that's what happened?"

I sigh. I've never had to tell anyone the full story before. Most people are willing to accept that I almost married someone who was crazy enough to fake an engagement. Naomi deserves to hear the truth, though.

"It was a misunderstanding."

"How?"

"I'm getting to that." I take a sip of water to clear my throat before I continue. "Penny and I got out of the military around the same time. She knew that I would never commit to going home to Dallas with her, so she followed me back to San Diego. I didn't know until I ran into her at the university. I guess she thought that she could win me over. I avoided her for a few weeks, but she was pushy. She managed to run into me on a daily basis. She wore me down. She lived in a dorm, and I had my own apartment. She started to spend more and more time at my apartment until one day I realized that she had moved in. When I confronted her about it, she offered to pay half the rent. I was living on the GI bill, and my apartment was expensive, so I caved. After a while, she started introducing herself to all my friends as my girlfriend.

"It was hard to argue with that. We were living together, we went to the store together, we drove together to school. Her family even came to visit us a few times. She talked about moving to Dallas when we were done with school, so I thought that it would be over by then. Turns out she wanted me to move with her. I was in vet school, which took longer than her degree, so I was able to put that conversation off for a while. I guess I should have just been honest with her. I used to tell her all the time that I wasn't ready to commit, but I guess after a while I assumed that she knew I still felt that way. I was wrong. She overheard me talking to Ben one day, and she thought that we were talking about her. She thought that we were going to get married."

"How did she get that from your conversation with Ben?" Naomi asks, frowning. "What were you talking about to make her think that?"

"That's…" I hesitate. "That's not important. After about a year, I guess she grew impatient with waiting for me to propose, so she started planning our wedding and used my credit card to buy herself a ring."

She turns her whole body on the couch so that she's facing me, her eyes narrowed. "That doesn't make any sense. I feel like you're missing an important detail."

I shrug, hoping to drop the subject. "She was crazy."

"It's what you were talking about with Ben, isn't it? Were you cheating on her?"

"No. No, no."

Her face turns serious. "Don't lie to me again, Luca. What were you talking about with Ben that made her think you two were engaged?"

I realize that if I tell her, she'll think I'm batshit crazy. If I don't, she'll never trust me again. I have to tell her. I pinch my lips together, bracing myself. "I was talking about you."

"Me?"

"Ben always knew about the letters. He's the closest thing I had to a best friend. He used to give me shit for writing such mean things to you in fifth grade. In middle school, I thought I was hot shit. I had a new girlfriend every other day. Same in high school – the first couple years, anyway." I pause, letting out a sigh. "You're going to think this is pathetic."

She raises an eyebrow. "More pathetic than accidentally getting engaged to someone?"

"Touché."

"Go on," she prods.

I stare at the coffee table because it's hard to look at her while I admit this. "Ben started making fun of me because I stopped dating junior year. He said it must have something to do with all those letters that I wrote to you. I don't think he realized how right he was. He and I weren't as close in high school, but we still had a few classes together, and he noticed that I was different. We didn't talk at all after I left for boot camp. I ran into him about three years after I came back to San Diego. Penny was all over me. He told me later that it was good to see I had finally moved on and wasn't all hung up on 'that girl from fifth grade' anymore."

I gesture to the last letter I read on the coffee table, the one with the married-by-twenty-five pact. "I had just written that letter to you two days earlier. I told Ben that we were going to get married, that I had already proposed to you, and I was going to let you pick out the perfect ring. I guess Penny was walking past the room at just the right time. She never heard me say your name. She thought that I was talking about her."

"But you hadn't proposed to her. Why would she think you had, based on overhearing a conversation with Ben?"

I shrug. "Don't know. I think she wanted so badly for it to be true that she made up a whole proposal in her head."

"Surely she heard the sarcasm in your tone when you were talking to Ben, though."

"I wasn't being sarcastic." When she narrows her eyes, I add, "Okay, maybe I just liked the idea of being married to you. I had every intention of convincing you to meet me. Getting married seemed like the next logical step."

344

"Come on," she says with a laugh. "You really thought that I was going to agree to marry you? I didn't even know you."

Her laugh does something to me. My heart beats a little faster, and I can feel the corners of my mouth stretching until I'm smiling. "Stranger things have happened. I never told Penny that I loved her, yet she thought that we were getting married."

Naomi yawns. "Really? You never said those three little words? Even out of obligation?"

"Are you tired? It's getting late."

She shakes her head. "We've already read so much. We only have a couple years left. It shouldn't take that long. And I want to know more about—" She cups her hand over her mouth, fighting another yawn. When she finishes her sentence, it comes out in an unintelligible mumble.

I laugh. She's cute when she's this tired. I want to reach over and hug her close to me, but I force myself to stay where I am. "What was that?"

"I want to know why you were so obsessed with me."

"We can talk about that later. We need to finish these letters before you fall asleep."

Chapter Thirty-Seven

PAPER CUT

Naomi

I wake up sandwiched between Luca and the back of the couch. My head is resting on his chest, and something hard is poking me in the stomach. I look down, and in the dark of the room, I see that Bruno is sleeping between us. His legs are stretched out as far as they will go. It's the puppy's back feet that are poking me.

I reach down to readjust Bruno so that he's not kicking me anymore. The puppy yawns and rolls over, stretching his feet out to kick Luca this time. Luca grunts. I sit up, careful not to bump anyone. The stacks of letters are sitting the way we left them on the coffee table. I look around the dark room, searching for a clock.

I guess my movement wakes Luca, because when I look back down at him, his eyes are open.

"Hey," he says.

"What time is it? I didn't mean to fall asleep."

He taps his phone, lighting it up. "Almost two."

"I should go home. I need to get ready for work."

He sits up so that I can get off the couch more easily, but I don't move just yet. We both watch as Bruno rolls from the middle to the back end of the couch in his sleep. I laugh, putting my hand over my mouth to try to keep myself quiet. Then I remember the puppy can't hear me. Luca meets my eyes and we exchange a smile.

In the dim light, his eyelids look heavy and his pupils are dark. His hair is tousled, and his face is peppered with a five o'clock shadow. It's really hard not to lean in a little closer to him, to remind myself of the way his stubble feels against my skin.

"It's great that you made so much progress on his training," he says, talking about the dog. "It will make it easier to find him a new home."

My smile dissolves. It's easy to forget that Bruno belongs to the shelter, and Luca is only fostering him. "How long until that happens?" I ask.

He shrugs. "Could be months. Weeks. Days. There's an adoption event this weekend. I didn't think he would be ready just yet, but I'm going to call the shelter in the morning and find out if they want him there."

"Oh." I look back down at the sleeping puppy. I don't know why I feel so sad. "I guess I thought I had more time with him."

I slide off the couch. Luca stands up behind me. I pick up my box of letters, then turn to face him.

"I liked reading them with you," he says.

I nod, too tired and conflicted to respond.

"Maybe we can finish reading them later?" he asks.

"Yeah. Sure."

He walks with me to his front door. "I can walk you home,"

he offers as he opens the door for me.

"Thanks, but I think I'll be fine. It's not like I have to leave the building. Plus," I add, gesturing to the box that I'm holding against my stomach, "if anyone tries anything, I can use this box of letters to defend myself."

"That gives a whole new meaning to using words as a weapon."

I step out into the hallway and then turn around to face him. Something has shifted between us. I'm not mad at him anymore. I want to go back to the way things were before he told me who he is. I want to trust him again.

He stands in the doorway, watching me as I readjust the box in my arms. I'm stalling. I could have turned around and headed for the stairwell by now, but something is keeping me here in this hallway.

"Goodnight," I say, even though this is the start of my morning. I know that he will be going back to bed.

I turn around and head for the stairwell. I'm almost there when I hear the sound of footsteps hurrying behind me. I look over my shoulder to see that Luca is following me.

"I told you I don't need you to walk me—"

Before I can finish my sentence, he cups my face in his hands and kisses me. I'm still holding the box against my stomach, so it's positioned awkwardly between us, and he has to lean over it to reach me. His lips are warm against mine, and his stubble scratches my face like I imagined it would. My heart is beating so fast I'm afraid I might drop my box.

When he lets go, he takes a step back and pushes the stairwell door open.

"Sorry," he says. "I was only coming to get the door for you, but..."

"But?" I prod when he trails off.

"I didn't want you to go home thinking that I didn't want to kiss you."

I smile, but I can't find the words to respond. I head downstairs to my own floor, thinking about him, about that kiss, about everything that happened tonight.

I make it back to my apartment and set the box down so that I can unlock the door. I hesitate before I turn the key. Maybe I'm overthinking things. I've been known to do that. We had such a great connection before, and after spending the night reading old letters with him, it doesn't feel like anything has changed. I want so badly to trust him, so maybe I should stop looking for reasons not to.

"Cheers to being a homeowner," Anne says, clinking her glass against mine. "Let me know if you need help with the mortgage. I've been told I make an excellent roommate."

It's Friday night. I just spent the afternoon doing one last walk-through of my new house and then signing a bunch of documents until my wrist was sore and I was pretty sure I was developing a case of carpal tunnel syndrome. When I was finished, they handed me the key to my new house and sent me on my way. I never knew that buying a new house would be so anticlimactic. Now I'm at a five-star restaurant with Anne, celebrating with an expensive dinner and a bottle of champagne.

"I already have two roommates lined up," I tell her. "Their names are Roland and Phoebe."

She rolls her eyes. "Cats don't count as roommates."

"Why not?"

"They don't pay the rent."

"I'm thinking about signing them up with an animal modeling agency. I'm sure they can get a good gig with all the tricks I've been teaching them."

"You are so weird," she says. She takes a sip of her champagne, and as she does, her phone buzzes on the table. She quickly turns it over so that I can't see what's on the screen, but it's too late.

"Patrick is texting you? I didn't know you had his number."

"I sent him that selfie of us in front of your new house," she says. I can tell that she's trying to maintain a sense of nonchalance, but her face is turning pink.

"Oh my God. You like him."

"What? No. Of course not. He's my boss, and he's practically bald."

I almost snort out my champagne. "You said that Maxwell was cute."

"Who?"

"Luca's old friend that we met in Georgia. He was bald."

She shrugs. "So what? That has nothing to do with Patrick."

I smile, deciding to let it go. She leaves her phone face down as we finish dinner.

"When are you moving into the new house?" she asks.

"I have movers coming next week. I'm going to start packing this weekend."

"Nice. And what about Luca?"

"What about him?"

"Don't play dumb. What are you going to do about him?"

I smile. "I have a plan."

Chapter Thirty-Eight

THE END OF THE ROAD

Luca

I'm in bed, half asleep, when I hear the knocking at my door. I climb out of bed, not bothering to put on a shirt as I make my way to the front door. Not many people visit me here, and the few that do would never come this late. There is only one person who I think it might be, but I'm still surprised when I open the door and it's her.

"Naomi."

She doesn't wait for me to invite her in. She steps through my doorway and stands on her tiptoes and kisses me. Her lips taste like wine. I don't ask where she's been all day. She's here now, and she's kissing me, and it feels like this is all that matters.

Without letting go of her, I reach behind her to push the door closed. She doesn't stop kissing me as we move through my apartment, backing into furniture and tripping over dog toys on the way to my bedroom. When we make it there, we end up on my bed. Her clothes come off gradually, in between kisses and light touches of fingertips against skin, the kind of touch that sends goosebumps over bare flesh even in a warm room.

When it's over, we lay there, her head against my chest. She's breathing deeply. I can't see her eyes, but I think she might be asleep. I could stay like this forever, but I don't know if she can. I hurt her, and I'm still trying to make up for it.

In the morning, she's still in my bed. I watch her sleep for a little while. It's rare that she gets to sleep in, so I don't wake her up. I get dressed quietly, then pack up Bruno and all of his belongings and bring him to the pet store. It's always hard giving up a foster animal. Before Roland and Phoebe, I had fostered an adult cat, and before the cat, there was an older dog. I try not to get too attached to the animals, but it happens every time, and then I go home feeling like a piece of me is missing until I bring the next animal home.

I think it's going to be even harder with Bruno. Not because he's more special than any of the other animals I've fostered, but because Naomi has grown attached to him too. Standing here at the pet supply store with Bruno in a pen, waiting for his first adoption applicant to show up, feels a little like giving away someone else's pet.

Now he's going to his new home, where Naomi won't hear him crying through her ceiling, and there won't be any reason for her to sneak into my apartment and leave little notes on my refrigerator.

It's raining this morning, so instead of having Bruno's pen outside like it was last time, we're crammed inside the store, his pen lined up with all the others through the center aisle. I hope that the heavy rain won't be enough to discourage people from coming in and adopting a pet.

I watch the front of the store as the doors slide open and a woman walks in wearing a heavy rain coat. She peels off her hood, and for a moment I think I'm imagining that fiery red hair. It feels like it did the first time I saw her coming out of the apartment building, when she held the door open for me. Except this time, I've memorized the way she walks and the way the little dimples appear on her cheeks when she smiles. There's no mistaking that the woman walking into the store is the one I fell in love with before I ever met her.

When she spots me and Bruno, she smiles wider, and her dimples look even deeper.

"What are you doing here?" I ask. I can't help but smile when I see her.

She looks down at Bruno, who is excitedly jumping at the gate, trying to get to her. Then she looks back up at me. "I'm here to adopt Bruno."

I wish that I could tell her yes, and let her jump the long list of people who already filled out applications, but that's not how this works. Her smile fades a little when she sees the look on my face.

"Bruno already has a bunch of applicants. There's a waitlist for him."

To my surprise, her smile gets bigger. "Oh, I know. I already filled out an application. I got the call this morning. My application was approved, and I'm first on the list."

I frown. I hadn't looked at the list of applicants, so I can't be sure. "You are?"

"I applied for him as soon as you told me he might get adopted this weekend." She reaches into the pen to pet him. "I couldn't let him go to just anyone."

I look down at the stack of papers on the table, and sift through it until I see her application.

"But you don't meet all the criteria," I tell her. "Bruno

needs a house with a yard. An apartment is fine while he's small, but he's going to be a big dog. He needs a lot of space."

She bends down and picks up the puppy, holding him against her chest. "I'm moving."

I frown. She never mentioned this before. "You are?"

She nods, that pretty smile still tugging up the corners of her lips. "Yes. I bought a house."

I can't tell if she's messing with me or not. "When?"

"It was finalized yesterday."

I'm at a loss for what to say. On the one hand, I'm happy that she's the one adopting Bruno. But hearing that she's moving and that she didn't tell me until now has me hesitant. A wave of emotion that I can't describe comes over me as I think about last night. I can't help but wonder if that was her way of saying goodbye, one last night together before she goes somewhere else. I don't even know if she'll still want to write to me after I screwed everything up.

"Where?" I ask. I can't seem to form any sentences longer than one word.

She smiles, but it doesn't reach her eyes this time. She pulls an envelope out of her bag and hands it to me. "Read it after I leave."

I stare at the envelope in my hand while she finalizes the adoption with one of the shelter employees. All that's on it is my name, handwritten in that familiar curvy handwriting of hers. No address. Not even a return address.

After she leaves, I head out to my car and sit inside it while the rain pelts down on the roof. I slide my finger under the envelope flap, opening it carefully.

Dear Luca,

Remember when you sent all those letters to me at the news

station without a return address? Consider this payback. I wonder if
you can figure out my new address faster than I figured out yours.
   Love,
   Naomi

I turn the page over, then check the envelope again. Then I look over my shoulder, checking the parking lot for her car. Of course she would tell me to read this after she's already gone. I read the letter again, hoping to find a clue I might have missed the first time, but there's nothing other than that taunting note.

I pull out my phone and I dial her number, but it goes straight to voicemail. I send a text, even though I already know she won't answer me. I'm supposed to look for her the same way she looked for me.

I stare through my rain-drenched windshield at the warped buildings on the other side, and I start to laugh. I wonder if this is how she felt when I sent her that first letter at the news station.

I turn the key in the ignition and head home. When I get there, I check my mailbox, but to my disappointment she hasn't left anything for me there. I head upstairs to the third floor. I knock on her door, but she doesn't answer. I listen for a minute, but it's quiet. She must have gone to her new home. I look up and down her hallway, as if that's going to give me clues, but still nothing.

Then I remember something. Naomi didn't just stand around waiting for a clue to drop into her lap. She went up and down the streets I used to live on, talking to old neighbors I don't even remember, like Carol Bell. Maybe that's what I'm supposed to do.

I run to the apartment next door and knock on the door. No one answers. I try the next apartment, and the next, until someone finally answers, but it turns out Naomi didn't talk much to any of her neighbors, and none of them know where she's going. After knocking on every single door on her floor, and talking to half a dozen people, I feel defeated, but I'm not ready to give up yet.

I'm about to head into the elevator when I have an idea. I need to think like Naomi. I take the stairs instead, hoping the stairwell will offer me a clue, but it's another dead-end. I make it to the lobby. Joel is sitting at his desk, ignoring me in favor of his newspaper. I already know the answer, but I have to ask.

"Naomi didn't tell you where she's moving, did she?"

He frowns over the top of his paper. "Thought you two made up or something."

"I'm guessing that's a no."

He nods in the direction of the front door. "I saw her talking to the kid earlier."

I look outside and spot Caitlin squatting on the wet sidewalk, searching a bush for caterpillars. The rain has stopped and the sun is out now.

"Thanks," I say to Joel. I step outside. "Hey, kid."

She spins around to face me, a bright smile on her face. "There's a cocoon in this bush!"

"Neat. Hey, did Naomi say anything to you about where she was moving?"

"No," she says without any hesitation. She starts to turn back to look at the cocoon, but pauses to face me again. "Oh. She wanted me to tell you that she was going to the diner."

"The diner?"

"Oops. I mean, she didn't want me to tell you that. She just..." The kid groans. "I'm messing it all up." She takes a deep breath, composing herself. When she speaks again, her tone is completely changed, like she's been practicing this: "She might have mentioned that she was going to the diner."

"The Spanish diner?"

Caitlin nods. "The one with the really yummy *huevos rancheros.*"

I smile, amused by her exaggerated accent. I thank her for the information and take off down the street. When I reach the restaurant, I glance around the dining room, looking for Naomi. I don't see her. I'm about to leave, but something holds me back. I head over to the booth where we had breakfast a few weeks ago.

On the table is an assortment of jelly packets and coffee creamers arranged in the shape of two big smiley faces. For a second, I think a kid must have left this here, but then I take a closer look. It's a replica of the faces I drew in the sand the day that Naomi and I went to the beach. She even used strawberry jelly packets to represent her own red hair.

"Can I clean this up now?"

I'm startled by the waitress. I didn't realize anyone was standing there watching me. She has her hands on her hips, her eyebrows raised.

"Yeah. I think I have what I need."

With this new clue, I head back across the street to the parking garage to get my car. I think I know where Naomi went next.

When I get to the beach, I don't bother taking my shoes off before I run into the sand. I think of Naomi and how she screeched while running over the hot sand barefoot, and I smile. By the time I reach the top of the dune, my shoes are filled with sand. There are a lot more people here today than when it was just me and Naomi. I scan the crowd for a minute, looking for her red hair, but she's not here.

I step closer to the water, weaving my way between families and children playing. I'm not sure what I'm looking for, but I know that I'm supposed to be here. I stop when I reach a pile of seaweed that seems to be separated from the mound of seaweed by the water. I take a step back so that I can see the whole thing. It's been arranged in the shape of a number: 1372.

There's no other context. Just the number. I frown, then look around the beach, searching for something to give this context, but I find nothing.

There's a woman lying on a towel nearby, sunbathing.

"Excuse me. Did you see who did this?" I ask her.

She looks my way, seeming annoyed that I'm addressing her. "I don't know," she says with a shrug.

I look back at the number. It's not part of her phone number. I already have that. Maybe an address? But there's no street name, no city, no zip code. I take my phone out and type '1372 Miami' into the address bar. A number of possible addresses pop up with several different street names.

I sigh, realizing that I'm going to have to visit every one of these properties to figure out where she is. I head back to my car and put the first address into my GPS. It takes me fourteen minutes from the beach to a store that looks like it's been closed for a while. I get out of my car anyway and walk up to the boarded-up front door, hoping to find a clue here, but there's nothing. I go back to my car. This time, instead of just driving to the next address on the list, I put each address into Google and check whether these are businesses or residential properties.

If Naomi gave me part of her new home address, I don't want to waste my time driving around to old stores.

I put each of the residential addresses into a real estate

website and search again. My new search narrows down my options. There's a house in a neighborhood about ten minutes from here that matches the address, and the real estate website has it marked as recently sold. I think this is it. I punch the address into my GPS and drive there.

The house has a green lawn and palm trees in the front yard. The backyard is fenced, the roof has red shingles, and there's a closed garage, so if Naomi is here, I won't be able to see her car. The real estate agent's sign is still in front of the house, marked with the word 'SOLD' in big red letters.

I stop my car in front of the house across the street and get out. I'm thinking about going up to the front door and knocking when I notice something taped to the mailbox. I step across the street and approach the mailbox. It's a white envelope with my name on it. I take it off the mailbox, then open it and unfold the small sheet of paper inside.

Dear Luca,

One of my favorite things about 'us' has always been going outside to check the mail and wondering if I had a new letter from you. I lived each week in anticipation of what ridiculous thing you would say next. You were always on my mind in one way or another. Usually, I was thinking up what I would write to you. Over the last two years, I mostly wondered where you went and why you weren't writing back. I don't want to lose contact again. This is my new address. I hope that you have a nice life. Maybe you can still write to me once in a while.

Love,
Naomi

I stare at the letter in my hand, completely dumfounded about why she would make me play this game and go through all this trouble just to tell me to have a nice life and we can write to each other. I had thought that things were getting better and that she had forgiven me, but this letter has me realizing I was wrong. I guess writing letters to her is better than nothing, but I hoped that this wasn't going to be all there ever was. I don't know if I'll be able to bring myself to write to her, knowing what it's like to have so much more than this, and also what it feels like to lose it.

Chapter Thirty-Nine

WRITE TO ME

Naomi

He's standing by my new mailbox, reading the letter I wrote for him as I approach from the corner of my house. I wait until I'm sure he's finished reading it before I speak up.

"Or we could stop wasting time and you can come inside with me." He turns around to look at me, eyes wide, and I know for sure that he didn't know I was behind him. "We don't have to move fast. You can come visit me, and maybe eventually you can move out of your apartment, and we can leave notes on the refrigerator and write letters to each other from opposite ends of the couch."

He stares at me for a moment, clutching the letter in his hand. When he doesn't move, I begin to wonder if I got it wrong. Maybe this isn't what he wanted after all. Maybe last night meant more to me than it did to him. I've never put myself out there like this before, and now that I have, it terrifies me that he isn't responding.

"I love you," I tell him.

Those three words seem to snap him out of his daze, and he steps toward me and lifts me off my feet as his lips meet mine.

When we separate, he sets me back down on the sidewalk and looks at me with a frown.

"This letter," he says, holding it up. "I thought…"

He doesn't finish his sentence, just shakes his head. I know that it was mean to write a letter like that, but then again, our letters have never been nice. I think that means I won this round.

Then he laughs, and I wonder if he realizes it too. He kisses me again, and when he pulls away, he says, "You can't keep adopting every single animal that I foster."

I think this means he's coming with me.

Epilogue

TWO YEARS LATER

Dear Naomi,

I feel like I should give you a heads up that there isn't an expensive bracelet inside this little box. I just don't want you to be disappointed, especially because what's inside is so much more important than any piece of jewelry. Before you open it, you should know that contrary to what you claim, adjusting your pillows has had absolutely no effect on the volume and intensity of your snoring. I'll give you a hint: it's a box of nose strips.

Oh, shit. I just gave it away, didn't I? I am terrible at surprises. I hope you still like my gift. I'll even help you put it on because I'm a gentleman.

Can you pick up cat food on your way home from work tomorrow? We're almost out, and you know how Roland gets when his bowl is half empty. Thank you so much. XOXOXO

Love,

Your Husband

I look up from the letter at Luca, who is watching me with a big smile on his face. He loves seeing my reaction as I read his letters, especially when he's done something to annoy me.

"You expect me to buy the cat food after you make fun of my snoring? Really?"

He shrugs. "They are your cats."

"That you tricked me into adopting," I remind him.

"I didn't trick you. Besides, I wasn't making fun of your snoring. I was doing us both a favor."

He nudges the box closer to me. I pick it up and carefully remove the ribbon from the small box, then tear off the wrapping paper. Inside is a box of nose strips with a note attached: *Just kidding. I'll buy the cat food.*

"See, I was counting on you to read the letter first. Otherwise the note wouldn't have made sense."

I roll my eyes, but I can't fight the smile tugging at the corners of my lips. I stand up on my tiptoes and kiss him.

"Besides, the snoring is my fault. You were such a quiet sleeper before all this." He waves his hand over my belly, distended from seven months of pregnancy.

"This was all your idea," I agree.

I walk with him to the front door to say goodbye as he heads back to work to finish his day. I give him another kiss, then watch him leave. I'm still smiling as he drives away. I'm already thinking of what I'll write in my next letter to him. I sit down on the couch, though there isn't much room for me with Bruno taking up half the space. I pick up my notebook and my pen and I begin to write.